THE
THREE PARTNERS

BRET HARTE

1ˢᵗ WORLD
LIBRARY
Literary Society

The Three Partners

Bret Harte

© 1st World Library, 2008
PO Box 2211
Fairfield, IA 52556
www.1stworldlibrary.com
First Edition

LCCN: 2007935363

Softcover ISBN: 978-1-4218-9317-4
Hardcover ISBN: 978-1-4218-9417-1
eBook ISBN: 978-1-4218-9217-7

Purchase *"The Three Partners"*
as a traditional bound book at:
www.1stWorldLibrary.com/purchase.asp?ISBN=978-1-4218-9317-4

1st World Library is a literary, educational organization
dedicated to:

- Creating a free internet library of downloadable ebooks

- Hosting writing competitions and offering book publishing
scholarships.

Interested in more 1st World Library books? contact:
literacy@1stworldlibrary.com
Check us out at: www.1stworldlibrary.com

1ˢᵗ World Library Literary Society

Giving Back to the World

"If you want to work on the core problem, it's early school literacy."

- James Barksdale, former CEO of Netscape

"No skill is more crucial to the future of a child, or to a democratic and prosperous society, than literacy."

- Los Angeles Times

"Literacy... means far more than learning how to read and write... The aim is to transmit... knowledge and promote social participation."

- UNESCO

"Literacy is not a luxury, it is a right and a responsibility. If our world is to meet the challenges of the twenty-first century we must harness the energy and creativity of all our citizens."

- President Bill Clinton

"Parents should be encouraged to read to their children, and teachers should be equipped with all available techniques for teaching literacy, so the varying needs and capacities of individual kids can be taken into account."

- Hugh Mackay

PROLOGUE

The sun was going down on the Black Spur Range. The red light it had kindled there was still eating its way along the serried crest, showing through gaps in the ranks of pines, etching out the interstices of broken boughs, fading away and then flashing suddenly out again like sparks in burnt-up paper. Then the night wind swept down the whole mountain side, and began its usual struggle with the shadows upclimbing from the valley, only to lose itself in the end and be absorbed in the all-conquering darkness. Yet for some time the pines on the long slope of Heavy Tree Hill murmured and protested with swaying arms; but as the shadows stole upwards, and cabin after cabin and tunnel after tunnel were swallowed up, a complete silence followed. Only the sky remained visible—a vast concave mirror of dull steel, in which the stars did not seem to be set, but only reflected.

A single cabin door on the crest of Heavy Tree Hill had remained open to the wind and darkness. Then it was slowly shut by an invisible figure, afterwards revealed by the embers of the fire it was stirring. At first only this figure brooding over the hearth was shown, but as the flames leaped up, two other figures could be seen sitting motionless before it. When the door was shut, they acknowledged that interruption by slightly changing their position; the one who had risen to shut the door sank back into an invisible seat, but the attitude of each man was one of profound reflection or reserve, and apparently upon some common subject which made them respect each other's silence. However, this was at last broken by a laugh. It was a boyish laugh, and came from the youngest of the party. The two others turned their profiles and glanced inquiringly towards him, but did not speak.

"I was thinking," he began in apologetic explanation, "how mighty queer it was that while we were working like niggers on grub wages, without the ghost of a chance of making a strike, how we used to sit here, night after night, and flapdoodle and speculate about what we'd do if we ever DID make one; and now, Great Scott! that we HAVE made it, and are just wallowing in gold, here we are sitting as glum and silent as if we'd had a washout! Why, Lord! I remember one night—not so long ago, either—that you two quarreled over the swell hotel you were going to stop at in 'Frisco, and whether you wouldn't strike straight out for London and Rome and Paris, or go away to Japan and China and round by India and the Red Sea."

"No, we didn't QUARREL over it," said one of the figures gently; "there was only a little discussion."

"Yes, but you did, though," returned the young fellow mischievously, "and you told Stacy, there, that we'd better learn something of the world before we tried to buy it or even hire it, and that it was just as well to get the hayseed out of our hair and the slumgullion off our boots before we mixed in polite society."

"Well, I don't see what's the matter with that sentiment now," returned the second speaker good-humoredly; "only," he added gravely, "we didn't quarrel—God forbid!"

There was something in the speaker's tone which seemed to touch a common chord in their natures, and this was voiced by Barker with sudden and almost pathetic earnestness. "I tell you what, boys, we ought to swear here to-night to always stand by each other—in luck and out of it! We ought to hold ourselves always at each other's call. We ought to have a kind of password or signal, you know, by which we could summon each other at any time from any quarter of the globe!"

"Come off the roof, Barker," murmured Stacy, without lifting his eyes from the fire. But Demorest smiled and glanced tolerantly at the younger man.

"Yes, but look here, Stacy," continued Barker, "comrades like us, in the old days, used to do that in times of trouble and adventures. Why shouldn't we do it in our luck?"

"There's a good deal in that, Barker boy," said Demorest, "though, as a general thing, passwords butter no parsnips, and the ordinary, every-day, single yelp from a wolf brings the whole pack together for business about as quick as a password. But you cling to that sentiment, and put it away with your gold-dust in your belt."

"What I like about Barker is his commodiousness," said Stacy. "Here he is, the only man among us that has his future fixed and his preemption lines laid out and registered. He's already got a girl that he's going to marry and settle down with on the strength of his luck. And I'd like to know what Kitty Carter, when she's Mrs. Barker, would say to her husband being signaled for from Asia or Africa. I don't seem to see her tumbling to any password. And when he and she go into a new partnership, I reckon she'll let the old one slide."

"That's just where you're wrong!" said Barker, with quickly rising color. "She's the sweetest girl in the world, and she'd be sure to understand our feelings. Why, she thinks everything of you two; she was just eager for you to get this claim, which has put us where we are, when I held back, and if it hadn't been for her, by Jove! we wouldn't have had it."

"That was only because she cared for YOU," returned Stacy, with a half-yawn; "and now that you've got YOUR share she isn't going to take a breathless interest in US. And, by the way, I'd rather YOU'D remind us that we owe our luck to her than that SHE should ever remind YOU of it."

"What do you mean?" said Barker quickly. But Demorest here rose lazily, and, throwing a gigantic shadow on the wall, stood between the two with his back to the fire. "He means," he said slowly, "that you're talking rot, and so is he. However, as yours comes from the heart and his from the head, I prefer yours. But you're both making me tired. Let's have a fresh deal."

Nobody ever dreamed of contradicting Demorest. Nevertheless, Barker persisted eagerly: "But isn't it better for us to look at this cheerfully and happily all round? There's nothing criminal in our having made a strike! It seems to me, boys, that of all ways of making money it's the squarest and most level; nobody is the poorer for it; our luck brings no misfortune to others. The gold was put there ages ago for anybody to find; we found it. It hasn't been tarnished by man's touch before. I don't know how it strikes you, boys, but it seems to me that of all gifts that are going it is the straightest. For whether we deserve it or not, it comes to us first-hand—from God!"

The two men glanced quickly at the speaker, whose face flushed and then smiled embarrassedly as if ashamed of the

Bret Harte

enthusiasm into which he had been betrayed. But Demorest did not smile, and Stacy's eyes shone in the firelight as he said languidly, "I never heard that prospecting was a religious occupation before. But I shouldn't wonder if you're right, Barker boy. So let's liquor up."

Nevertheless he did not move, nor did the others. The fire leaped higher, bringing out the rude rafters and sternly economic details of the rough cabin, and making the occupants in their seats before the fire look gigantic by contrast.

"Who shut the door?" said Demorest after a pause.

"I did," said Barker. "I reckoned it was getting cold."

"Better open it again, now that the fire's blazing. It will light the way if any of the men from below want to drop in this evening."

Stacy stared at his companion. "I thought that it was understood that we were giving them that dinner at Boomville tomorrow night, so that we might have the last evening here by ourselves in peace and quietness?"

"Yes, but if any one DID want to come it would seem churlish to shut him out," said Demorest.

"I reckon you're feeling very much as I am," said Stacy, "that this good fortune is rather crowding to us three alone. For myself, I know," he continued, with a backward glance towards a blanketed, covered pile in the corner of the cabin, "that I feel rather oppressed by—by its specific gravity, I calculate—and sort of crampy and twitchy in the legs, as if I ought to 'lite' out and do something, and yet it holds me here. All the same, I doubt if anybody will come up—except from curiosity. Our luck has made them rather sore down the hill, for all they're coming to the dinner to-morrow."

"That's only human nature," said Demorest.

"But," said Barker eagerly, "what does it mean? Why, only this afternoon, when I was passing the 'Old Kentuck' tunnel, where those Marshalls have been grubbing along for four years without making a single strike, I felt ashamed to look at them, and as they barely nodded to me I slinked by as if I had done them an injury. I don't understand it."

"It somehow does not seem to square with this 'gift of God' idea of yours, does it?" said Stacy. "But we'll open the door and give them a show."

As he did so it seemed as if the night were their only guest, and had been waiting on the threshold to now enter bodily and pervade all things with its presence. With that cool, fragrant inflow of air they breathed freely. The red edge had gone from Black Spur, but it was even more clearly defined against the sky in its towering blackness. The sky itself had grown lighter, although the stars still seemed mere reflections of the solitary pin-points of light scattered along the concave valley below. Mingling with the cooler, restful air of the summit, yet penetratingly distinct from it, arose the stimulating breath of the pines below, still hot and panting from the day-long sun. The silence was intense. The far-off barking of a dog on the invisible river-bar nearly a mile beneath them came to them like a sound in a dream. They had risen, and, standing in the doorway, by common consent turned their faces to the east. It was the frequent attitude of the home-remembering miner, and it gave him the crowning glory of the view. For, beyond the pine-hearsed summits, rarely seen except against the evening sky, lay a thin, white cloud like a dropped portion of the Milky Way. Faint with an indescribable pallor, remote yet distinct enough to assert itself above and beyond all surrounding objects, it was always there. It was the snow-line of the Sierras.

They turned away and silently reseated themselves, the same thought in the minds of each. Here was something they could not take away, something to be left forever and irretrievably behind,—left with the healthy life they had been leading, the cheerful endeavor, the undying hopefulness which it had fostered and blessed. Was what they WERE taking away worth it? And oddly enough, frank and outspoken as they had always been to each other, that common thought remained unuttered. Even Barker was silent; perhaps he was also thinking of Kitty.

Suddenly two figures appeared in the very doorway of the cabin. The effect was startling upon the partners, who had only just reseated themselves, and for a moment they had forgotten that the narrow band of light which shot forth from the open door rendered the darkness on either side of it more impenetrable, and that out of this darkness, although themselves guided by the light, the figures had just emerged. Yet one was familiar enough. It was the Hill drunkard, Dick Hall, or, as he was called, "Whiskey Dick," or, indicated still more succinctly by the Hill humorists, "Alky Hall."

Everybody had seen that sodden, puffy, but good-humored face; everybody had felt the fiery exhalations of that enormous red beard, which always seemed to be kept in a state of moist, unkempt luxuriance by liquor; everybody knew the absurd dignity of manner and attempted precision of statement with which he was wont to disguise his frequent excesses. Very few, however, knew, or cared to know, the pathetic weariness and chilling horror that sometimes looked out of those bloodshot eyes.

He was evidently equally unprepared for the three silent seated figures before the door, and for a moment looked at them blankly with the doubts of a frequently deceived perception. Was he sure that they were quite real? He had not dared to look at his companion for verification, but smiled vaguely.

"Good-evening," said Demorest pleasantly.

Whiskey Dick's face brightened. "Good-evenin', good-evenin' yourselves, boys—and see how you like it! Lemme interdrush my ole frien' William J. Steptoe, of Red Gulch. Stepsho—Steptoe—is shtay—ish stay—" He stopped, hiccupped, waved his hand gravely, and with an air of reproachful dignity concluded, "sojourning for the present on the Bar. We wish to offer our congrashulashen and felish—felish—" He paused again, and, leaning against the door-post, added severely, "—itations."

His companion, however, laughed coarsely, and, pushing past Dick, entered the cabin. He was a short, powerful man, with a closely cropped crust of beard and hair that seemed to adhere to his round head like moss or lichen. He cast a glance—furtive rather than curious around the cabin, and said, with a familiarity that had not even good humor to excuse it, "So you're the gay galoots who've made the big strike? Thought I'd meander up the Hill with this old bloat Alky, and drop in to see the show. And here you are, feeling your oats, eh? and not caring any particular G-d d—n if school keeps or not."

"Show Mr. Steptoe—the whiskey," said Demorest to Stacy. Then quietly addressing Dick, but ignoring Steptoe as completely as Steptoe had ignored his unfortunate companion, he said, "You quite startled us at first. We did not see you come up the trail."

"No. We came up the back trail to please Steptoe, who wanted to see round the cabin," said Dick, glancing nervously yet with a forced indifference towards the whiskey which Stacy was offering to the stranger.

"What yer gettin' off there?" said Steptoe, facing Dick almost brutally. "YOU know your tangled legs wouldn't take you straight up the trail, and you had to make a circumbendibus. Gosh! if you hadn't scented this licker at the top you'd have never found it."

"No matter! I'm glad you DID find it, Dick," said Demorest, "and I hope you'll find the liquor good enough to pay you for the trouble."

Barker stared at Demorest. This extraordinary tolerance of the drunkard was something new in his partner. But at a glance from Demorest he led Dick to the demijohn and tin cup which stood on a table in the corner. And in another moment Dick had forgotten his companion's rudeness.

Demorest remained by the door, looking out into the darkness.

"Well," said Steptoe, putting down his emptied cup, "trot out your strike. I reckon our eyes are strong enough to bear it now." Stacy drew the blanket from the vague pile that stood in the corner, and discovered a deep tin prospecting-pan. It was heaped with several large fragments of quartz. At first the marble whiteness of the quartz and the glittering crystals of mica in its veins were the most noticeable, but as they drew closer they could see the dull yellow of gold filling the decomposed and honeycombed portion of the rock as if still liquid and molten. The eyes of the party sparkled like the mica—even those of Barker and Stacy, who were already familiar with the treasure.

"Which is the richest chunk?" asked Steptoe in a thickening voice.

Stacy pointed it out.

"Why, it's smaller than the others."

"Heft it in your hand," said Barker, with boyish enthusiasm.

The short, thick fingers of Steptoe grasped it with a certain aquiline suggestion; his whole arm strained over it until his face grew purple, but he could not lift it.

"Thar useter be a little game in the 'Frisco Mint," said Dick, restored to fluency by his liquor, "when thar war ladies visiting it, and that was to offer to give 'em any of those little boxes of gold coin, that contained five thousand dollars, ef they would kindly lift it from the counter and take it away! It wasn't no bigger than one of these chunks; but Jiminy! you oughter have seed them gals grip and heave on it, and then hev to give it up! You see they didn't know anything about the paci—(hic) the speshif—" He stopped with great dignity, and added with painful precision, "the specific gravity of gold."

"Dry up!" said Steptoe roughly. Then turning to Stacy he said abruptly, "But where's the rest of it? You've got more than that."

"We sent it to Boomville this morning. You see we've sold out our claim to a company who take it up to-morrow, and put up a mill and stamps. In fact, it's under their charge now. They've got a gang of men on the claim already."

"And what mout ye hev got for it, if it's a fair question?" said Steptoe, with a forced smile.

Stacy smiled also. "I don't know that it's a business question," he said.

"Five hundred thousand dollars," said Demorest abruptly from the doorway, "and a treble interest."

The eyes of the two men met. There was no mistaking the dull fire of envy in Steptoe's glance, but Demorest received it with a certain cold curiosity, and turned away as the sound of arriving voices came from without.

"Five hundred thousand's a big figger," said Steptoe, with a coarse laugh, "and I don't wonder it makes you feel so d—d sassy. But it WAS a fair question."

Unfortunately it here occurred to the whiskey-stimulated brain of Dick that the friend he had introduced was being treated with scant courtesy, and he forgot his own treatment by Steptoe. Leaning against the wall he waved a dignified rebuke. "I'm sashified my ole frien' is akshuated by only businesh principles." He paused, recollected himself, and added with great precision: "When I say he himself has a valuable claim in Red Gulch, and to my shertain knowledge has received offers—I have said enough."

The laugh that broke from Stacy and Barker, to whom the infelicitous reputation of Red Gulch was notorious, did not allay Steptoe's irritation. He darted a vindictive glance at the unfortunate Dick, but joined in the laugh. "And what was ye goin' to do with that?" he said, pointing to the treasure.

"Oh, we're taking that with us. There's a chunk for each of us as a memento. We cast lots for the choice, and Demorest won,—that one which you couldn't lift with one hand, you know," said Stacy.

"Oh, couldn't I? I reckon you ain't goin' to give me the same chance that they did at the Mint, eh?"

Although the remark was accompanied with his usual coarse, familiar laugh, there was a look in his eye so inconsequent in its significance that Stacy would have made some reply, but at this moment Demorest re-entered the cabin, ushering in a half dozen miners from the Bar below. They were, although youngish men, some of the older locators in the vicinity, yet, through years of seclusion and uneventful labors, they had acquired a certain childish simplicity of thought and manner that was alternately amusing and pathetic. They had never intruded upon the reserve of the three partners of Heavy Tree Hill before; nothing but an infantine curiosity, a shy recognition of the partners' courtesy in inviting them with the whole population of Heavy Tree to the dinner the next day, and the never-to-be-resisted temptation of an evening of "free liquor" and forgetfulness of the past had brought them there now. Among them, and yet not of them, was a young man who, although speaking English without accent, was distinctly of a different nationality and race. This, with a certain neatness of dress and artificial suavity of address, had gained him the nickname of "the Count" and "Frenchy," although he was really of Flemish extraction. He was the Union Ditch Company's agent on the Bar, by virtue of his knowledge of languages.

Barker uttered an exclamation of pleasure when he saw him. Himself the incarnation of naturalness, he had always secretly admired this young foreigner, with his lacquered smoothness, although a vague consciousness that neither Stacy nor Demorest shared his feelings had restricted their acquaintance. Nevertheless, he was proud now to see the bow with which Paul Van Loo entered the cabin as if it were a drawing-room, and perhaps did not reflect upon that want of real feeling in an act which made the others uncomfortable.

Bret Harte

The slight awkwardness their entrance produced, however, was quickly forgotten when the blanket was again lifted from the pan of treasure. Singularly enough, too, the same feverish light came into the eyes of each as they all gathered around this yellow shrine. Even the polite Paul rudely elbowed his way between the others, though his artificial "Pardon" seemed to Barker to condone this act of brutal instinct. But it was more instructive to observe the manner in which the older locators received this confirmation of the fickle Fortune that had overlooked their weary labors and years of waiting to lavish her favors on the new and inexperienced amateurs. Yet as they turned their dazzled eyes upon the three partners there was no envy or malice in their depths, no reproach on their lips, no insincerity in their wondering satisfaction. Rather there was a touching, almost childlike resumption of hope as they gazed at this conclusive evidence of Nature's bounty. The gold had been there—THEY had only missed it! And if there, more could be found! Was it not a proof of the richness of Heavy Tree Hill? So strongly was this reflected on their faces that a casual observer, contrasting them with the thoughtful countenances of the real owners, would have thought them the lucky ones. It touched Barker's quick sympathies, it puzzled Stacy, it made Demorest more serious, it aroused Steptoe's active contempt. Whiskey Dick alone remained stolid and impassive in a desperate attempt to pull himself once more together. Eventually he succeeded, even to the ambitious achievement of mounting a chair and lifting his tin cup with a dangerously unsteady hand, which did not, however, affect his precision of utterance, and said:—

"Order, gentlemen! We'll drink success to—to"—

"The next strike!" said Barker, leaping impetuously on another chair and beaming upon the old locators—"and may it come to those who have so long deserved it!"

His sincere and generous enthusiasm seemed to break the spell of silence that had fallen upon them. Other toasts quickly followed. In the general good feeling Barker attached himself to Van Loo with his usual boyish effusion, and in a burst of confidence imparted the secret of his engagement to Kitty Carter. Van Loo listened with polite attention, formal congratulations, but inscrutable eyes, that occasionally wandered to Stacy and again to the treasure. A slight chill of disappointment came over Barker's quick sensitiveness. Perhaps his enthusiasm had bored this superior man of the world. Perhaps his confidences were in bad taste! With a new sense of his inexperience he turned sadly away. Van Loo took that opportunity to approach Stacy.

"What's all this I hear of Barker being engaged to Miss Carter?" he said, with a faintly superior smile. "Is it really true?"

"Yes. Why shouldn't it be?" returned Stacy bluntly.

Van Loo was instantly deprecating and smiling. "Why not, of course? But isn't it sudden?"

"They have known each other ever since he's been on Heavy Tree Hill," responded Stacy.

"Ah, yes! True," said Van Loo. "But now"—

"Well—he's got money enough to marry, and he's going to marry."

"Rather young, isn't he?" said Van Loo, still deprecatingly. "And she's got nothing. Used to wait on the table at her father's hotel in Boomville, didn't she?"

"Yes. What of that? We all know it."

"Of course. It's an excellent thing for her—and her father. He'll have a rich son-in-law. About two hundred thousand is his share, isn't it? I suppose old Carter is delighted?"

Stacy had thought this before, but did not care to have it corroborated by this superfine young foreigner. "And I don't reckon that Barker is offended if he is," he said curtly as he turned away. Nevertheless, he felt irritated that one of the three superior partners of Heavy Tree Hill should be thought a dupe.

Suddenly the conversation dropped, the laughter ceased. Every one turned round, and, by a common instinct, looked towards the door. From the obscurity of the hill slope below came a wonderful tenor voice, modulated by distance and spiritualized by the darkness:—

"When at some future day
I shall be far away,
Thou wilt be weeping,
Thy lone watch keeping."

The men looked at one another. "That's Jack Hamlin," they said. "What's he doing here?"

"The wolves are gathering around fresh meat," said Steptoe, with his coarse laugh and a glance at the treasure. "Didn't ye know he came over from Red Dog yesterday?"

"Well, give Jack a fair show and his own game," said one of the old locators, "and he'd clean out that pile afore sunrise."

"And lose it next day," added another.

"But never turn a hair or change a muscle in either case," said a third. "Lord! I've heard him sing away just like that when he's been leaving the board with five thousand dollars in his pocket, or going away stripped of his last red cent."

Van Loo, who had been listening with a peculiar smile, here said in his most deprecating manner, "Yes, but did you never consider the influence that such a man has on the hard-working tunnelmen, who are ready to gamble their whole week's earnings to him? Perhaps not. But I know the difficulties of getting the Ditch rates from these men when he has been in camp."

He glanced around him with some importance, but only a laugh followed his speech. "Come, Frenchy," said an old locator, "you only say that because your little brother wanted to play with Jack like a grown man, and when Jack ordered him off the board and he became sassy, Jack scooted him outer the saloon."

Van Loo's face reddened with an anger that had the apparent effect of removing every trace of his former polished repose, and leaving only a hard outline beneath. At which Demorest interfered:—

"I can't say that I see much difference in gambling by putting money into a hole in the ground and expecting to take more from it than by putting it on a card for the same purpose."

Here the ravishing tenor voice, which had been approaching, ceased, and was succeeded by a heart-breaking and equally melodious whistling to finish the bar of the singer's song. And the next moment Jack Hamlin appeared in the doorway.

Whatever was his present financial condition, in perfect self-possession and charming sang-froid he fully bore out his previous description. He was as clean and refreshing looking as a madrono-tree in the dust-blown forest. An odor of scented soap and freshly ironed linen was wafted from him; there was scarcely a crease in his white waistcoat, nor a speck upon his varnished shoes. He might have been an auditor of the previous conversation, so quickly and completely did he seem to take in the whole situation at a glance. Perhaps there was an extra tilt to his black-ribboned Panama hat, and a certain dancing devilry in his brown eyes—which might also have been an answer to adverse criticism.

"When I, his truth to prove, would trifle with my love," he warbled in general continuance from the doorway. Then dropping cheerfully into speech, he added, "Well, boys, I am here to welcome the little stranger, and to trust that the family are doing as well as can be expected. Ah! there it is! Bless it!" he went on, walking leisurely to the treasure. "Triplets, too!—and plump at that. Have you had 'em weighed?"

Frankness was an essential quality of Heavy Tree Hill. "We were just saying, Jack," said an old locator, "that, giving you a fair show and your own game, you could manage to get away with that pile before daybreak."

"And I'm just thinking," said Jack cheerfully, "that there were some of you here that could do that without any such useless preliminary." His brown eyes rested for a moment on Steptoe, but turning quite abruptly to Van Loo, he held out his hand. Startled and embarrassed before the others, the young man at last advanced his, when Jack coolly put his own, as if forgetfully, in his pocket. "I thought you might like to know what that little brother of yours is doing," he said to Van Loo, yet looking at Steptoe. "I found him wandering about the Hill here quite drunk."

"I have repeatedly warned him"—began Van Loo, reddening.

"Against bad company—I know," suggested Jack gayly; "yet in spite of all that, I think he owes some of his liquor to Steptoe yonder."

"I never supposed the fool would get drunk over a glass of whiskey offered in fun," said Steptoe harshly, yet evidently quite as much disconcerted as angry.

"The trouble with Steptoe," said Hamlin, thoughtfully spanning his slim waist with both hands as he looked down at his polished shoes, "is that he has such a soft-hearted liking for all weaknesses. Always wanting to protect chaps that can't look after themselves, whether it's Whiskey Dick there when he has a pull on, or some nigger when he's made a little strike, or that straying lamb of Van Loo's when he's puppy drunk. But you're wrong about me, boys. You can't draw me in any game to-night. This is one of my nights off, which I devote exclusively to contemplation and song. But," he added, suddenly turning to his three hosts with a bewildering and fascinating change of expression, "I couldn't resist coming up here to see you and your pile, even if I never saw the one or the other before, and am not likely to see either again. I believe in luck! And it comes a mighty sight oftener than a fellow thinks it does. But it doesn't come to stay. So I'd advise you to keep your eyes skinned, and hang on to it while it's with you, like grim death. So long!"

Resisting all attempts of his hosts—who had apparently fallen as suddenly and unaccountably under the magic of his manner—to detain him longer, he stepped lightly away, his voice presently rising again in melody as he descended the hill. Nor was it at all remarkable that the others, apparently drawn by the same inevitable magnetism, were impelled to follow him, naturally joining their voices with his, leaving Steptoe and Van Loo so markedly behind them alone that they were compelled at last in sheer embarrassment to close up the rear of the procession. In another moment the cabin and the three partners again relapsed into the peace and quiet of the night. With the dying away of the last voices on the hillside the old solitude reasserted itself.

But since the irruption of the strangers they had lost their former sluggish contemplation, and now busied themselves in preparation for their early departure from the cabin the next morning. They had arranged to spend the following day and night at Boomville and Carter's Hotel, where they were to give their farewell dinner to Heavy Tree Hill. They talked but little together: since the rebuff his enthusiastic confidences had received from Van Loo, Barker had been grave and thoughtful, and Stacy, with the irritating recollection of Van Loo's criticisms in his mind, had refrained from his usual rallying of Barker. Oddly enough, they spoke chiefly of Jack Hamlin,—till then personally a stranger to them, on account of his infelix reputation,—and even the critical Demorest expressed a wish they had known him before. "But you never know the real value of anything until you're quitting it or it's quitting you," he added sententiously.

Barker and Stacy both stared at their companion. It was unlike Demorest to regret anything—particularly a mere social diversion.

"They say," remarked Stacy, "that if you had known Jack Hamlin earlier and professionally, a great deal of real value would have quitted you before he did."

"Don't repeat that rot flung out by men who have played Jack's game and lost," returned Demorest derisively. "I'd rather trust him than"—He stopped, glanced at the meditative Barker, and then concluded abruptly, "the whole caboodle of his critics."

They were silent for a few moments, and then seemed to have fallen into their former dreamy mood as they relapsed into their old seats again. At last Stacy drew a long breath. "I wish we had sent those nuggets off with the others this morning."

"Why?" said Demorest suddenly.

"Why? Well, d—n it all! they kind of oppress me, don't you see. I seem to feel 'em here, on my chest—all the three," returned Stacy only half jocularly. "It's their d—d specific gravity, I suppose. I don't like the idea of sleeping in the same room with 'em. They're altogether too much for us three men to be left alone with."

"You don't mean that you think that anybody would attempt"—said Demorest.

Stacy curled a fighting lip rather superciliously. "No; I don't think THAT—I rather wish I did. It's the blessed chunks of solid gold that seem to have got US fast, don't you know, and are going to stick to us for good or ill. A sort of Frankenstein monster that we've picked out of a hole from below."

"I know just what Stacy means," said Barker breathlessly, rounding his gray eyes. "I've felt it, too. Couldn't we make a sort of cache of it—bury it just outside the cabin for to-night? It would be sort of putting it back into its old place, you know, for the time being. IT might like it."

The other two laughed. "Rather rough on Providence, Barker boy," said Stacy, "handing back the Heaven-sent gift so soon! Besides, what's to keep any prospector from coming along and making a strike of it? You know that's mining law—if you haven't preempted the spot as a claim."

But Barker was too staggered by this material statement to make any reply, and Demorest arose. "And I feel that you'd both better be turning in, as we've got to get up early." He went to the corner of the cabin, and threw the blanket back over the pan and its treasure. "There that'll keep the chunks from getting up to ride astride of you like a nightmare." He shut the door and gave a momentary glance at its cheap hinges and the absence of bolt or bar. Stacy caught his eye. "We'll miss this security in San Francisco—perhaps even in Boomville," he sighed.

It was scarcely ten o'clock, but Stacy and Barker had begun to undress themselves with intervals of yawning and desultory talk, Barker continuing an amusing story, with one stocking off and his trousers hanging on his arm, until at last both men were snugly curled up in their respective bunks. Presently Stacy's voice came from under the blankets:—

"Hallo! aren't you going to turn in too?"

"Not yet," said Demorest from his chair before the fire. "You see it's the last night in the old shanty, and I reckon I'll see the rest of it out."

"That's so," said the impulsive Barker, struggling violently with his blankets. "I tell you what, boys: we just ought to make a watch-night of it—a regular vigil, you know—until twelve at least. Hold on! I'll get up, too!" But here Demorest arose, caught his youthful partner's bare foot which went searching painfully for the ground in one hand, tucked it back under the blankets, and heaping them on the top of him, patted the bulk with an authoritative, paternal air.

"You'll just say your prayers and go to sleep, sonny. You'll want to be fresh as a daisy to appear before Miss Kitty to-morrow early, and you can keep your vigils for to-morrow night, after dinner, in the back drawing-room. I said 'Good-night,' and I mean it!"

Protesting feebly, Barker finally yielded in a nestling shiver and a sudden silence. Demorest walked back to his chair. A prolonged snore came from Stacy's bunk; then everything was quiet. Demorest stirred up the fire, cast a huge root upon it, and, leaning back in his chair, sat with half-closed eyes and dreamed.

It was an old dream that for the past three years had come to him daily, sometimes even overtaking him under the shade of a buckeye in his noontide rest on his claim,—a dream that had never yet failed to wait for him at night by the fireside when his partners were at rest; a dream of the past, but so real that it always made the present seem the dream through which he was moving towards some sure awakening.

It was not strange that it should come to him to-night, as it had often come before, slowly shaping itself out of the obscurity as the vision of a fair young girl seated in one of the empty chairs before him. Always the same pretty, child-like face, fraught with a half-frightened, half-wondering trouble; always the same slender, graceful figure, but always glimmering in diamonds and satin, or spiritual in lace and pearls, against his own rude and sordid surroundings; always silent with parted lips, until the night wind smote some chord of recollection, and then mingled a remembered voice with his own. For at those times he seemed to speak also, albeit with closed lips, and an utterance inaudible to all but her.

"Well?" he said sadly.

"Well?" the voice repeated, like a gentle echo blending with his own.

"You know it all now," he went on. "You know that it has come at last,—all that I had worked for, prayed for; all that would have made us happy here; all that would have saved you to me has come at last, and all too late!"

"Too late!" echoed the voice with his.

"You remember," he went on, "the last day we were together. You remember your friends and family would have you give me up—a penniless man. You remember when they reproached you with my poverty, and told you that it was only your wealth that I was seeking, that I then determined to go away and never to return to claim you until that reproach could be removed. You remember, dearest, how you clung to me and bade me stay with you, even fly with you, but not to leave you alone with them. You wore the same dress that day, darling; your eyes had the same wondering childlike fear and trouble in them; your jewels glittered on you as you trembled, and I refused. In my pride, or rather in my weakness and cowardice, I refused. I came away and broke my heart among these rocks and ledges, yet grew strong; and you, my love, YOU, sheltered and guarded by those you loved, YOU"—He stopped and buried his face in his hands. The night wind breathed down the chimney, and from the stirred ashes on the hearth came the soft whisper, "I died."

"And then," he went on, "I cared for nothing. Sometimes my heart awoke for this young partner of mine in his innocent, trustful love for a girl that even in her humble station was far beyond his hopes, and I pitied myself in him. Home, fortune, friends, I no longer cared for—all were forgotten. And now they are returning to me—only that I may see the hollowness and vanity of them, and taste the bitterness for which I have sacrificed you. And here, on this last night of my exile, I am confronted with only the jealousy, the doubt, the meanness and selfishness that is to come. Too late! Too late!"

The wondering, troubled eyes that had looked into his here appeared to clear and brighten with a sweet prescience. Was it the wind moaning in the chimney that seemed to whisper to him: "Too late, beloved, for ME, but not for you. I died, but Love still lives. Be happy, Philip. And in your happiness I too may live again"?

He started. In the flickering firelight the chair was empty. The wind that had swept down the chimney had stirred the ashes with a sound like the passage of a rustling skirt. There was a chill in the air and a smell like that of opened earth. A nervous shiver passed over him. Then he sat upright. There was no mistake; it was no superstitious fancy, but a faint, damp current of air was actually flowing across his feet towards the fireplace. He was about to rise when he stopped suddenly and became motionless.

He was actively conscious now of a strange sound which had affected him even in the preoccupation of his vision. It was a gentle brushing of some yielding substance like that made by a soft broom on sand, or the sweep of a gown. But to his mountain ears, attuned to every woodland sound, it was not like the gnawing of gopher or squirrel, the scratching of wildcat, nor the hairy rubbing of bear. Nor was it human; the long, deep respirations of his sleeping companions were distinct from that monotonous sound. He could not even tell if it were IN the cabin or without. Suddenly his eye fell upon the pile in the corner. The blanket that covered the treasure was actually moving!

He rose quickly, but silently, alert, self-contained, and menacing. For this dreamer, this bereaved man, this scornful philosopher of riches had disappeared with that midnight trespass upon the sacred treasure. The movement of the blanket ceased; the soft, swishing sound recommenced. He drew a glittering bowie-knife from his boot-leg, and in three noiseless strides was beside the pile. There he saw what he fully expected to see,—a narrow, horizontal gap between the log walls of the cabin and the adobe floor, slowly widening and deepening by the burrowing of unseen hands from without. The cold outer air which he had felt before was now plainly flowing into the heated cabin through the opening. The swishing sound recommenced, and stopped. Then the four fingers of a hand, palm downwards, were cautiously introduced between the bottom log and the denuded floor. Upon that intruding hand the bowie-knife of Demorest descended like a flash of lightning. There was no outcry. Even in that supreme moment Demorest felt a pang of admiration for the stoicism of the unseen trespasser. But the maimed hand was quickly withdrawn, and as quickly Demorest rushed to the door and dashed into the outer darkness.

For an instant he was dazed and bewildered by the sudden change. But the next moment he saw a dodging, doubling figure running before him, and threw himself upon it. In the shock both men fell, but even in that contact Demorest felt the tangled beard and alcoholic fumes of Whiskey Dick, and felt also that the hands which were thrown up against his breast, the palms turned outward with the instinctive move-ment of a timid, defenseless man, were unstained with soil or blood. With an oath he threw the drunkard from him and dashed to the rear of the cabin. But too late! There, indeed, was the scattered earth, there the widened burrow as it had been excavated apparently by that mutilated hand—but nothing else!

He turned back to Whiskey Dick. But the miserable man, although still retaining a look of dazed terror in his eyes, had recovered his feet in a kind of angry confidence and a forced sense of injury. What did Demorest mean by attacking "innoshent" gentlemen on the trail outside his cabin? Yes!

OUTSIDE his cabin, he would swear it!

"What were you doing here at midnight?" demanded Demorest.

What was he doing? What was any gentleman doing? He wasn't any molly-coddle to go to bed at ten o'clock! What was he doing? Well—he'd been with men who didn't shut their doors and turn the boys out just in the shank of the evening. He wasn't any Barker to be wet-nursed by Demorest.

"Some one else was here!" said Demorest sternly, with his eyes fixed on Whiskey Dick. The dull glaze which seemed to veil the outer world from the drunkard's pupils shifted suddenly with such a look of direct horror that Demorest was fain to turn away his own. But the veil mercifully returned, and with it Dick's worked-up sense of injury. Nobody was there—not "a shole." Did Demorest think if there had been any of his friends there they would have stood by like "dogsh" and seen him insulted?

Demorest turned away and re-entered the cabin as Dick lurched heavily forward, still muttering, down the trail. The excitement over, a sickening repugnance to the whole incident took the place of Demorest's resentment and indignation. There had been a cowardly attempt to rob them of their miserable treasure. He had met it and frustrated it in almost as brutal a fashion: the gold was already tarnished with blood. To his surprise, yet relief, he found his partners unconscious of the outrage, still sleeping with the physical immobility of over-excited and tired men. Should he awaken them? No! He should have to awaken also their suspicions and desire for revenge. There was no danger of a further attack; there was no fear that the culprit would disclose himself, and to-morrow they would be far away. Let oblivion rest upon that night's stain on the honor of Heavy Tree Hill.

He rolled a small barrel before the opening, smoothed the dislodged earth, replaced the pan with its treasure, and trusted that in the bustle of the early morning departure his partners might not notice any change. Stopping before the bunk of Stacy he glanced at the sleeping man. He was lying on his back, but breathing heavily, and his hands were moving towards his chest as if, indeed, his strange fancy of the golden incubus were being realized. Demorest would have wakened him, but presently, with a sigh of relief, the sleeper turned over on his side. It was pleasanter to look at Barker, whose damp curls were matted over his smooth, boyish forehead, and whose lips were parted in a smile under the silken wings of his brown mustache. He, too, seemed to be trying to speak, and remembering some previous revelations which had amused them, Demorest leaned over him fraternally with an answering smile, waiting for the beloved one's name to pass the young man's lips. But he only murmured, "Three—hundred—thousand dollars!" The elder man turned away with a grave face. The influence of the treasure was paramount.

When he had placed one of the chairs against the unprotected door at an angle which would prevent any easy or noiseless intrusion, Demorest threw himself on his bunk without undressing, and turned his face towards the single window of the cabin that looked towards the east. He did not apprehend another covert attempt against the gold. He did not fear a robbery with force and arms, although he was satisfied that there was more than one concerned in it, but this he attributed only to the encumbering weight of their expected booty. He simply waited for the dawn. It was some time before his eyes were greeted with the vague opaline brightness of the firmament which meant the vanishing of the pallid snow-line before the coming day. A bird twittered on the roof. The air was chill; he drew his blanket around him. Then he closed his eyes, he fancied only for a moment, but when he opened them the door was standing open in the strong daylight. He sprang to his feet, but the next moment he saw it was only Stacy who had passed out, and was returning fully dressed, bringing water from the spring to fill the kettle. But Stacy's face was so grave that, recalling his disturbed sleep, Demorest laughingly inquired if he had been haunted by the treasure. But to his surprise Stacy put down the kettle, and, with a hurried glance at the still sleeping Barker, said in a low voice:—

"I want you to do something for me without asking why. Later I will tell you."

Demorest looked at him fixedly. "What is it?" he said.

"The pack-mules will be here in a few moments. Don't wait to close up or put away anything here, but clap that gold in the saddle-bags, and take Barker with you and 'lite' out for Boomville AT ONCE. I will overtake you later."

"Is there no time to discuss this?" asked Demorest.

"No," said Stacy bluntly. "Call me a crank, say I'm in a blue funk"—his compressed lips and sharp black eyes did not lend themselves much to that hypothesis—"only get out of this with that stuff, and take Barker with you! I'm not responsible for myself while it's here."

Demorest knew Stacy to be combative, but practical. If he had not been assured of his partner's last night slumbers he might have thought he knew of the attempt. Or if he had discovered the turned-up ground in the rear of the cabin his curiosity would have demanded an explanation. Demorest paused only for a moment, and said, "Very well, I will go."

Bret Harte

"Good! I'll rouse out Barker, but not a word to him—except that he must go."

The rousing out of Barker consisted of Stacy's lifting that young gentleman bodily from his bunk and standing him upright in the open doorway. But Barker was accustomed to this Spartan process, and after a moment's balancing with closed lids like an unwrapped mummy, he sat down in the doorway and began to dress. He at first demurred to their departure except all together—it was so unfraternal; but eventually he allowed himself to be persuaded out of it and into his clothes. For Barker had also had HIS visions in the night, one of which was that they should build a beautiful villa on the site of the old cabin and solemnly agree to come every year and pass a week in it together. "I thought at first," he said, sliding along the floor in search of different articles of his dress, or stopping gravely to catch them as they were thrown to him by his partners, "that we'd have it at Boomville, as being handier to get there; but I've concluded we'd better have it here, a little higher up the hill, where it could be seen over the whole Black Spur Range. When we weren't here we could use it as a Hut of Refuge for broken-down or washed-out miners or weary travelers, like those hospices in the Alps, you know, and have somebody to keep it for us. You see I've thought even of THAT, and Van Loo is the very man to take charge of it for us. You see he's got such good manners and speaks two languages. Lord! if a German or Frenchman came along, poor and distressed, Van Loo would just chip in his own language. See? You've got to think of all these details, you see, boys. And we might call it 'The Rest of the Three Partners,' or 'Three Partners' Rest.'"

"And you might begin by giving us one," said Stacy. "Dry up and drink your coffee."

"I'll draw out the plans. I've got it all in my head," continued the enthusiastic Barker, unheeding the interruption. "I'll just run out and take a look at the site, it's only right back of the cabin." But here Stacy caught him by his dangling belt as he was flying out of the door with one boot on, and thrust him down in a chair with a tin cup of coffee in his hand.

"Keep the plans in your head, Barker boy," said Demorest, "for here are the pack mules and packer." This was quite enough to divert the impressionable young man, who speedily finished his dressing, as a mule bearing a large pack-saddle and two enormous saddle-bags or pouches drove up before the door, led by a muleteer on a small horse. The transfer of the treasure to the saddle-bags was quickly made by their united efforts, as the first rays of the sun were beginning to paint the hillside. Shading his keen eyes with his hand, Stacy stood in the doorway and handed Demorest the two rifles. Demorest hesitated. "Hadn't YOU better keep one?" he said, looking in his partner's eyes with his first challenge of curiosity. The sun seemed to put a humorous twinkle into Stacy's glance as he returned, "Not much! And you'd better take my revolver with you, too. I'm feeling a little better now," he said, looking at the saddlebags, "but I'm not fit to be trusted yet with carnal weapons. When the other mule comes and is packed I'll overtake you on the horse."

A little more satisfied, although still wondering and perplexed, Demorest shouldered one rifle, and with Barker, who was carrying the other, followed the muleteer and his equipage down the trail. For a while he was a little ashamed of his part in this unusual spectacle of two armed men convoying a laden mule in broad daylight, but, luckily, it was too early for the Bar miners to be going to work, and as the tunnelmen were now at breakfast the trail was free of wayfarers. At the point where it crossed the main road Demorest, however, saw Steptoe and Whiskey Dick emerge from the thicket, apparently in earnest conversation.

Demorest felt his repugnance and half-restrained suspicions suddenly return. Yet he did not wish to betray them before Barker, nor was he willing, in case of an emergency, to allow the young man to be entirely unprepared. Calling him to follow, he ran quickly ahead of the laden mule, and was relieved to find that, looking back, his companion had brought his rifle to a "ready," through some instinctive feeling of defense. As Steptoe and Whiskey Dick, a moment later discovering them, were evidently surprised, there seemed, however, to be no reason for fearing an outbreak. Suddenly, at a whisper from Steptoe, he and Whiskey Dick both threw up their hands, and stood still on the trail a few yards from them in a burlesque of the usual recognized attitude of helplessness, while a hoarse laugh broke from Steptoe.

"D—d if we didn't think you were road-agents! But we see you're only guarding your treasure. Rather fancy style for Heavy Tree Hill, ain't it? Things must be gettin' rough up thar to hev to take out your guns like that!"

Demorest had looked keenly at the four hands thus exhibited, and was more concerned that they bore no trace of wounds or mutilation than at the insult of the speech, particularly as he had a distinct impression that the action was intended to show him the futility of his suspicions.

"I am glad to see that if you haven't any arms in your hands you're not incapable of handling them," said Demorest coolly, as he passed by them and again fell into the rear of the muleteer.

But Barker had thought the incident very funny, and laughed effusively at Whiskey Dick. "I didn't know that Steptoe was up to that kind of fun," he said, "and I suppose we DID look rather rough with these guns as we ran on ahead of the mule.

But then you know that when you called to me I really thought you were in for a shindy. All the same, Whiskey Dick did that 'hands up' to perfection: how he managed it I don't know, but his knees seemed to knock together as if he was in a real funk."

Demorest had thought so too, but he made no reply. How far that miserable drunkard was a forced or willing accomplice of the events of last night was part of a question that had become more and more repugnant to him as he was leaving the scene of it forever. It had come upon him, desecrating the dream he had dreamt that last night and turning its hopeful climax to bitterness. Small wonder that Barker, walking by his side, had his quick sympathies aroused, and as he saw that shadow, which they were all familiar with, but had never sought to penetrate, fall upon his companion's handsome face, even his youthful spirits yielded to it. They were both relieved when the clatter of hoofs behind them, as they reached the valley, announced the approach of Stacy. "I started with the second mule and the last load soon after you left," he explained, "and have just passed them. I thought it better to join you and let the other load follow. Nobody will interfere with THAT."

"Then you are satisfied?" said Demorest, regarding him steadfastly.

"You bet! Look!"

He turned in his saddle and pointed to the crest of the hill they had just descended. Above the pines circling the lower slope above the bare ledges of rock and outcrop, a column of thick black smoke was rising straight as a spire in the windless air.

"That's the old shanty passing away," said Stacy complacently.

"I reckon there won't be much left of it before we get to Boomville."

Demorest and Barker stared. "You fired it?" said Barker, trembling with excitement.

"Yes," said Stacy. "I couldn't bear to leave the old rookery for coyotes and wild-cats to gather in, so I touched her off before I left."

"But"—said Barker.

"But," repeated Stacy composedly. "Hallo! what's the matter with that new plan of 'The Rest' that you're going to build, eh? You don't want them BOTH."

"And you did this rather than leave the dear old cabin to strangers?" said Barker, with kindling eyes. "Stacy, I didn't think you had that poetry in you!"

"There's heaps in me, Barker boy, that you don't know, and I don't exactly sabe myself."

"Only," continued the young fellow eagerly, "we ought to have ALL been there! We ought to have made a solemn rite of it, you know,—a kind of sacrifice. We ought to have poured a kind of libation on the ground!"

"I did sprinkle a little kerosene over it, I think," returned Stacy, "just to help things along. But if you want to see her flaming, Barker, you just run back to that last corner on the road beyond the big red wood. That's the spot for a view."

As Barker—always devoted to a spectacle—swiftly disappeared the two men faced each other. "Well, what does it all mean?" said Demorest gravely.

"It means, old man," said Stacy suddenly, "that if we hadn't had nigger luck, the same blind luck that sent us that strike, you and I and that Barker over there would have been swirling in that smoke up to the sky about two hours ago!" He stopped and added in a lower, but earnest voice, "Look here, Phil! When I went out to fetch water this morning I smelt something queer. I went round to the back of the cabin and found a hole dug under the floor, and piled against the corner wall a lot of brush-wood and a can of kerosene. Some of the kerosene had been already poured on the brush. Everything was ready to light, and only my coming out an hour earlier had frightened the devils away. The idea was to set the place on fire, suffocate us in the smoke of the kerosene poured into the hole, and then to rush in and grab the treasure. It was a systematic plan!"

"No!" said Demorest quietly.

"No?" repeated Stacy. "I told you I saw the whole thing and took away the kerosene, which I hid, and after you had gone used it to fire the cabin with, to see if the ones I suspected would gather to watch their work."

"It was no part of their FIRST plan'" said Demorest, "which was only robbery. Listen!" He hurriedly recounted his experience of the preceding night to the astonished Stacy. "No, the fire was an afterthought and revenge," he added sternly.

"But you say you cut the robber in the hand; there would be no difficulty in identifying him by that."

"I wounded only a HAND," said Demorest. "But there was a HEAD in that attempt that I never saw." He then revealed his own half-suspicions, but how they were apparently refuted by the bravado of Steptoe and Whiskey Dick.

Bret Harte

"Then that was the reason THEY didn't gather at the fire," said Stacy quickly.

"Ah!" said Demorest, "then YOU too suspected them?"

Stacy hesitated, and then said abruptly, "Yes."

Demorest was silent for a moment.

"Why didn't you tell me this this morning?" he said gently.

Stacy pointed to the distant Barker. "I didn't want you to tell him. I thought it better for one partner to keep a secret from two than for the two to keep it from one. Why didn't you tell me of your experience last night?"

"I am afraid it was for the same reason," said Demorest, with a faint smile. "And it sometimes seems to me, Jim, that we ought to imitate Barker's frankness. In our dread of tainting him with our own knowledge of evil we are sending him out into the world very poorly equipped, for all his three hundred thousand dollars."

"I reckon you're right," said Stacy briefly, extending his hand. "Shake on that!"

The two men grasped each other's hands.

"And he's no fool, either," continued Demorest. "When we met Steptoe on the road, without a word from me, he closed up alongside, with his hand on the lock of his rifle. And I hadn't the heart to praise him or laugh it off."

Nevertheless they were both silent as the object of their criticism bounded down the trail towards them. He had seen the funeral pyre. It was awfully sad, it was awfully lovely, but there was something grand in it! Who could have thought Stacy could be so poetic? But he wanted to tell them something else that was mighty pretty.

"What was it?" said Demorest.

"Well," said Barker, "don't laugh! But you know that Jack Hamlin? Well, boys, he's been hovering around us on his mustang, keeping us and that pack-mule in sight ever since we left. Sometimes he's on a side trail off to the right, sometimes off to the left, but always at the same distance. I didn't like to tell you, boys, for I thought you'd laugh at me; but I think, you know, he's taken a sort of shine to us since he dropped in last night. And I fancy, you see, he's sort of hanging round to see that we get along all right. I'd have pointed him out before only I reckoned you and Stacy would say he was making up to us for our money."

"And we'd have been wrong, Barker boy," said Stacy, with a heartiness that surprised Demorest, "for I reckon your instinct's the right one."

"There he is now," said the gratified Barker, "just abreast of us on the cut-off. He started just after we did, and he's got a horse that could have brought him into Boomville hours ago. It's just his kindness."

He pointed to a distant fringe of buckeye from which Jack Hamlin had just emerged. Although evidently holding in a powerful mustang, nothing could be more unconscious and utterly indifferent than his attitude. He did not seem to know of the proximity of any other traveler, and to care less. His handsome head was slightly thrown back, as if he was caroling after his usual fashion, but the distance was too great to make his melody audible to them, or to allow Barker's shout of invitation to reach him. Suddenly he lowered his tightened rein, the mustang sprang forward, and with a flash of silver spurs and bridle fripperies he had disappeared. But as the trail he was pursuing crossed theirs a mile beyond, it seemed quite possible that they should again meet him.

They were now fairly into the Boomville valley, and were entering a narrow arroyo bordered with dusky willows which effectually excluded the view on either side. It was the bed of a mountain torrent that in winter descended the hillside over the trail by which they had just come, but was now sunk into the thirsty plain between banks that varied from two to five feet in height. The muleteer had advanced into the narrow channel when he suddenly cast a hurried glance behind him, uttered a "Madre de Dios!" and backed his mule and his precious freight against the bank. The sound of hoofs on the trail in their rear had caught his quicker ear, and as the three partners turned they beheld three horsemen thundering down the hill towards them. They were apparently Mexican vaqueros of the usual common swarthy type, their faces made still darker by the black silk handkerchief tied round their heads under their stiff sombreros. Either they were unable or unwilling to restrain their horses in their headlong speed, and a collision in that narrow passage was imminent, but suddenly, before reaching its entrance, they diverged with a volley of oaths, and dashing along the left bank of the arroyo, disappeared in the intervening willows. Divided between relief at their escape and indignation at what seemed to be a drunken, feast-day freak of these roystering vaqueros, the little party re-formed, when a cry from Barker arrested them. He had just perceived a horseman motionless in the arroyo who, although unnoticed by them, had evidently been seen by the Mexicans. He had apparently leaped into it from the bank, and had halted as if to witness this singular incident. As the clatter of the vaqueros' hoofs died away he lightly leaped the bank again and disappeared. But in that single glimpse of him they recognized Jack Hamlin. When they reached the spot where he had halted, they could see that he must have approached it from the trail where they had previously seen him, but which they now found crossed it at right angles. Barker was right. He had really kept them at easy distance the whole length of the journey.

But they were now reaching its end. When they issued at last from the arroyo they came upon the outskirts of Boomville and the great stage-road. Indeed, the six horses of the Pioneer coach were just panting along the last half mile of the steep upgrade as they approached. They halted mechanically as the heavy vehicle swayed and creaked by them. In their ordinary working dress, sunburnt with exposure, covered with dust, and carrying their rifles still in their hands, they, perhaps, presented a sufficiently characteristic appearance to draw a few faces—some of them pretty and intelligent—to the windows of the coach as it passed. The sensitive Barker was quickest to feel that resentment with which the Pioneer usually met the wide-eyed criticism of the Eastern tourist or "greenhorn," and reddened under the bold scrutiny of a pair of black inquisitive eyes behind an eyeglass. That annoyance was communicated, though in a lesser degree, even to the bearded Demorest and Stacy. It was an unexpected contact with that great world in which they were so soon to enter. They felt ashamed of their appearance, and yet ashamed of that feeling. They felt a secret satisfaction when Barker said, "They'd open their eyes wider if they knew what was in that pack-saddle," and yet they corrected him for what they were pleased to call his "snobbishness." They hurried a little faster as the road became more frequented, as if eager to shorten their distance to clean clothes and civilization.

Only Demorest began to linger in the rear. This contact with the stagecoach had again brought him face to face with his buried past. He felt his old dream revive, and occasionally turned to look back upon the dark outlines of Black Spur, under whose shadow it had returned so often, and wondered if he had left it there forever, and it were now slowly exhaling with the thinned and dying smoke of their burning cabin.

His companions, knowing his silent moods, had preceded him at some distance, when he heard the soft sound of ambling hoofs on the thick dust, and suddenly the light touch of Jack Hamlin's gauntlet on his shoulder. The mustang Jack bestrode was reeking with grime and sweat, but Jack himself was as immaculate and fresh as ever. With a delightful affectation of embarrassment and timidity he began flicking the side buttons of his velvet vaquero trousers with the thong of his riata. "I reckoned to sling a word along with you before you went," he said, looking down, "but I'm so shy that I couldn't do it in company. So I thought I'd get it off on you while you were alone."

"We've seen you once or twice before, this morning," said Demorest pleasantly, "and we were sorry you didn't join us."

"I reckon I might have," said Jack gayly, "if my horse had only made up his mind whether he was a bird or a squirrel, and hadn't been so various and promiscuous about whether he wanted to climb a tree or fly. He's not a bad horse for a Mexican plug, only when he thinks there is any devilment around he wants to wade in and take a hand. However, I reckoned to see the last of you and your pile into Boomville. And I DID. When I meet three fellows like you that are clean white all through I sort of cotton to 'em, even if I'M a little of a brunette myself. And I've got something to give you."

He took from a fold of his scarlet sash a small parcel neatly folded in white paper as fresh and spotless as himself.

Holding it in his fingers, he went on: "I happened to be at Heavy Tree Hill early this morning before sun-up. In the darkness I struck your cabin, and I reckon—I struck somebody else! At first I thought it was one of you chaps down on your knees praying at the rear of the cabin, but the way the fellow lit out when he smelt me coming made me think it wasn't entirely fasting and prayer. However, I went to the rear of the cabin, and then I reckoned some kind friend had been bringing you kindlings and firewood for your early breakfast. But that didn't satisfy me, so I knelt down as he had knelt, and then I saw—well, Mr. Demorest, I reckon I saw JUST WHAT YOU HAVE SEEN! But even then I wasn't quite satisfied, for that man had been grubbing round as if searching for something. So I searched too—and I found IT. I've got it here. I'm going to give it to you, for it may some day come in handy, and you won't find anything like it among the folks where you're going. It's something unique, as those fine-art-collecting sharps in 'Frisco say— something quite matchless, unless you try to match it one day yourself! Don't open the paper until I run on and say 'So long' to your partners. Good-by."

He grasped Demorest's hand and then dropped the little packet into his palm, and ambled away towards Stacy and Barker. Holding the packet in his hand with an amused yet puzzled smile, Demorest watched the gambler give Stacy's hand a hearty farewell shake and a supplementary slap on the back to the delighted Barker, and then vanish in a flash of red sash and silver buttons. At which Demorest, walking slowly towards his partners, opened the packet, and stood suddenly still. It contained the dried and bloodless second finger of a human hand cut off at the first joint!

For an instant he held it at arm's length, as if about to cast it away. Then he grimly replaced it in the paper, put it carefully in his pocket, and silently walked after his companions.

CHAPTER I

A strong southwester was beating against the windows and doors of Stacy's Bank in San Francisco, and spreading a film of rain between the regular splendors of its mahogany counters and sprucely dressed clerks and the usual passing pedestrian. For Stacy's new banking-house had long since received the epithet of "palatial" from an enthusiastic local press fresh from the "opening" luncheon in its richly decorated directors' rooms, and it was said that once a homely would-be depositor from One Horse Gulch was so cowed by its magnificence that his heart failed him at the last moment, and mumbling an apology to the elegant receiving teller, fled with his greasy chamois pouch of gold-dust to deposit his treasure in the dingy Mint around the corner. Perhaps there was something of this feeling, mingled with a certain simple-minded fascination, in the hesitation of a stranger of a higher class who entered the bank that rainy morning and finally tendered his card to the important negro messenger.

The card preceded him through noiselessly swinging doors and across heavily carpeted passages until it reached the inner core of Mr. James Stacy's private offices, and was respectfully laid before him. He was not alone. At his side, in an attitude of polite and studied expectancy, stood a correct-looking young man, for whom Mr. Stacy was evidently writing a memorandum. The stranger glanced furtively at the card with a curiosity hardly in keeping with his suggested good breeding; but Stacy did not look at it until he had finished his memorandum.

"There," he said, with business decision, "you can tell your people that if we carry their new debentures over our limit we will expect a larger margin. Ditches are not what they were three years ago when miners were willing to waste their money over your rates. They don't gamble THAT WAY any more, and your company ought to know it, and not gamble themselves over that prospect." He handed the paper to the stranger, who bowed over it with studied politeness, and backed towards the door. Stacy took up the waiting card, read it, said to the messenger, "Show him in," and in the same breath turned to his guest: "I say, Van Loo, it's George Barker! You know him."

"Yes," said Van Loo, with a polite hesitation as he halted at the door. "He was—I think—er—in your employ at Heavy Tree Hill."

"Nonsense! He was my partner. And you must have known him since at Boomville. Come! He got forty shares of Ditch stock—through you—at 110, which were worth about 80! SOMEBODY must have made money enough by it to remember him."

"I was only speaking of him socially," said Van Loo, with a deprecating smile. "You know he married a young woman—the hotel-keeper's daughter, who used to wait at the table—and after my mother and sister came out to keep house for me at Boomville it was quite impossible for me to see much of him, for he seldom went out without his wife, you know."

"Yes," said Stacy dryly, "I think you didn't like his marriage.

But I'm glad your disinclination to see him isn't on account of that deal in stocks."

"Oh no," said Van Loo. "Good-by."

But, unfortunately, in the next passage he came upon Barker, who with a cry of unfeigned pleasure, none the less sincere that he was feeling a little alien in these impressive surroundings, recognized him. Nothing could exceed Van Loo's protest of delight at the meeting; nothing his equal desolation at the fact that he was hastening to another engagement. "But your old partner," he added, with a smile, "is waiting for you; he has just received your card, and I should be only keeping you from him. So glad to see you; you're looking so well. Good-by! Good-by!"

Reassured, Barker no longer hesitated, but dashed with his old impetuousness into his former partner's room. Stacy, already deeply absorbed in other business, was sitting with his back towards him, and Barker's arms were actually encircling his neck before the astonished and half-angry man looked up. But when his eyes met the laughing gray ones of Barker above him he gently disengaged himself with a quick return of the caress, rose, shut the door of an inner office, and returning pushed Barker into an armchair in quite the old suppressive fashion of former days. Yes; it was the same Stacy that Barker looked at, albeit his brown beard was now closely cropped around his determined mouth and jaw in a kind of grave decorum, and his energetic limbs already attuned to the rigor of clothes of fashionable cut and still more rigorous sombreness of color.

"Barker boy," he began, with the familiar twinkle in his keen eyes which the younger partner remembered, "I don't encourage stag dancing among my young men during bank hours, and you'll please to remember that we are not on

Heavy Tree Hill"—

"Where," broke in Barker enthusiastically, "we were only overlooked by the Black Spur Range and the Sierran snowline; where the nearest voice that came to you was quarter of a mile away as the crow flies and nearly a mile by the trail."

"And was generally an oath!" said Stacy. "But you're in San Francisco NOW. Where are you stopping?" He took up a pencil and held it over a memorandum pad awaitingly.

"At the Brook House. It's"—

"Hold on! 'Brook House,'" Stacy repeated as he jotted it down. "And for how long?"

"Oh, a day or two. You see, Kitty"—

Stacy checked him with a movement of his pencil in the air, and then wrote down, "'Day or two.' Wife with you?"

"Yes; and oh, Stacy, our boy! Ah!" he went on, with a laugh, knocking aside the remonstrating pencil, "you must listen! He's just the sweetest, knowingest little chap living. Do you know what we're going to christen him? Well, he'll be Stacy Demorest Barker. Good names, aren't they? And then it perpetuates the dear old friendship."

Stacy picked up the pencil again, wrote "Wife and child S. D. B.," and leaned back in his chair. "Now, Barker," he said briefly, "I'm coming to dine with you tonight at 7.30 sharp. THEN we'll talk Heavy Tree Hill, wife, baby, and S. D. B. But here I'm all for business. Have you any with me?"

Barker, who was easily amused, had extracted a certain entertainment out of Stacy's memorandum, but he straightened himself with a look of eager confidence and said, "Certainly; that's just what it is—business. Lord! Stacy, I'm ALL business now. I'm in everything. And I bank with you, though perhaps you don't know it; it's in your Branch at Marysville. I didn't want to say anything about it to you before. But Lord! you don't suppose that I'd bank anywhere else while you are in the business—checks, dividends, and all that; but in this matter I felt you knew, old chap. I didn't want to talk to a banker nor to a bank, but to Jim Stacy, my old partner."

"Barker," said Stacy curtly, "how much money are you short of?"

At this direct question Barker's always quick color rose, but, with an equally quick smile, he said, "I don't know yet that I'm short at all."

"But I do!"

"Look here, Jim: why, I'm just overloaded with shares and stocks," said Barker, smiling.

"Not one of which you could realize on without sacrifice. Barker, three years ago you had three hundred thousand dollars put to your account at San Francisco."

"Yes," said Barker, with a quiet reminiscent laugh. "I remember I wanted to draw it out in one check to see how it would look."

"And you've drawn out all in three years, and it looks d—d bad."

"How did you know it?" asked Barker, his face beaming only with admiration of his companion's omniscience.

"How did I know it?" retorted Stacy. "I know YOU, and I know the kind of people who have unloaded to you."

"Come, Stacy," said Barker, "I've only invested in shares and stocks like everybody else, and then only on the best advice I could get: like Van Loo's, for instance,—that man who was here just now, the new manager of the Empire Ditch Company; and Carter's, my own Kitty's father. And when I was offered fifty thousand Wide West Extensions, and was hesitating over it, he told me YOU were in it too—and that was enough for me to buy it."

"Yes, but we didn't go into it at his figures."

"No," said Barker, with an eager smile, "but you SOLD at his figures, for I knew that when I found that YOU, my old partner, was in it; don't you see, I preferred to buy it through your bank, and did at 110. Of course, you wouldn't have sold it at that figure if it wasn't worth it then, and neither I nor you are to blame if it dropped the next week to 60, don't you see?"

Stacy's eyes hardened for a moment as he looked keenly into his former partner's bright gray ones, but there was no trace of irony in Barker's. On the contrary, a slight shade of sadness came over them. "No," he said reflectively, "I don't think I've ever been foolish or followed out my OWN ideas, except once, and that was extravagant, I admit. That was my idea of building a kind of refuge, you know, on the site of our old cabin, where poor miners and played-out prospectors waiting for a strike could stay without paying anything. Well, I sunk twenty thousand dollars in that, and might have lost more, only Carter—Kitty's father—persuaded me—he's an awful clever old fellow—into turning it into a kind of branch hotel of Boomville, while using it as a hotel to take poor chaps who couldn't pay, at half prices, or quarter prices,

PRIVATELY, don't you see, so as to spare their pride,—awfully pretty, wasn't it?—and make the hotel profit by it."

"Well?" said Stacy as Barker paused.

"They didn't come," said Barker.

"But," he added eagerly, "it shows that things were better than I had imagined. Only the others did not come, either."

"And you lost your twenty thousand dollars," said Stacy curtly.

"FIFTY thousand," said Barker, "for of course it had to be a larger hotel than the other. And I think that Carter wouldn't have gone into it except to save me from losing money."

"And yet made you lose fifty thousand instead of twenty. For I don't suppose HE advanced anything."

"He gave his time and experience," said Barker simply.

"I don't think it worth thirty thousand dollars," said Stacy dryly. "But all this doesn't tell me what your business is with me to-day."

"No," said Barker, brightening up, "but it is business, you know. Something in the old style—as between partner and partner—and that's why I came to YOU, and not to the 'banker.' And it all comes out of something that Demorest once told us; so you see it's all us three again! Well, you know, of course, that the Excelsior Ditch Company have abandoned the Bar and Heavy Tree Hill. It didn't pay."

"Yes; nor does the company pay any dividends now. You ought to know, with fifty thousand of their stock on your hands."

Barker laughed. "But listen. I found that I could buy up their whole plant and all the ditching along the Black Spur Range for ten thousand dollars."

"And Great Scott! you don't think of taking up their business?" said Stacy, aghast.

Barker laughed more heartily. "No. Not their business. But I remember that once Demorest told us, in the dear old days, that it cost nearly as much to make a water ditch as a railroad, in the way of surveying and engineering and levels, you know. And here's the plant for a railroad. Don't you see?"

"But a railroad from Black Spur to Heavy Tree Hill—what's the good of that?"

"Why, Black Spur will be in the line of the new Divide Railroad they're trying to get a bill for in the legislature."

"An infamous piece of wildcat jobbing that will never pass," said Stacy decisively.

"They said BECAUSE it was that, it would pass," said Barker simply. "They say that Watson's Bank is in it, and is bound to get it through. And as that is a rival bank of yours, don't you see, I thought that if WE could get something real good or valuable out of it,—something that would do the Black Spur good,—it would be all right."

"And was your business to consult me about it?" said Stacy bluntly.

"No," said Barker, "it's too late to consult you now, though I wish I had. I've given my word to take it, and I can't back out. But I haven't the ten thousand dollars, and I came to you."

Stacy slowly settled himself back in his chair, and put both hands in his pockets. "Not a cent, Barker, not a cent."

"I'm not asking it of the BANK," said Barker, with a smile, "for I could have gone to the bank for it. But as this was something between us, I am asking you, Stacy, as my old partner."

"And I am answering you, Barker, as your old partner, but also as the partner of a hundred other men, who have even a greater right to ask me. And my answer is, not a cent!"

Barker looked at him with a pale, astonished face and slightly parted lips. Stacy rose, thrust his hands deeper in his pockets, and standing before him went on:—

"Now look here! It's time you should understand me and yourself. Three years ago, when our partnership was dissolved by accident, or mutual consent, we will say, we started afresh, each on our own hook. Through foolishness and bad advice you have in those three years hopelessly involved yourself as you never would have done had we been partners, and yet in your difficulty you ask me and my new partners to help you out of a difficulty in which they have no concern."

"Your NEW partners?" stammered Barker.

"Yes, my new partners; for every man who has a share, or a deposit, or an interest, or a dollar in this bank is my PARTNER—even you, with your securities at the Branch, are one; and you may say that in THIS I am protecting you against yourself."

"But you have money—you have private means."

"None to speculate with as you wish me to—on account of my position; none to give away foolishly as you expect me to—on account of precedent and example. I am a soulless machine taking care of capital intrusted to me and my brains, but decidedly NOT to my heart nor my sentiment. So my answer is, not a cent!"

Barker's face had changed; his color had come back, but with an older expression. Presently, however, his beaming smile returned, with the additional suggestion of an affectionate toleration which puzzled Stacy.

"I believe you're right, old chap," he said, extending his hand to the banker, "and I wish I had talked to you before. But it's too late now, and I've given my word."

"Your WORD!" said Stacy. "Have you no written agreement?"

"No. My word was accepted." He blushed slightly as if conscious of a great weakness.

"But that isn't legal nor business. And you couldn't even hold the Ditch Company to it if THEY chose to back out."

"But I don't think they will," said Barker simply. "And you see my word wasn't given entirely to THEM. I bought the thing through my wife's cousin, Henry Spring, a broker, and he makes something by it, from the company, on commission. And I can't go back on HIM. What did you say?"

Stacy had only groaned through his set teeth. "Nothing," he

said briefly, "except that I'm coming, as I said before, to dine with you to-night; but no more BUSINESS. I've enough of that with others, and there are some waiting for me in the outer office now."

Barker rose at once, but with the same affectionate smile and tender gravity of countenance, and laid his hand caressingly on Stacy's shoulder. "It's like you to give up so much of your time to me and my foolishness and be so frank with me. And I know it's mighty rough on you to have to be a mere machine instead of Jim Stacy. Don't you bother about me. I'll sell some of my Wide West Extension and pull the thing through myself. It's all right, but I'm sorry for you, old chap." He glanced around the room at the walls and rich paneling, and added, "I suppose that's what you have to pay for all this sort of thing?"

Before Stacy could reply, a waiting visitor was announced for the second time, and Barker, with another hand-shake and a reassuring smile to his old partner, passed into the hall, as if the onus of any infelicity in the interview was upon himself alone. But Stacy did not seem to be in a particularly accessible mood to the new caller, who in his turn appeared to be slightly irritated by having been kept waiting over some irksome business. "You don't seem to follow me," he said to Stacy after reciting his business perplexity. "Can't you suggest something?"

"Well, why don't you get hold of one of your board of directors?" said Stacy abstractedly. "There's Captain Drummond; you and he are old friends. You were comrades in the Mexican War, weren't you?"

"That be d—d!" said his visitor bitterly. "All his interests are the other way, and in a trade of this kind, you know, Stacy, that a man would sacrifice his own brother. Do you suppose that he'd let up on a sure thing that he's got just because he and I fought side by side at Cerro Gordo? Come! what are you giving us? You're the last man I ever expected to hear that kind of flapdoodle from. If it's because your bank has got some other interest and you can't advise me, why don't you say so?" Nevertheless, in spite of Stacy's abrupt disclaimer, he left a few minutes later, half convinced that Stacy's lukewarmness was due to some adverse influence. Other callers were almost as quickly disposed of, and at the end of an hour Stacy found himself again alone.

But not apparently in a very satisfied mood. After a few moments of purely mechanical memoranda-making, he rose abruptly and opened a small drawer in a cabinet, from which he took a letter still in its envelope. It bore a foreign postmark. Glancing over it hastily, his eyes at last became fixed on a concluding paragraph. "I hope," wrote his correspondent, "that even in the rush of your big business you will sometimes look after Barker. Not that I think the dear old chap will ever go wrong—indeed, I often wish I was as certain of myself as of him and his insight; but I am afraid we were more inclined to be merely amused and tolerant of his wonderful trust and simplicity than to really understand it for his own good and ours. I know you did not like his marriage, and were inclined to believe he was the victim of a rather unscrupulous father and a foolish, unequal girl; but are you satisfied that he would have been the happier without it, or lived his perfect life under other and what you may think wiser conditions? If he WROTE the poetry that he LIVES everybody would think him wonderful; for being what he is we never give him sufficient credit." Stacy smiled grimly, and penciled on his memorandum, "He wants it to the amount of ten thousand dollars." "Anyhow," continued the writer, "look after him, Jim, for his sake, your sake, and the sake of—PHIL DEMOREST."

Stacy put the letter back in its envelope, and tossing it grimly aside went on with his calculations. Presently he stopped, restored the letter to his cabinet, and rang a bell on his table. "Send Mr. North here," he said to the negro messenger. In a few moments his chief book-keeper appeared in the doorway.

"Turn to the Branch ledger and bring me a statement of Mr. George Barker's account."

"He was here a moment ago," said North, essaying a confidential look towards his chief.

"I know it," said Stacy coolly, without looking up.

"He's been running a good deal on wildcat lately," suggested North.

"I asked for his account, and not your opinion of it," said Stacy shortly.

The subordinate withdrew somewhat abashed but still curious, and returned presently with a ledger which he laid before his chief. Stacy ran his eyes over the list of Barker's securities; it seemed to him that all the wildest schemes of the past year stared him in the face. His finger, however, stopped on the Wide West Extension. "Mr. Barker will be wanting to sell some of this stock. What is it quoted at now?"

"Sixty."

"But I would prefer that Mr. Barker should not offer in the open market at present. Give him seventy for it—private sale; that will be ten thousand dollars paid to his credit. Advise the Branch of this at once, and to keep the transaction quiet."

"Yes, sir," responded the clerk as he moved towards the door. But he hesitated, and with another essay at confidence said insinuatingly, "I always thought, sir, that Wide West would recover."

Stacy, perhaps not displeased to find what had evidently passed in his subordinate's mind, looked at him and said dryly, "Then I would advise you also to keep that opinion to yourself." But, clever as he was, he had not anticipated the result. Mr. North, though a trusted employee, was human. On arriving in the outer office he beckoned to one of the lounging brokers, and in a low voice said, "I'll take two shares of Wide West, if you can get it cheap."

The broker's face became alert and eager. "Yes, but I say, is anything up?"

"I'm not here to give the business of the bank away," retorted North severely; "take the order or leave it."

The man hurried away. Having thus vindicated his humanity by also passing the snub he had received from Stacy to an inferior, he turned away to carry out his master's instructions, yet secure in the belief that he had profited by his superior discernment of the real reason of that master's singular conduct. But when he returned to the private room, in hopes of further revelations, Mr. Stacy was closeted with another financial magnate, and had apparently divested his mind of the whole affair.

CHAPTER II

When George Barker returned to the outer ward of the financial stronghold he had penetrated, with its curving sweep of counters, brass railings, and wirework screens defended by the spruce clerks behind them, he was again impressed with the position of the man he had just quitted, and for a moment hesitated, with an inclination to go back. It was with no idea of making a further appeal to his old comrade, but—what would have been odd in any other nature but his—he was affected by a sense that HE might have been unfair and selfish in his manner to the man panoplied by these defenses, and who was in a measure forced to be a part of them. He would like to have returned and condoled with him. The clerks, who were heartlessly familiar with the anxious bearing of the men who sought interviews with their chief, both before and after, smiled with the whispered conviction that the fresh and ingenuous young stranger had been "chucked" like others until they met his kindly, tolerant, and even superior eyes, and were puzzled. Meanwhile Barker, who had that sublime, natural quality of abstraction over small impertinences which is more exasperating than studied indifference, after his brief hesitation passed out unconcernedly through the swinging mahogany doors into the blowy street. Here the wind and rain revived him; the bank and its curt refusal were forgotten; he walked onward with only a smiling memory of his partner as in the old days. He remembered how Stacy had burned down their old cabin rather than have it fall into sordid or unworthy hands—this Stacy who was now condemned to sink his impulses and become a mere machine. He had never known Stacy's real motive for that act,—both Demorest and Stacy had kept their knowledge of the attempted robbery from their younger partner,—it always seemed to him to be a precious revelation of Stacy's inner nature. Facing the wind and rain, he recalled how Stacy, though never so enthusiastic about his marriage as Demorest, had taken up Van Loo sharply for some foolish sneer about his own youthfulness. He was affectionately tolerant of even Stacy's dislike to his wife's relations, for Stacy did not know them as he did. Indeed, Barker, whose own father and mother had died in his infancy, had accepted his wife's relations with a loving trust and confidence that was supreme, from the fact that he had never known any other.

At last he reached his hotel. It was a new one, the latest creation of a feverish progress in hotel-building which had covered five years and as many squares with large showy erections, utterly beyond the needs of the community, yet each superior in size and adornment to its predecessor. It struck him as being the one evidence of an abiding faith in the future of the metropolis that he had seen in nothing else. As he entered its frescoed hall that afternoon he was suddenly reminded, by its challenging opulency, of the bank he had just quitted, without knowing that the bank had really furnished its capital and its original design. The gilded bar-rooms, flashing with mirrors and cut glass; the saloons, with their desert expanse of Turkey carpet and oasis of clustered divans and gilded tables; the great dining-room, with porphyry columns, and walls and ceilings shining with allegory—all these things which had attracted his youthful wonder without distracting his correct simplicity of taste he now began to comprehend. It was the bank's money "at work." In the clatter of dishes in the dining-room he even seemed to hear again the chinking of coin.

It was a short cut to his apartments to pass through a smaller public sitting-room popularly known as "Flirtation Camp," where eight or ten couples generally found refuge on chairs and settees by the windows, half concealed by heavy curtains. But the occupants were by no means youthful spinsters or bachelors; they were generally married women, guests of the hotel, receiving other people's husbands whose wives were "in the States," or responsible middle-aged leaders of the town. In the elaborate toilettes of the women, as compared with the less formal business suits of the men, there was an odd mingling of the social attitude with perhaps more mysterious confidences. The idle gossip about them had never affected Barker; rather he had that innate respect for the secrets of others which is as inseparable from simplicity as it is from high breeding, and he scarcely glanced at the different couples in his progress through the room. He did not even notice a rather striking and handsome woman, who, surrounded by two or three admirers, yet looked up at Barker as he passed with self-conscious lids as if seeking a return of her glance. But he moved on abstractedly, and only stopped when he suddenly saw the familiar skirt of his wife at a further window, and halted before it.

"Oh, it's YOU," said Mrs. Barker, with a half-nervous, half-impatient laugh. "Why, I thought you'd certainly stay half the afternoon with your old partner, considering that you haven't met for three years."

There was no doubt she HAD thought so; there was equally no doubt that the conversation she was carrying on with her companion—a good-looking, portly business man—was effectually interrupted. But Barker did not notice it. "Captain

Heath, my husband," she went on, carelessly rising and smoothing her skirts. The captain, who had risen too, bowed vaguely at the introduction, but Barker extended his hand frankly. "I found Stacy busy," he said in answer to his wife, "but he is coming to dine with us to-night."

"If you mean Jim Stacy, the banker," said Captain Heath, brightening into greater ease, "he's the busiest man in California. I've seen men standing in a queue outside his door as in the old days at the post-office. And he only gives you five minutes and no extension. So you and he were partners once?" he said, looking curiously at the still youthful Barker.

But it was Mrs. Barker who answered, "Oh yes! and always such good friends. I was awfully jealous of him." Nevertheless, she did not respond to the affectionate protest in Barker's eyes nor to the laugh of Captain Heath, but glanced indifferently around the room as if to leave further conversation to the two men. It was possible that she was beginning to feel that Captain Heath was as de trop now as her husband had been a moment before. Standing there, however, between them both, idly tracing a pattern on the carpet with the toe of her slipper, she looked prettier than she had ever looked as Kitty Carter. Her slight figure was more fully developed. That artificial severity covering a natural virgin coyness with which she used to wait at table in her father's hotel at Boomville had gone, and was replaced by a satisfied consciousness of her power to please. Her glance was freer, but not as frank as in those days. Her dress was undoubtedly richer and more stylish; yet Barker's loyal heart often reverted fondly to the chintz gown, coquettishly frilled apron, and spotless cuffs and collar in which she had handed him his coffee with a faint color that left his own face crimson.

Captain Heath's tact being equal to her indifference, he had excused himself, although he was becoming interested in this youthful husband. But Mrs. Barker, after having asserted her husband's distinction as the equal friend of the millionaire, was by no means willing that the captain should be further interested in Barker for himself alone, and did not urge him to stay. As he departed she turned to her husband, and, indicating the group he had passed the moment before, said:—

"That horrid woman has been staring at us all the time. I don't see what you see in her to admire."

Poor Barker's admiration had been limited to a few words of civility in the enforced contact of that huge caravansary and in his quiet, youthful recognition of her striking personality. But he was just then too preoccupied with his interview with Stacy to reply, and perhaps he did not quite understand his wife. It was odd how many things he did not quite understand now about Kitty, but that he knew must be HIS fault. But Mrs. Barker apparently did not require, after the fashion of her sex, a reply. For the next moment, as they moved towards their rooms, she said impatiently, "Well, you don't tell what Stacy said. Did you get the money?"

I grieve to say that this soul of truth and frankness lied—only to his wife. Perhaps he considered it only lying to HIMSELF, a thing of which he was at times miserably conscious. "It wasn't necessary, dear," he said; "he advised me to sell my securities in the bank; and if you only knew how dreadfully busy he is."

Mrs. Barker curled her pretty lip. "It doesn't take very long to lend ten thousand dollars!" she said. "But that's what I always tell you. You have about made me sick by singing the praises of those wonderful partners of yours, and here you ask a favor of one of them and he tells you to sell your securities! And you know, and he knows, they're worth next to nothing."

"You don't understand, dear"—began Barker.

"I understand that you've given your word to poor Harry," said Mrs. Barker in pretty indignation, "who's responsible for the Ditch purchase."

"And I shall keep it. I always do," said Barker very quietly, but with that same singular expression of face that had puzzled Stacy. But Mrs. Barker, who, perhaps, knew her husband better, said in an altered voice:—

"But HOW can you, dear?"

"If I'm short a thousand or two I'll ask your father."

Mrs. Barker was silent. "Father's so very much harried now, George. Why don't you simply throw the whole thing up?"

"But I've given my word to your cousin Henry."

"Yes, but only your WORD. There was no written agreement. And you couldn't even hold him to it."

Barker opened his frank eyes in astonishment. Her own cousin, too! And they were Stacy's very words!

"Besides," added Mrs. Barker audaciously, "he could get rid of it elsewhere. He had another offer, but he thought yours the best. So don't be silly."

By this time they had reached their rooms. Barker, apparently dismissing the subject from his mind with characteristic buoyancy, turned into the bedroom and walked smilingly towards a small crib which stood in the corner. "Why, he's gone!" he said in some dismay.

"Well," said Mrs. Barker a little impatiently, "you didn't expect me to take him into the public parlor, where I was seeing visitors, did you? I sent him out with the nurse into the lower hall to play with the other children."

A shade momentarily passed over Barker's face. He always looked forward to meeting the child when he came back. He had a belief, based on no grounds whatever, that the little creature understood him. And he had a father's doubt of the wholesomeness of other people's children who were born into the world indiscriminately and not under the exceptional conditions of his own. "I'll go and fetch him," he said.

"You haven't told me anything about your interview; what you did and what your good friend Stacy said," said Mrs. Barker, dropping languidly into a chair. "And really if you are simply running away again after that child, I might just as well have asked Captain Heath to stay longer."

"Oh, as to Stacy," said Barker, dropping beside her and taking her hand; "well, dear, he was awfully busy, you know, and shut up in the innermost office like the agate in one of the Japanese nests of boxes. But," he continued, brightening up, "just the same dear old Jim Stacy of Heavy Tree Hill, when I first knew you. Lord! dear, how it all came back to me! That day I proposed to you in the belief that I was unexpectedly rich and even bought a claim for the boys on the strength of it, and how I came back to them to find that they had made a big strike on the very claim. Lord! I remember how I was so afraid to tell them about you—and how they guessed it—that dear old Stacy one of the first."

"Yes," said Mrs. Barker, "and I hope your friend Stacy remembered that but for ME, when you found out that you were not rich, you'd have given up the claim, but that I really deceived my own father to make you keep it. I've often worried over that, George," she said pensively, turning a diamond bracelet around her pretty wrist, "although I never said anything about it."

"But, Kitty darling," said Barker, grasping his wife's hand, "I gave my note for it; you know you said that was bargain enough, and I had better wait until the note was due, and until I found I couldn't pay, before I gave up the claim. It was very clever of you, and the boys all said so, too. But you never deceived your father, dear," he said, looking at her gravely, "for I should have told him everything."

"Of course, if you look at it in that way," said his wife languidly, "it's nothing; only I think it ought to be remembered when people go about saying papa ruined you with his hotel schemes."

"Who dares say that?" said Barker indignantly.

"Well, if they don't SAY it they look it," said Mrs. Barker, with a toss of her pretty head, "and I believe that's at the bottom of Stacy's refusal."

"But he never said a word, Kitty," said Barker, flushing.

"There, don't excite yourself, George," said Mrs. Barker resignedly, "but go for the baby. I know you're dying to go, and I suppose it's time Norah brought it upstairs."

At any other time Barker would have lingered with explanations, but just then a deeper sense than usual of some misunderstanding made him anxious to shorten this domestic colloquy. He rose, pressed his wife's hand, and went out. But yet he was not entirely satisfied with himself for leaving her. "I suppose it isn't right my going off as soon as I come in," he murmured reproachfully to himself, "but I think she wants the baby back as much as I; only, womanlike, she didn't care to let me know it."

He reached the lower hall, which he knew was a favorite promenade for the nurses who were gathered at the farther end, where a large window looked upon Montgomery Street. But Norah, the Irish nurse, was not among them; he passed through several corridors in his search, but in vain. At last, worried and a little anxious, he turned to regain his rooms through the long saloon where he had found his wife previously. It was deserted now; the last caller had left— even frivolity had its prescribed limits. He was consequently startled by a gentle murmur from one of the heavily curtained window recesses. It was a woman's voice—low, sweet, caressing, and filled with an almost pathetic tenderness. And it was followed by a distinct gurgling satisfied crow.

Barker turned instantly in that direction. A step brought him to the curtain, where a singular spectacle presented itself.

Seated on a lounge, completely absorbed and possessed by her treasure, was the "horrid woman" whom his wife had indicated only a little while ago, holding a baby—Kitty's sacred baby—in her wanton lap! The child was feebly grasping the end of the slender jeweled necklace which the woman held temptingly dangling from a thin white jeweled finger above it. But its eyes were beaming with an intense delight, as if trying to respond to the deep, concentrated love in the handsome face that was bent above it.

At the sudden intrusion of Barker she looked up. There was a faint rise in her color, but no loss of sell-possession.

"Please don't scold the nurse," she said, "nor say anything to Mrs. Barker. It is all my fault. I thought that both the nurse and child looked dreadfully bored with each other, and I borrowed the little fellow for a while to try and amuse him. At least I haven't made him cry, have I, dear?" The last epithet, it is needless to say, was addressed to the little creature in her lap, but in its tender modulation it touched the father's quick sympathies as if he had shared it with the child. "You see," she said softly, disengaging the baby fingers from her necklace, "that OUR sex is not the only one tempted by jewelry and glitter."

Barker hesitated; the Madonna-like devotion of a moment ago was gone; it was only the woman of the world who laughingly looked up at him. Nevertheless he was touched. "Have you—ever—had a child, Mrs. Horncastle?" he asked gently and hesitatingly. He had a vague recollection that she passed for a widow, and in his simple eyes all women were virgins or married saints.

"No," she said abruptly. Then she added with a laugh, "Or perhaps I should not admire them so much. I suppose it's the same feeling bachelors have for other people's wives. But I know you're dying to take that boy from me. Take him, then, and don't be ashamed to carry him yourself just because I'm here; you know you would delight to do it if I weren't."

Barker bent over the silken lap in which the child was comfortably nestling, and in that attitude had a faint consciousness that Mrs. Horncastle was mischievously breathing into his curls a silent laugh. Barker lifted his firstborn with proud skillfulness, but that sagacious infant evidently knew when he was comfortable, and in a paroxysm of objection caught his father's curls with one fist, while with the other he grasped Mrs. Horncastle's brown braids and brought their heads into contact. Upon which humorous situation Norah, the nurse, entered.

"It's all right, Norah," said Mrs. Horncastle, laughing, as she disengaged herself from the linking child. "Mr. Barker has claimed the baby, and has agreed to forgive you and me and say nothing to Mrs. Barker." Norah, with the inscrutable criticism of her sex on her sex, thought it extremely probable, and halted with exasperating discretion. "There," continued Mrs. Horncastle, playfully evading the child's further advances, "go with papa, that's a dear. Mr. Barker prefers to carry him back, Norah."

"But," said the ingenuous and persistent Barker, still lingering in hopes of recalling the woman's previous expression, "you DO love children, and you think him a bright little chap for his age?"

"Yes," said Mrs. Horncastle, putting back her loosened braid, "so round and fat and soft. And such a discriminating eye for jewelry. Really you ought to get a necklace like mine for Mrs. Barker—it would please both, you know." She moved slowly away, the united efforts of Norah and Barker scarcely sufficing to restrain the struggling child from leaping after her as she turned at the door and blew him a kiss.

When Barker regained his room he found that Mrs. Barker had dismissed Stacy from her mind except so far as to invoke Norah's aid in laying out her smartest gown for dinner. "But why take all this trouble, dear?" said her simple-minded husband; "we are going to dine in a private room so that we can talk over old times all by ourselves, and any dress would suit him. And, Lord, dear!" he added, with a quick brightening at the fancy, "if you could only just rig yourself up in that pretty lilac gown you used to wear at Boomville—

it would be too killing, and just like old times. I put it away myself in one of our trunks—I couldn't bear to leave it behind; I know just where it is. I'll"—But Mrs. Barker's restraining scorn withheld him.

"George Barker, if you think I am going to let you throw away and utterly WASTE Mr. Stacy on us, alone, in a private room with closed doors—and I dare say you'd like to sit in your dressing-gown and slippers—you are entirely mistaken. I know what is due, not to your old partner, but to the great Mr. Stacy, the financier, and I know what is due FROM HIM TO US! No! We dine in the great dining-room, publicly, and, if possible, at the very next table to those stuck-up Peterburys and their Eastern friends, including that horrid woman, which, I'm sure, ought to satisfy you. Then you can talk as much as you like, and as loud as you like, about old times,—and the louder and the more the better,—but I don't think HE'LL like it."

"But the baby!" expostulated Barker. "Stacy's just wild to see him—and we can't bring him down to the table—though we MIGHT," he added, momentarily brightening.

"After dinner," said Mrs. Barker severely, "we will walk through the big drawing-rooms, and THEN Mr. Stacy may come upstairs and see him in his crib; but not before. And now, George, I do wish that to-night, FOR ONCE, you would not wear a turn-down collar, and that you would go to the barber's and have him cut your hair and smooth out the curls. And, for Heaven's sake! let him put some wax or gum or SOMETHING on your mustache and twist it up on your cheek like Captain Heath's, for it positively droops over your mouth like a girl's ringlet. It's quite enough for me to hear people talk of your inexperience, but really I don't want you to look as if I had run away with a pretty schoolboy. And, considering the size of that child, it's positively disgraceful.

And, one thing more, George. When I'm talking to anybody, please don't sit opposite to me, beaming with delight, and your mouth open. And don't roar if by chance I say something funny. And—whatever you do—don't make eyes at me in company whenever I happen to allude to you, as I did before Captain Heath. It is positively too ridiculous."

Nothing could exceed the laughing good humor with which her husband received these cautions, nor the evident sincerity with which he promised amendment. Equally sincere was he, though a little more thoughtful, in his severe self-examination of his deficiencies, when, later, he seated himself at the window with one hand softly encompassing his child's chubby fist in the crib beside him, and, in the instinctive fashion of all loneliness, looked out of the window. The southern trades were whipping the waves of the distant bay and harbor into yeasty crests. Sheets of rain swept the sidewalks with the regularity of a fusillade, against which a few pedestrians struggled with flapping waterproofs and slanting umbrellas. He could look along the deserted length of Montgomery Street to the heights of Telegraph Hill and its long-disused semaphore. It seemed lonelier to him than the mile-long sweep of Heavy Tree Hill, writhing against the mountain wind and its aeolian song. He had never felt so lonely THERE. In his rigid self-examination he thought Kitty right in protesting against the effect of his youthfulness and optimism. Yet he was also right in being himself. There is an egoism in the highest simplicity; and Barker, while willing to believe in others' methods, never abandoned his own aims. He was right in loving Kitty as he did; he knew that she was better and more lovable than she could believe herself to be; but he was willing to believe it pained and discomposed her if he showed it before company. He would not have her change even this peculiarity—it was part of herself—no more than he would have changed himself. And behind what he had conceived was her clear, practical common sense, all this time had been her belief that she had deceived her father! Poor dear, dear Kitty! And she had suffered because stupid people had conceived that her father had led him away in selfish speculations. As if he—Barker—would not have first discovered it, and as if anybody—even dear Kitty herself—was responsible for HIS convictions and actions but himself. Nevertheless, this gentle egotist was unusually serious, and when the child awoke at last, and with a fretful start and vacant eyes pushed his caressing hand away, he felt lonelier than before. It was with a slight sense of humiliation, too, that he saw it stretch its hands to the mere hireling, Norah, who had never given it the love that he had seen even in the frivolous Mrs. Horncastle's eyes. Later, when his wife came in, looking very pretty in her elaborate dinner toilette, he had the same conflicting emotions. He knew that they had already passed that phase of their married life when she no longer dressed to please him, and that the dictates of fashion or the rivalry of another woman she held superior to his tastes; yet he did not blame her. But he was a little surprised to see that her dress was copied from one of Mrs. Horncastle's most striking ones, and that it did not suit her. That which adorned the maturer woman did not agree with the demure and slightly austere prettiness of the young wife.

But Barker forgot all this when Stacy—reserved and somewhat severe-looking in evening dress—arrived with business punctuality. He fancied that his old partner received the announcement that they would dine in the public room with something of surprise, and he saw him glance keenly at Kitty in her fine array, as if he had suspected it was her choice, and understood her motives. Indeed, the young husband had found himself somewhat nervous in regard to Stacy's estimate of Kitty; he was conscious that she was not looking and acting like the old Kitty that Stacy had known; it did not enter his honest heart that Stacy had, perhaps, not appreciated her then, and that her present quality might accord more with his worldly tastes and experience. It was, therefore, with a kind of timid delight that he saw Stacy apparently enter into her mood, and with a still more timorous amusement to notice that he seemed to sympathize not only with her, but with her half-rallying, half-serious attitude towards his (Barker's) inexperience and simplicity. He was glad that she had made a friend of Stacy, even in this way. Stacy would understand, as he did, her pretty willfulness at last; she would understand what a true friend Stacy was to him. It was with unfeigned satisfaction that he followed them in to dinner as she leaned upon his guest's arm, chatting confidentially. He was only uneasy because her manner had a slight ostentation.

The entrance of the little party produced a quick sensation throughout the dining-room. Whispers passed from table to table; all heads were turned towards the great financier as towards a magnet; a few guests even shamelessly faced round in their chairs as he passed. Mrs. Barker was pink, pretty, and voluble with excitement; Stacy had a slight mask of reserve; Barker was the only one natural and unconscious.

As the dinner progressed Barker found that there was little chance for him to invoke his old partner's memories of the past. He found, however, that Stacy had received a letter from Demorest, and that he was coming home from Europe. His letters were still sad; they both agreed upon that. And then for the first time that day Stacy looked intently at Barker with the look that he had often worn on Heavy Tree Hill.

"Then you think it is the same old trouble that worries him?" said Barker in an awed and sympathetic voice.

"I believe it is," said Stacy, with an equal feeling. Mrs.

Barker pricked up her pretty ears; her husband's ready sympathy was familiar enough; but that this cold, practical Stacy should be moved at anything piqued her curiosity.

"And you believe that he has never got over it?" continued Barker.

"He had one chance, but he threw it away," said Stacy energetically. "If, instead of going off to Europe by himself to brood over it, he had joined me in business, he'd have been another man."

"But not Demorest," said Barker quickly.

"What dreadful secret is this about Demorest?" said Mrs. Barker petulantly. "Is he ill?"

Both men were silent by their old common instinct. But it was Stacy who said "No" in a way that put any further questioning at an end, and Barker was grateful and for the moment disloyal to his Kitty.

It was with delight that Mrs. Barker had seen that the attention of the next table was directed to them, and that even Mrs. Horncastle had glanced from time to time at Stacy. But she was not prepared for the evident equal effect that Mrs. Horncastle had created upon Stacy. His cold face warmed, his critical eye softened; he asked her name. Mrs. Barker was voluble, prejudiced, and, it seemed, misinformed.

"I know it all," said Stacy, with didactic emphasis. "Her husband was as bad as they make them. When her life had become intolerable WITH HIM, he tried to make it shameful WITHOUT HIM by abandoning her. She could get a divorce a dozen times over, but she won't."

"I suppose that's what makes her so very attractive to gentlemen," said Mrs. Barker ironically.

"I have never seen her before," continued Stacy, with business precision, "although I and two other men are guardians of her property, and have saved it from the clutches of her husband. They told me she was handsome—and so she is."

Pleased with the sudden human weakness of Stacy, Barker glanced at his wife for sympathy. But she was looking studiously another way, and the young husband's eyes, still full of his gratification, fell upon Mrs. Horncastle's. She looked away with a bright color. Whereupon the sanguine Barker—perfectly convinced that she returned Stacy's admiration—was seized with one of his old boyish dreams of the future, and saw Stacy happily united to her, and was only recalled to the dinner before him by its end. Then Stacy duly promenaded the great saloon with Mrs. Barker on his arm, visited the baby in her apartments, and took an easy leave. But he grasped Barker's hand before parting in quite his old fashion, and said, "Come to lunch with me at the bank any day, and we'll talk of Phil Demorest," and left Barker as happy as if the appointment were to confer the favor he had that morning refused. But Mrs. Barker, who had overheard, was more dubious.

"You don't suppose he asks you to talk with you about Demorest and his stupid secret, do you?" she said scornfully.

"Perhaps not only about that," said Barker, glad that she had not demanded the secret.

"Well," returned Mrs. Barker as she turned away, "he might just as well lunch here and talk about HER—and see her, too."

Meantime Stacy had dropped into his club, only a few squares distant. His appearance created the same interest that it had produced at the hotel, but with less reserve among his fellow members.

"Have you heard the news?" said a dozen voices. Stacy had not; he had been dining out.

"That infernal swindle of a Divide Railroad has passed the legislature."

Stacy instantly remembered Barker's absurd belief in it and his reasons. He smiled and said carelessly, "Are you quite sure it's a swindle?"

There was a dead silence at the coolness of the man who had been most outspoken against it.

"But," said a voice hesitatingly, "you know it goes nowhere and to no purpose."

"But that does not prevent it, now that it's a fact, from going anywhere and to some purpose," said Stacy, turning away. He passed into the reading-room quietly, but in an instant turned and quickly descended by another staircase into the hall, hurriedly put on his overcoat, and slipping out was a moment later re-entering the hotel. Here he hastily summoned Barker, who came down, flushed and excited. Laying his hand on Barker's arm in his old dominant way, he said:—

"Don't delay a single hour, but get a written agreement for that Ditch property."

Barker smiled. "But I have. Got it this afternoon."

"Then you know?" ejaculated Stacy in surprise.

"I only know," said Barker, coloring, "that you said I could back out of it if it wasn't signed, and that's what Kitty said, too. And I thought it looked awfully mean for me to hold a man to that kind of a bargain. And so—you won't be mad, old fellow, will you?—I thought I'd put it beyond any question of my own good faith by having it in black and white." He stopped, laughing and blushing, but still earnest and sincere. "You don't think me a fool, do you?" he said pathetically.

Stacy smiled grimly. "I think, Barker boy, that if you go to the Branch you'll have no difficulty in paying for the Ditch property. Good-night."

In a few moments he was back at the club again before any one knew he had even left the building. As he again re-entered the smoking-room he found the members still in eager discussion about the new railroad. One was saying, "If they could get an extension, and carry the road through Heavy Tree Hill to Boomville they'd be all right."

"I quite agree with you," said Stacy.

CHAPTER III

The swaying, creaking, Boomville coach had at last reached the level ridge, and sank forward upon its springs with a sigh of relief and the slow precipitation of the red dust which had hung in clouds around it. The whole coach, inside and out, was covered with this impalpable powder; it had poured into the windows that gaped widely in the insufferable heat; it lay thick upon the novel read by the passenger who had for the third or fourth time during the ascent made a gutter of the half-opened book and blown the dust away in a single puff, like the smoke from a pistol. It lay in folds and creases over the yellow silk duster of the handsome woman on the back seat, and when she endeavored to shake it off enveloped her in a reddish nimbus. It grimed the handkerchiefs of others, and left sanguinary streaks on their mopped foreheads. But as the coach had slowly climbed the summit the sun was also sinking behind the Black Spur Range, and with its ultimate disappearance a delicious coolness spread itself like a wave across the ridge. The passengers drew a long breath, the reader closed his book, the lady lifted the edge of her veil and delicately wiped her forehead, over which a few damp tendrils of hair were clinging. Even a distinguished-looking man who had sat as impenetrable and remote as a statue in one of the front seats moved and turned his abstracted face to the window. His deeply tanned cheek and clearly cut features harmonized with the red dust that lay in the curves of his brown linen dust-cloak, and completed his resemblance to a bronze figure. Yet it was Demorest, changed only in coloring. Now, as five years ago, his abstraction had a certain quality which the most familiar stranger shrank from disturbing. But in the general relaxation of relief the novel-reader addressed him.

"Well, we ain't far from Boomville now, and it's all down-grade the rest of the way. I reckon you'll be as glad to get a 'wash up' and a 'shake' as the rest of us."

"I am afraid I won't have so early an opportunity," said Demorest, with a faint, grave smile, "for I get off at the cross-road to Heavy Tree Hill."

"Heavy Tree Hill!" repeated the other in surprise. "You ain't goin' to Heavy Tree Hill? Why, you might have gone there direct by railroad, and have been there four hours ago. You know there's a branch from the Divide Railroad goes there straight to the hotel at Hymettus."

"Where?" said Demorest, with a puzzled smile.

"Hymettus. That's the fancy name they've given to the watering-place on the slope. But I reckon you're a stranger here?"

"For five years," said Demorest. "I fancy I've heard of the railroad, although I prefer to go to Heavy Tree this way. But I never heard of a watering-place there before."

"Why, it's the biggest boom of the year. Folks that are tired of the fogs of 'Frisco and the heat of Sacramento all go there. It's four thousand feet up, with a hotel like Saratoga, dancing, and a band plays every night. And it all sprang out of the Divide Railroad and a crank named George Barker, who bought up some old Ditch property and ran a branch line along its levels, and made a junction with the Divide. You can come all the way from 'Frisco or Sacramento by rail. It's a mighty big thing!"

"Yet," said Demorest, with some animation, "you call the man who originated this success a crank. I should say he was a genius."

The other passenger shook his head. "All sheer nigger luck. He bought the Ditch plant afore there was a ghost of a chance for the Divide Railroad, just out o' pure d—d foolishness. He expected so little from it that he hadn't even got the agreement done in writin', and hadn't paid for it, when the Divide Railroad passed the legislature, as it never oughter done! For, you see, the blamedest cur'ous thing about the whole affair was that this 'straw' road of a Divide, all pure wildcat, was only gotten up to frighten the Pacific Railroad sharps into buying it up. And the road that nobody ever calculated would ever have a rail of it laid was pushed on as soon as folks knew that the Ditch plant had been bought up, for they thought there was a big thing behind it. Even the hotel was, at first, simply a kind of genteel alms-house that this yer Barker had built for broken-down miners!"

"Nevertheless," continued Demorest, smiling, "you admit that it is a great success?"

"Yes," said the other, a little irritated by some complacency in Demorest's smile, "but the success isn't HIS'N. Fools has ideas, and wise men profit by them, for that hotel now has Jim Stacy's bank behind it, and is even a kind of country branch of the Brook House in 'Frisco. Barker's out of it, I reckon. Anyhow, HE couldn't run a hotel, for all that his wife—she that's one of the big 'Frisco swells now—used to help serve in her father's. No, sir, it's just a fool's luck, gettin' the first taste and leavin' the rest to others."

"I'm not sure that it's the worst kind of luck," returned Demorest, with persistent gravity; "and I suppose he's satisfied with it." But so heterodox an opinion only irritated his antagonist the more, especially as he noticed that the handsome woman in the back seat appeared to be interested in the conversation, and even sympathetic with Demorest. The man was in the main a good-natured fellow and loyal to his friends; but this did not preclude any virulent criticism of others, and for a moment he hated this bronze-faced stranger, and even saw blemishes in the handsome woman's beauty. "That may be YOUR idea of an Eastern man," he said bluntly, "but I kin tell ye that Californy ain't run on those lines. No, sir." Nevertheless, his curiosity got the better of his ill humor, and as the coach at last pulled up at the cross-road for Demorest to descend he smiled affably at his departing companion.

"You allowed just now that you'd bin five years away. Whar mout ye have bin?"

"In Europe," said Demorest pleasantly.

"I reckoned ez much," returned his interrogator, smiling significantly at the other passengers. "But in what place?"

"Oh, many," said Demorest, smiling also.

"But what place war ye last livin' at?"

"Well," said Demorest, descending the steps, but lingering for a moment with his hand on the door of the coach, "oddly enough, now you remind me of it—at Hymettus!"

He closed the door, and the coach rolled on. The passenger reddened, glanced indignantly after the departing figure of Demorest and suspiciously at the others. The lady was looking from the window with a faint smile on her face.

"He might hev given me a civil answer," muttered the passenger, and resumed his novel.

When the coach drew up before Carter's Hotel the lady got down, and the curiosity of her susceptible companions was gratified to the extent of learning from the register that her name was Horncastle.

She was shown to a private sitting-room, which chanced to be the one which had belonged to Mrs. Barker in the days of her maidenhood, and was the sacred, impenetrable bower to which she retired when her daily duties of waiting upon her father's guests were over. But the breath of custom had passed through it since then, and but little remained of its former maiden glories, except a few schoolgirl crayon drawings on the wall and an unrecognizable portrait of herself in oil, done by a wandering artist and still preserved as a receipt for his unpaid bill. Of these facts Mrs. Horncastle knew nothing; she was evidently preoccupied, and after she had removed her outer duster and entered the room, she glanced at the clock on the mantel-shelf and threw herself with an air of resigned abstraction in an armchair in the corner. Her traveling-dress, although unostentatious, was tasteful and well-fitting; a slight pallor from her fatiguing journey, and, perhaps, from some absorbing thought, made her beauty still more striking. She gave even an air of elegance to the faded, worn adornments of the room, which it is to be feared it never possessed in Miss Kitty's occupancy. Again she glanced at the clock. There was a tap at the door.

Bret Harte

"Come in."

The door opened to a Chinese servant bearing a piece of torn paper with a name written on it in lieu of a card.

Mrs. Horncastle took it, glanced at the name, and handed the paper back.

"There must be some mistake," she said, "it do not know Mr. Steptoe."

"No, but you know ME all the same," said a voice from the doorway as a man entered, coolly took the Chinese servant by the elbows and thrust him into the passage, closing the door upon him. "Steptoe and Horncastle are the same man, only I prefer to call myself Steptoe HERE. And I see YOU'RE down on the register as 'Horncastle.' Well, it's plucky of you, and it's not a bad name to keep; you might be thankful that I have always left it to you. And if I call myself Steptoe here it's a good blind against any of your swell friends knowing you met your HUSBAND here."

In the half-scornful, half-resigned look she had given him when he entered there was no doubt that she recognized him as the man she had come to see. He had changed little in the five years that had elapsed since he entered the three partners' cabin at Heavy Tree Hill. His short hair and beard still clung to his head like curled moss or the crisp flocculence of Astrakhan. He was dressed more pretentiously, but still gave the same idea of vulgar strength. She listened to him without emotion, but said, with even a deepening of scorn in her manner:—

"What new shame is this?"

"Nothing NEW," he replied. "Only five years ago I was livin' over on the Bar at Heavy Tree Hill under the name of Steptoe, and folks here might recognize me. I was here when your particular friend, Jim Stacy, who only knew me as Steptoe, and doesn't know me as Horncastle, your HUSBAND,—for all he's bound up my property for you,—made his big strike with his two partners. I was in his cabin that very night, and drank his whiskey. Oh, I'm all right there! I left everything all right behind me—only it's just as well he doesn't know I'm Horncastle. And as the boy happened to be there with me"—He stopped, and looked at her significantly.

The expression of her face changed. Eagerness, anxiety, and even fear came into it in turn, but always mingling with some scorn that dominated her. "The boy!" she said in a voice that had changed too; "well, what about him? You promised to tell me all,—all!"

"Where's the money?" he said. "Husband and wife are ONE, I know," he went on with a coarse laugh, "but I don't trust MYSELF in these matters."

She took from a traveling-reticule that lay beside her a roll of notes and a chamois leather bag of coin, and laid them on the table before him. He examined both carefully.

"All right," he said. "I see you've got the checks made out 'to bearer.' Your head's level, Conny. Pity you and me can't agree."

"I went to the bank across the way as soon as I arrived," she said, with contemptuous directness. "I told them I was going over to Hymettus and might want money."

He dropped into a chair before her with his broad heavy hands upon his knees, and looked at her with an equal, though baser, contempt: for his was mingled with a certain pride of mastery and possession.

"And, of course, you'll go to Hymettus and cut a splurge as you always do. The beautiful Mrs. Horncastle! The helpless victim of a wretched, dissipated, disgraced, gambling husband. So dreadfully sad, you know, and so interesting! Could get a divorce from the brute if she wanted, but won't, on account of her religious scruples. And so while the brute is gambling, swindling, disgracing himself, and dodging a shot here and a lynch committee there, two or three hundred miles away, you're splurging round in first-class hotels and watering-places, doing the injured and abused, and run after by a lot of men who are ready to take my place, and, maybe, some of my reputation along with it."

"Stop!" she said suddenly, in a voice that made the glass chandelier ring. He had risen too, with a quick, uneasy glance towards the door. But her outbreak passed as suddenly, and sinking back into her chair, she said, with her previous scornful resignation, "Never mind. Go on. You KNOW you're lying!"

He sat down again and looked at her critically. "Yes, as far as you're concerned I WAS lying! I know your style. But as you know, too, that I'd kill you and the first man I suspected, and there ain't a judge or a jury in all Californy that wouldn't let me go free for it, and even consider, too, that it had wiped off the whole slate agin me—it's to my credit!"

"I know what you men call chivalry," she said coldly, "but I did not come here to buy a knowledge of that. So now about the child?" she ended abruptly, leaning forward again with the same look of eager solicitude in her eyes.

"Well, about the child—our child—though, perhaps, I prefer

to say MY child," he began, with a certain brutal frankness. "I'll tell you. But first, I don't want you to talk about BUYING your information of me. If I haven't told you anything before, it's because I didn't think you oughter know. If I didn't trust the child to YOU, it's because I didn't think you could go shashaying about with a child that was three years old when I"—he stopped and wiped his mouth with the back of his hand—"made an honest woman of you—I think that's what they call it."

"But," she said eagerly, ignoring the insult, "I could have hidden it where no one but myself would have known it. I could have sent it to school and visited it as a relation."

"Yes," he said curtly, "like all women, and then blurted it out some day and made it worse."

"But," she said desperately, "even THEN, suppose I had been willing to take the shame of it! I have taken more!"

"But I didn't intend that you should," he said roughly.

"You are very careful of my reputation," she returned scornfully.

"Not by a d—d sight," he burst out; "but I care for HIS! I'm not goin' to let any man call him a bastard!"

Callous as she had become even under this last cruel blow, she could not but see something in his coarse eyes she had never seen before; could not but hear something in his brutal voice she had never heard before! Was it possible that somewhere in the depths of his sordid nature he had his own contemptible sense of honor? A hysterical feeling came over her hitherto passive disgust and scorn, but it disappeared with his next sentence in a haze of anxiety. "No!" he said hoarsely, "he had enough wrong done him already."

"What do you mean?" she said imploringly. "Or are you again lying? You said, four years ago, that he had 'got into trouble;' that was your excuse for keeping him from me. Or was that a lie, too?"

His manner changed and softened, but not for any pity for his companion, but rather from some change in his own feelings. "Oh, that," he said, with a rough laugh, "that was only a kind o' trouble any sassy kid like him was likely to get into. You ain't got no call to hear that, for," he added, with a momentary return to his previous manner, "the wrong that was done him is MY lookout! You want to know what I did with him, how he's been looked arter, and where he is? You want the worth of your money. That's square enough. But first I want you to know, though you mayn't believe it, that every red cent you've given me to-night goes to HIM. And don't you forget it."

For all his vulgar frankness she knew he had lied to her many times before,—maliciously, wantonly, complacently, but never evasively; yet there was again that something in his manner which told her he was now telling the truth.

"Well," he began, settling himself back in his chair, "I told you I brought him to Heavy Tree Hill. After I left you I wasn't going to trust him to no school; he knew enough for me; but when I left those parts where nobody knew you, and got a little nearer 'Frisco, where people might have known us both, I thought it better not to travel round with a kid o' that size as his FATHER. So I got a young fellow here to pass him off as HIS little brother, and look after him and board him; and I paid him a big price for it, too, you bet! You wouldn't think it was a man who's now swelling around here, the top o' the pile, that ever took money from a brute like me, and for such schoolmaster work, too; but he did, and his name was Van Loo, a clerk of the Ditch Company."

"Van Loo!" said the woman, with a movement of disgust; "THAT man!"

"What's the matter with Van Loo?" he said, with a coarse laugh, enjoying his wife's discomfiture. "He speaks French and Spanish, and you oughter hear the kid roll off the lingo he's got from him. He's got style, and knows how to dress, and you ought to see the kid bow and scrape, and how he carries himself. Now, Van Loo wasn't exactly my style, and I reckon I don't hanker after him much, but he served my purpose."

"And this man knows"—she said, with a shudder.

"He knows Steptoe and the boy, but he don't know Horncastle nor YOU. Don't you be skeert. He's the last man in the world who would hanker to see me or the kid again, or would dare to say that he ever had! Lord! I'd like to see his fastidious mug if me and Eddy walked in upon him and his high-toned mother and sister some arternoon." He threw himself back and laughed a derisive, spasmodic, choking laugh, which was so far from being genial that it even seemed to indicate a lively appreciation of pain in others rather than of pleasure in himself. He had often laughed at her in the same way.

"And where is he now?" she said, with a compressed lip.

"At school. Where, I don't tell you. You know why. But he's looked after by me, and d—d well looked after, too."

She hesitated, composed her face with an effort, parted her lips, and looked out of the window into the gathering darkness. Then after a moment she said slowly, yet with a certain precision:—

"And his mother? Do you ever talk to him of HER? Does—does he ever speak of ME?"

"What do you think?" he said comfortably, changing his position in the chair, and trying to read her face in the shadow. "Come, now. You don't know, eh? Well—no! NO! You understand. No! He's MY friend—MINE! He's stood by me through thick and thin. Run at my heels when everybody else fled me. Dodged vigilance committees with me, laid out in the brush with me with his hand in mine when the sheriff's deputies were huntin' me; shut his jaw close when, if he squealed, he'd have been called another victim of the brute Horncastle, and been as petted and canoodled as you."

It would have been difficult for any one but the woman who knew the man before her to have separated his brutish delight in paining her from another feeling she had never dreamt him capable of,—an intense and fierce pride in his affection for his child. And it was the more hopeless to her that it was not the mere sentiment of reciprocation, but the material instinct of paternity in its most animal form. And it seemed horrible to her that the only outcome of what had been her own wild, youthful passion for this brute was this love for the flesh of her flesh, for she was more and more conscious as he spoke that her yearning for the boy was the yearning of an equally dumb and unreasoning maternity. They had met again as animals—in fear, contempt, and anger of each other; but the animal had triumphed in both.

When she spoke again it was as the woman of the world,—the woman who had laughed two years ago at the irrepressible Barker. "It's a new thing," she said, languidly turning her rings on her fingers, "to see you in the role of a doting father. And may I ask how long you have had this amiable weakness, and how long it is to last?"

To her surprise and the keen retaliating delight of her sex, a conscious flush covered his face to the crisp edges of his black and matted beard. For a moment she hoped that he had lied. But, to her greater surprise, he stammered in equal frankness: "It's growed upon me for the last five years—ever since I was alone with him." He stopped, cleared his throat, and then, standing up before her, said in his former voice, but with a more settled and intense deliberation: "You wanter know how long it will last, do ye? Well, you know your special friend, Jim Stacy—the big millionaire—the great Jim of the Stock Exchange—the man that pinches the money market of Californy between his finger and thumb and makes it squeal in New York—the man who shakes the stock market when he sneezes? Well, it will go on until that man is a beggar; until he has to borrow a dime for his breakfast, and slump out of his lunch with a cent's worth of rat poison or a bullet in his head! It'll go on until his old partner—that softy George Barker—comes to the bottom of his d—d fool luck and is a penny-a-liner for the papers and a hanger-round at free lunches, and his scatter-brained wife runs away with another man! It'll go on until the high-toned Demorest, the last of those three little tin gods of Heavy Tree Hill, will have to climb down, and will know what I feel and what he's made me feel, and will wish himself in hell before he ever made the big strike on Heavy Tree! That's me! You hear me! I'm shoutin'! It'll last till then! It may be next week, next month, next year. But it'll come. And when it does come you'll see me and Eddy just waltzin' in and takin' the chief seats in the synagogue! And you'll have a free pass to the show!"

Either he was too intoxicated with his vengeful vision, or the shadows of the room had deepened, but he did not see the quick flush that had risen to his wife's face with this allusion to Barker, nor the after-settling of her handsome features into a dogged determination equal to his own. His blind fury against the three partners did not touch her curiosity; she was only struck with the evident depth of his emotion. He had never been a braggart; his hostility had always been lazy and cynical. Remembering this, she had a faint stirring of respect for the undoubted courage and consciousness of strength shown in this wild but single-handed crusade against wealth and power; rather, perhaps, it seemed to her to condone her own weakness in her youthful and inexplicable passion for him. No wonder she had submitted.

"Then you have nothing more to tell me?" she said after a pause, rising and going towards the mantel.

"You needn't light up for me," he returned, rising also. "I am going. Unless," he added, with his coarse laugh, "you think it wouldn't look well for Mrs. Horncastle to have been sitting in the dark with—a stranger!" He paused as she contemptuously put down the candlestick and threw the unlit match into the grate. "No, I've nothing more to tell. He's a fancy-looking pup. You'd take him for twenty-one, though he's only sixteen—clean-limbed and perfect—but for one thing"—He stopped. He met her quick look of interrogation, however, with a lowering silence that, nevertheless, changed again as he surveyed her erect figure by the faint light of the window with a sardonic smile. "He favors you, I think, and in all but one thing, too."

"And that?" she queried coldly, as he seemed to hesitate.

"He ain't ashamed of ME," he returned, with a laugh.

The door closed behind him; she heard his heavy step descend the creaking stairs; he was gone. She went to the window and threw it open, as if to get rid of the atmosphere charged with his presence,—a presence still so potent that she now knew that for the last five minutes she had been, to her horror, struggling against its magnetism. She even recoiled now at the thought of her child, as if, in these new confidences over it, it had revived the old intimacy in this link of their common flesh. She looked down from her window on the square shoulders, thick throat, and crisp matted hair of her husband as he vanished in the darkness, and drew a breath of freedom,—a freedom not so much from him as from her own weakness that he was bearing away with him into the exonerating night.

She shut the window and sank down in her chair again, but in the encompassing and compassionate obscurity of the room. And this was the man she had loved and for whom she had wrecked her young life! Or WAS it love? and, if NOT, how was she better than he? Worse; for he was more loyal to that passion that had brought them together and its responsibilities than she was. She had suffered the perils and pangs of maternity, and yet had only the mere animal yearning for her offspring, while he had taken over the toil and duty, and even the devotion, of parentage himself. But then she remembered also how he had fascinated her—a simple schoolgirl—by his sheer domineering strength, and how the objections of her parents to this coarse and common man had forced her into a clandestine intimacy that ended in her complete subjection to him. She remembered the birth of an infant whose concealment from her parents and friends was compassed by his low cunning; she remembered the late atonement of marriage preferred by the man she had already begun to loathe and fear, and who she now believed was eager only for her inheritance. She remembered her abject compliance through the greater fear of the world, the stormy scenes that followed their ill-omened union, her final abandonment of her husband, and the efforts of her friends and family who had rescued the last of her property from him. She was glad she remembered it; she dwelt upon it, upon his cruelty, his coarseness and vulgarity, until she saw, as she honestly believed, the hidden springs of his affection for their child. It was HIS child in nature, however it might have favored her in looks; it was HIS own brutal SELF he was worshiping in his brutal progeny. How else could it have ignored HER—its own mother? She never doubted the truth of what he had told her—she had seen it in his own triumphant eyes. And yet she would have made a kind mother; she remembered with a smile and a slight rising of color the affection of Barker's baby for her; she remembered with a deepening of that color the thrill of satisfaction she had felt in her husband's fulmination against Mrs. Barker, and, more than all, she felt in his blind and foolish hatred of Barker himself a delicious condonation of the strange feeling that had sprung up in her heart for Barker's simple, straightforward nature. How could HE understand, how could THEY understand (by the plural she meant Mrs. Barker and Horncastle), a character so innately noble. In her strange attraction towards him she had felt a charming sense of what she believed was a superior and even matronly protection; in the utter isolation of her life now—and with her husband's foolish abuse of him ringing in her ears—it seemed a sacred duty. She had lost a son. Providence had sent her an ideal friend to replace him. And this was quite consistent, too, with a faint smile that began to play about her mouth as she recalled some instances of Barker's delightful and irresistible youthfulness.

There was a clatter of hoofs and the sound of many voices from the street. Mrs. Horncastle knew it was the down coach changing horses; it would be off again in a few moments, and, no doubt, bearing her husband away with it. A new feeling of relief came over her as she at last heard the warning "All aboard!" and the great vehicle clattered and rolled into the darkness, trailing its burning lights across her walls and ceiling. But now she heard steps on the staircase, a pause before her room, a whisper of voices, the opening of the door, the rustle of a skirt, and a little feminine cry of protest as a man apparently tried to follow the figure into the room. "No, no! I tell you NO!" remonstrated the woman's voice in a hurried whisper. "It won't do. Everybody knows me here. You must not come in now. You must wait to be announced by the servant. Hush! Go!"

There was a slight struggle, the sound of a kiss, and the woman succeeded in finally shutting the door. Then she walked slowly, but with a certain familiarity towards the mantel, struck a match and lit the candle. The light shone upon the bright eyes and slightly flushed face of Mrs. Barker. But the motionless woman in the chair had recognized her voice and the voice of her companion at once. And then their eyes met.

Mrs. Barker drew back, but did not utter a cry. Mrs. Horncastle, with eyes even brighter than her companion's, smiled. The red deepened in Mrs. Barker's cheek.

"This is my room!" she said indignantly, with a sweeping gesture around the walls.

"I should judge so," said Mrs. Horncastle, following the gesture; "but," she added quietly, "they put ME into it. It appears, however, they did not expect you."

Mrs. Barker saw her mistake. "No, no," she said apologetically, "of course not." Then she added, with nervous volubility, sitting down and tugging at her gloves, "You see, I just ran down from Marysville to take a look at my father's old house on my way to Hymettus. I hope I haven't disturbed you. Perhaps," she said, with sudden eagerness, "you were asleep when I came in!"

"No," said Mrs. Horncastle, "I was not sleeping nor dreaming. I heard you come in."

"Some of these men are such idiots," said Mrs. Barker, with a half-hysterical laugh. "They seem to think if a woman accepts the least courtesy from them they've a right to be familiar. But I fancy that fellow was a little astonished when I shut the door in his face."

"I fancy he WAS," returned Mrs. Horncastle dryly. "But I shouldn't call Mr. Van Loo an idiot. He has the reputation of being a cautious business man."

Mrs. Barker bit her lip. Her companion had been recognized. She rose with a slight flirt of her skirt. "I suppose I must go and get a room; there was nobody in the office when I came. Everything is badly managed here since my father took away the best servants to Hymettus." She moved with affected carelessness towards the door, when Mrs. Horncastle, without rising from her seat, said:—

"Why not stay here?"

Mrs. Barker brightened for a moment. "Oh," she said, with polite deprecation, "I couldn't think of turning you out."

"I don't intend you shall," said Mrs. Horncastle. "We will stay here together until you go with me to Hymettus, or until Mr. Van Loo leaves the hotel. He will hardly attempt to come in here again if I remain."

Mrs. Barker, with a half-laugh, sat down irresolutely. Mrs. Horncastle gazed at her curiously; she was evidently a novice in this sort of thing. But, strange to say,—and I leave the ethics of this for the sex to settle,—the fact did not soften Mrs. Horncastle's heart, nor in the least qualify her attitude towards the younger woman. After an awkward pause Mrs. Barker rose again. "Well, it's very good of you, and—and—I'll just run out and wash my hands and get the dust off me, and come back."

"No, Mrs. Barker," said Mrs. Horncastle, rising and approaching her, "you will first wash your hands of this Mr. Van Loo, and get some of the dust of the rendezvous off you before you do anything else. You CAN do it by simply telling him, SHOULD YOU MEET HIM IN THE HALL, that I was sitting here when he came in, and heard EVERYTHING! Depend upon it, he won't trouble you again."

But Mrs. Barker, though inexperienced in love, was a good fighter. The best of the sex are. She dropped into the rocking-chair, and began rocking backwards and forwards while still tugging at her gloves, and said, in a gradually warming voice, "I certainly shall not magnify Mr. Van Loo's silliness to that importance. And I have yet to learn what you mean by talking about a rendezvous! And I want to know," she continued, suddenly stopping her rocking and tilting the rockers impertinently behind her, as, with her elbows squared on the chair arms, she tilted her own face defiantly up into Mrs. Horncastle's, "how a woman in your position—who doesn't live with her husband—dares to talk to ME!"

There was a lull before the storm. Mrs. Horncastle approached nearer, and, laying her hand on the back of the chair, leaned over her, and, with a white face and a metallic ring in her voice, said: "It is just because I am a woman IN MY POSITION that I do! It is because I don't live with my husband that I can tell you what it will be when you no longer live with yours—which will be the inevitable result of what you are now doing. It is because I WAS in this position that the very man who is pursuing you, because he thinks you are discontented with YOUR husband, once thought he could pursue me because I had left MINE. You are here with him alone, without the knowledge of your husband; call it folly, caprice, vanity, or what you like, it can have but one end—to put you in my place at last, to be considered the fair game afterwards for any man who may succeed him. You can test him and the truth of what I say by telling him now that I heard all."

"Suppose he doesn't care what you have heard," said Mrs. Barker sharply. "Suppose he says nobody would believe you, if 'telling' is your game. Suppose he is a friend of my husband and he thinks him a much better guardian of my reputation than a woman like you. Suppose he should be the first one to tell my husband of the foul slander invented by you!"

For an instant Mrs. Horncastle was taken aback by the audacity of the woman before her. She knew the simple confidence and boyish trust of Barker in his wife in spite of their sometimes strained relations, and she knew how difficult it would be to shake it. And she had no idea of betraying Mrs. Barker's secret to him, though she had made this scene in his interest. She had wished to save Mrs. Barker from a compromising situation, even if there was a certain vindictiveness in her exposing her to herself. Yet she knew it was quite possible now, if Mrs. Barker had immediate access to her husband, that she would convince him of her perfect innocence. Nevertheless, she had still great confidence in Van Loo's fear of scandal and his utter unmanliness. She knew he was not in love with Mrs. Barker, and this puzzled her when she considered the evident risk he was running now. Her face, however, betrayed nothing. She drew back from Mrs. Barker, and, with an indifferent and graceful gesture towards the door, said, as she leaned against the mantel, "Go, then, and see this much-abused gentleman, and then go together with him and make peace with your husband—even on those terms. If I have saved you from the consequences of your folly I shall be willing to bear even HIS blame."

"Whatever I do," said Mrs. Barker, rising hotly, "I shall not stay here any longer to be insulted." She flounced out of the room and swept down the staircase into the office. Here she found an overworked clerk, and with crimson cheeks and flashing eyes wanted to know why in her own father's hotel she had found her own sitting-room engaged, and had been obliged to wait half an hour before she could be shown into a decent apartment to remove her hat and cloak in; and how it was that even the gentleman who had kindly escorted her had evidently been unable to procure her any assistance. She said this in a somewhat high voice, which might have reached the ears of that gentleman had he been in the vicinity. But he was not, and she was forced to meet the somewhat dazed apologies of the clerk alone, and to accompany the chambermaid to a room only a few paces distant from the one she had quitted. Here she hastily removed her outer duster and hat, washed her hands, and consulted her excited face in the mirror, with the door ajar and an ear sensitively attuned to any step in the corridor. But all this was effected so rapidly that she was at last obliged to sit down in a chair near the half-opened door, and wait. She waited five minutes—ten—but still no footstep. Then she went out into the corridor and listened, and then, smoothing her face, she slipped downstairs, past the door of that hateful room, and reappeared before the clerk with a smiling but somewhat pale and languid face. She had found the room very comfortable, but it was doubtful whether she would stay over night or go on to Hymettus. Had anybody been inquiring for her? She expected to meet friends. No! And her escort—the gentleman who came with her—was possibly in the billiard-room or the bar?

"Oh no! He was gone," said the clerk.

"Gone!" echoed Mrs. Barker. "Impossible! He was—he was here only a moment ago."

The clerk rang a bell sharply. The stableman appeared.

"That tall, smooth-faced man, in a high hat, who came with the lady," said the clerk severely and concisely,—"didn't you tell me he was gone?"

"Yes, sir," said the stableman.

"Are you sure?" interrupted Mrs. Barker, with a dazzling smile that, however, masked a sudden tightening round her heart.

"Quite sure, miss," said the stableman, "for he was in the yard when Steptoe came, after missing the coach. He wanted a buggy to take him over to the Divide. We hadn't one, so he went over to the other stables, and he didn't come back, so I reckon he's gone. I remember it, because Steptoe came by a minute after he'd gone, in another buggy, and as he was going to the Divide, too, I wondered why the gentleman hadn't gone with him."

"And he left no message for me? He said nothing?" asked Mrs. Barker, quite breathless, but still smiling.

"He said nothin' to me but 'Isn't that Steptoe over there?' when Steptoe came in. And I remember he said it kinder suddent—as if he was reminded o' suthin' he'd forgot; and then he asked for a buggy. Ye see, miss," added the man, with a certain rough consideration for her disappointment, "that's mebbe why he clean forgot to leave a message."

Mrs. Barker turned away, and ascended the stairs. Selfishness is quick to recognize selfishness, and she saw in a flash the reason of Van Loo's abandonment of her. Some fear of discovery had alarmed him; perhaps Steptoe knew her husband; perhaps he had heard of Mrs. Horncastle's possession of the sitting-room; perhaps—for she had not seen him since their playful struggle at the door—he had recognized the woman who was there, and the selfish coward had run away. Yes; Mrs. Horncastle was right: she had been only a miserable dupe.

Her cheeks blazed as she entered the room she had just quitted, and threw herself in a chair by the window. She bit her lip as she remembered how for the last three months she had been slowly yielding to Van Loo's cautious but insinuating solicitation, from a flirtation in the San Francisco hotel to a clandestine meeting in the street; from a ride in the suburbs to a supper in a fast restaurant after the theatre. Other women did it who were fashionable and rich, as Van Loo had pointed out to her. Other fashionable women also gambled in stocks, and had their private broker in a "Charley" or a "Jack." Why should not Mrs. Barker have business with a "Paul" Van Loo, particularly as this fast craze permitted secret meetings?—for business of this kind could not be conducted in public, and permitted the fair gambler to call at private offices without fear and without reproach. Mrs. Barker's vanity, Mrs. Barker's love of ceremony and form, Mrs. Barker's snobbishness, were flattered by the attentions of this polished gentleman with a foreign name, which even had the flavor of nobility, who never picked up her fan and handed it to her without bowing, and always rose when she entered the room. Mrs. Barker's scant schoolgirl knowledge was touched by this gentleman, who spoke French fluently, and delicately explained to her the libretto of a risky opera bouffe. And now she had finally yielded to a meeting out of San Francisco—and an ostensible visit—still as a speculator—to one or two mining districts—with HER BROKER. This was the boldest of her steps—an original idea of the fashionable Van Loo—which, no doubt, in time would become a craze, too. But it was a long step—and there was a streak of rustic decorum in Mrs. Barker's nature—the instinct that made Kitty Carter keep a perfectly secluded and distinct sitting-room in the days when she served her father's guests—that now had impelled her to make it a proviso that the first step of her journey should be from her old home in her father's hotel. It was this instinct of the proprieties that had revived in her suddenly at the door of the old sitting-room.

Then a new phase of the situation flashed upon her. It was hard for her vanity to accept Van Loo's desertion as voluntary and final. What if that hateful woman had lured him away by some trick or artfully designed message? She was capable of such meanness to insure the fulfillment of her prophecy. Or, more dreadful thought, what if she had some hold on his affections—she had said that he had pursued her; or, more infamous still, there were some secret understanding between them, and that she—Mrs. Barker—was the dupe of them both! What was she doing in the hotel at such a moment? What was her story of going to Hymettus but a lie as transparent as her own? The tortures of jealousy, which is as often the incentive as it is the result of passion, began to rack her. She had probably yet known no real passion for this man; but with the thought of his abandoning her, and the conception of his faithlessness, came the wish to hold and keep him that was dangerously near it. What if he were even then in that room, the room where she had said she would not stay to be insulted, and they, thus secured against her intrusion, were laughing at her now? She half rose at the thought, but a sound of a horse's hoofs in the stable-yard arrested her. She ran to the window which gave upon it, and, crouching down beside it, listened eagerly. The clatter of hoofs ceased; the stableman was talking to some one; suddenly she heard the stableman say, "Mrs. Barker is here." Her heart leaped,—Van Loo had returned.

But here the voice of the other man which she had not yet heard arose for the first time clear and distinct. "Are you quite sure? I didn't know she left San Francisco."

The room reeled around her. The voice was George Barker's, her husband! "Very well," he continued. "You needn't put up my horse for the night. I may take her back a little later in the buggy."

In another moment she had swept down the passage, and burst into the other room. Mrs. Horncastle was sitting by the table with a book in her hand. She started as the half-maddened woman closed the door, locked it behind her, and cast herself on her knees at her feet.

"My husband is here," she gasped. "What shall I do? In heaven's name help me!"

"Is Van Loo still here?" said Mrs. Horncastle quickly.

"No; gone. He went when I came."

Mrs. Horncastle caught her hand and looked intently into her frightened face. "Then what have you to fear from your husband?" she said abruptly.

"You don't understand. He didn't know I was here. He thought me in San Francisco."

"Does he know it now?"

"Yes. I heard the stableman tell him. Couldn't you say I came here with you; that we were here together; that it was just a little freak of ours? Oh, do!"

Mrs. Horncastle thought a moment. "Yes," she said, "we'll see him here together."

"Oh no! no!" said Mrs. Barker suddenly, clinging to her dress and looking fearfully towards the door. "I couldn't, COULDN'T see him now. Say I'm sick, tired out, gone to my room."

"But you'll have to see him later," said Mrs. Horncastle wonderingly.

"Yes, but he may go first. I heard him tell them not to put up his horse."

"Good!" said Mrs. Horncastle suddenly. "Go to your room and lock the door, and I'll come to you later. Stop! Would Mr. Barker be likely to disturb you if I told him you would like to be alone?"

"No, he never does. I often tell him that."

Mrs. Horncastle smiled faintly. "Come, quick, then," she said, "for he may come HERE first."

Opening the door she passed into the half-dark and empty hall. "Now run!" She heard the quick rustle of Mrs. Barker's skirt die away in the distance, the opening and shutting of a door—silence—and then turned back into her own room.

She was none too soon. Presently she heard Barker's voice saying, "Thank you, I can find the way," his still buoyant step on the staircase, and then saw his brown curls rising above the railing. The light streaming through the open door of the sitting room into the half-lit hall had partially dazzled him, and, already bewildered, he was still more dazzled at the unexpected apparition of the smiling face and bright eyes of Mrs. Horncastle standing in the doorway.

"You have fairly caught us," she said, with charming composure; "but I had half a mind to let you wander round the hotel a little longer. Come in." Barker followed her in mechanically, and she closed the door. "Now, sit down," she said gayly, "and tell me how you knew we were here, and what you mean by surprising us at this hour."

Barker's ready color always rose on meeting Mrs. Horncastle, for whom he entertained a respectful admiration, not without some fear of her worldly superiority. He flushed, bowed, and stared somewhat blankly around the room, at the familiar walls, at the chair from which Mrs. Horncastle had just risen, and finally at his wife's glove, which Mrs. Horncastle had a moment before ostentatiously thrown on the table. Seeing which she pounced upon it with assumed archness, and pretended to conceal it.

"I had no idea my wife was here," he said at last, "and I was quite surprised when the man told me, for she had not written to me about it." As his face was brightening, she for the first time noticed that his frank gray eyes had an abstracted look, and there was a faint line of contraction on his youthful forehead. "Still less," he added, "did I look for the pleasure of meeting you. For I only came here to inquire about my old partner, Demorest, who arrived from Europe a few days ago, and who should have reached Hymettus early this afternoon. But now I hear he came all the way by coach instead of by rail, and got off at the cross-road, and we must have passed each other on the different trails. So my journey would have gone for nothing, only that I now shall have the pleasure of going back with you and Kitty. It will be a lovely drive by moonlight."

Relieved by this revelation, it was easy work for Mrs. Horncastle to launch out into a playful, tantalizing, witty—but, I grieve to say, entirely imaginative—account of her escapade with Mrs. Barker. How, left alone at the San Francisco hotel while their gentlemen friends were enjoying themselves at Hymettus, they resolved upon a little trip, partly for the purpose of looking into some small investments of their own, and partly for the fun of the thing. What funny experiences they had! How, in particular, one horrid inquisitive, vulgar wretch had been boring a European fellow passenger who was going to Hymettus, finally asking him where he had come from last, and when he answered "Hymettus," thought the man was insulting him—

"But," interrupted the laughing Barker, "that passenger may have been Demorest, who has just come from Greece, and surely Kitty would have recognized him."

Mrs. Horncastle instantly saw her blunder, and not only retrieved it, but turned it to account. Ah, yes! but by that time poor Kitty, unused to long journeys and the heat, was utterly fagged out, was asleep, and perfectly unrecognizable in veils and dusters on the back seat of the coach. And this brought her to the point—which was, that she was sorry to say, on arriving, the poor child was nearly wild with a headache from fatigue and had gone to bed, and she had promised not to disturb her.

The undisguised amusement, mingled with relief, that had overspread Barker's face during this lively recital might have pricked the conscience of Mrs. Horncastle, but for some reason I fear it did not. But it emboldened her to go on. "I said I promised her that I would see she wasn't disturbed;

but, of course, now that YOU, her HUSBAND, have come, if"—

"Not for worlds," interrupted Barker earnestly. "I know poor Kitty's headaches, and I never disturb her, poor child, except when I'm thoughtless." And here one of the most thoughtful men in the world in his sensitive consideration of others beamed at her with such frank and wonderful eyes that the arch hypocrite before him with difficulty suppressed a hysterical desire to laugh, and felt the conscious blood flush her to the root of her hair. "You know," he went on, with a sigh, half of relief and half of reminiscence, "that I often think I'm a great bother to a clear-headed, sensible girl like Kitty. She knows people so much better than I do. She's wonderfully equipped for the world, and, you see, I'm only 'lucky,' as everybody says, and I dare say part of my luck was to have got her. I'm very glad she's a friend of yours, you know, for somehow I fancied always that you were not interested in her, or that you didn't understand each other until now. It's odd that nice women don't always like nice women, isn't it? I'm glad she was with you; I was quite startled to learn she was here, and couldn't make it out. I thought at first she might have got anxious about our little Sta, who is with me and the nurse at Hymettus. But I'm glad it was only a lark. I shouldn't wonder," he added, with a laugh, "although she always declares she isn't one of those 'doting, idiotic mothers,' that she found it a little dull without the boy, for all she thought it was better for ME to take him somewhere for a change of air."

The situation was becoming more difficult for Mrs. Horncastle than she had conceived. There had been a certain excitement in its first direct appeal to her tact and courage, and even, she believed, an unselfish desire to save the relations between husband and wife if she could. But she had not calculated upon his unconscious revelations, nor upon their effect upon herself. She had concluded to believe that Kitty had, in a moment of folly, lent herself to this hare-brained escapade, but it now might be possible that it had been deliberately planned. Kitty had sent her husband and child away three weeks before. Had she told the whole truth? How long had this been going on? And if the soulless Van Loo had deserted her now, was it not, perhaps, the miserable ending of an intrigue rather than its beginning? Had she been as great a dupe of this woman as the husband before her? A new and double consciousness came over her that for a moment prevented her from meeting his honest eyes. She felt the shame of being an accomplice mingled with a fierce joy at the idea of a climax that might separate him from his wife forever.

Luckily he did not notice it, but with a continued sense of relief threw himself back in his chair, and glancing familiarly round the walls broke into his youthful laugh. "Lord! how I remember this room in the old days. It was Kitty's own private sitting-room, you know, and I used to think it looked just as fresh and pretty as she. I used to think her crayon drawing wonderful, and still more wonderful that she should have that unnecessary talent when it was quite enough for her to be just 'Kitty.' You know, don't you, how you feel at those times when you're quite happy in being inferior"—He stopped a moment with a sudden recollection that Mrs. Horncastle's marriage had been notoriously unhappy. "I mean," he went on with a shy little laugh and an innocent attempt at gallantry which the very directness of his simple nature made atrociously obvious,—"I mean what you've made lots of young fellows feel. There used to be a picture of Colonel Brigg on the mantelpiece, in full uniform, and signed by himself 'for Kitty;' and Lord! how jealous I was of it, for Kitty never took presents from gentlemen, and nobody even was allowed in here, though she helped her father all over the hotel. She was awfully strict in those days," he interpolated, with a thoughtful look and a half-sigh; "but then she wasn't married. I proposed to her in this very room! Lord! I remember how frightened I was." He stopped for an instant, and then said with a certain timidity, "Do you mind my telling you something about it?"

Mrs. Horncastle was hardly prepared to hear these ingenuous domestic details, but she smiled vaguely, although she could not suppress a somewhat impatient movement with her hands. Even Barker noticed it, but to her surprise moved a little nearer to her, and in a half-entreating way said, "I hope I don't bore you, but it's something confidential. Do you know that she first REFUSED me?"

Mrs. Horncastle smiled, but could not resist a slight toss of her head. "I believe they all do when they are sure of a man."

"No!" said Barker eagerly, "you don't understand. I proposed to her because I thought I was rich. In a foolish moment I thought I had discovered that some old stocks I had had acquired a fabulous value. She believed it, too, but because she thought I was now a rich man and she only a poor girl— a mere servant to her father's guests—she refused me. Refused me because she thought I might regret it in the future, because she would not have it said that she had taken advantage of my proposal only when I was rich enough to make it."

"Well?" said Mrs. Horncastle incredulously, gazing straight before her; "and then?"

"In about an hour I discovered my error, that my stocks were worthless, that I was still a poor man. I thought it only honest to return to her and tell her, even though I had no hope. And then she pitied me, and cried, and accepted me. I tell it to you as her friend." He drew a little nearer and quite fraternally laid his hand upon her own. "I know you won't betray me, though you may think it wrong for me to have told it; but I wanted you to know how good she was and true."

For a moment Mrs. Horncastle was amazed and discomfited, although she saw, with the inscrutable instinct of her sex, no inconsistency between the Kitty of those days and the Kitty now shamefully hiding from her husband in the same hotel. No doubt Kitty had some good reason for her chivalrous act. But she could see the unmistakable effect of that act upon the more logically reasoning husband, and that it might lead him to be more merciful to the later wrong. And there was a keener irony that his first movement of unconscious kindliness towards her was the outcome of his affection for his undeserving wife.

"You said just now she was more practical than you," she said dryly. "Apart from this evidence of it, what other reasons have you for thinking so? Do you refer to her independence or her dealings in the stock market?" she added, with a laugh.

"No," said Barker seriously, "for I do not think her quite practical there; indeed, I'm afraid she is about as bad as I am. But I'm glad you have spoken, for I can now talk confidentially with you, and as you and she are both in the same ventures, perhaps she will feel less compunction in hearing from you—as your own opinion—what I have to tell you than if I spoke to her myself. I am afraid she trusts implicitly to Van Loo's judgment as her broker. I believe he is strictly honorable, but the general opinion of his business insight is not high. They—perhaps I ought to say HE—have been at least so unlucky that they might have learned prudence. The loss of twenty thousand dollars in three months"—

"Twenty thousand!" echoed Mrs. Horncastle.

"Yes. Why, you knew that; it was in the mine you and she visited; or, perhaps," he added hastily, as he flushed at his indiscretion, "she didn't tell you that."

But Mrs. Horncastle as hastily said, "Yes—yes—of course, only I had forgotten the amount;" and he continued:—

"That loss would have frightened any man; but you women are more daring. Only Van Loo ought to have withdrawn. Don't you think so? Of course I couldn't say anything to him without seeming to condemn my own wife; I couldn't say anything to HER because it's her own money."

"I didn't know that Mrs. Barker had any money of her own," said Mrs. Horncastle.

"Well, I gave it to her," said Barker, with sublime simplicity, "and that would make it all the worse for me to speak about it."

Mrs. Horncastle was silent. A new theory flashed upon her which seemed to reconcile all the previous inconsistencies of the situation. Van Loo, under the guise of a lover, was really possessing himself of Mrs. Barker's money. This accounted for the risks he was running in this escapade, which were so incongruous to the rascal's nature. He was calculating that the scandal of an intrigue would relieve him of the perils of criminal defalcation. It was compatible with Kitty's innocence, though it did not relieve her vanity of the part it played in this despicable comedy of passion. All that Mrs. Horncastle thought of now was the effect of its eventful revelation upon the man before her. Of course, he would overlook his wife's trustfulness and business ignorance—it would seem so like his own unselfish faith! That was the fault of all unselfish goodness; it even took the color of adjacent evil, without altering the nature of either. Mrs. Horncastle set her teeth tightly together, but her beautiful mouth smiled upon Barker, though her eyes were bent upon the tablecloth before her.

"I shall do all I can to impress your views upon her," she said at last, "though I fear they will have little weight if given as my own. And you overrate my general influence with her."

Her handsome head drooped in such a thoughtful humility that Barker instinctively drew nearer to her. Besides, she had not lifted her dark lashes for some moments, and he had the still youthful habit of looking frankly into the eyes of those he addressed.

"No," he said eagerly; "how could I? She could not help but love you and do as you would wish. I can't tell you how glad and relieved I am to find that you and she have become such friends. You know I always thought you beautiful, I always thought you so clever—I was even a little frightened of you; but I never until now knew you were so GOOD. No, stop! Yes, I DID know it. Do you remember once in San Francisco, when I found you with Sta in your lap in the drawing-room? I knew it then. You tried to make me think it was a whim—the fancy of a bored and worried woman. But I knew better. And I knew what you were thinking then. Shall I tell you?"

As her eyes were still cast down, although her mouth was still smiling, in his endeavors to look into them his face was quite near hers. He fancied that it bore the look she had worn once before.

"You were thinking," he said in a voice which had grown suddenly quite hesitating and tremulous,—he did not know why,—"that the poor little baby was quite friendless and alone. You were pitying it—you know you were—because there was no one to give it the loving care that was its due, and because it was intrusted to that hired nurse in that great hotel. You were thinking how you would love it if it were yours, and how cruel it was that Love was sent without an object to waste itself upon. You were: I saw it in your face."

She suddenly lifted her eyes and looked full into his with a look that held and possessed him. For a moment his whole soul seemed to tremble on the verge of their lustrous depths, and he drew back dizzy and frightened. What he saw there he never clearly knew; but, whatever it was, it seemed to suddenly change his relations to her, to the room, to his wife, to the world without. It was a glimpse of a world of which he knew nothing. He had looked frankly and admiringly into the eyes of other pretty women; he had even gazed into her own before, but never with this feeling. A sudden sense that what he had seen there he had himself evoked, that it was an answer to some question he had scarcely yet formulated, and that they were both now linked by an understanding and consciousness that was irretrievable, came over him. He rose awkwardly and went to the window. She rose also, but more leisurely and easily, moved one of the books on the table, smoothed out her skirts, and changed her seat to a little sofa. It is the woman who always comes out of these crucial moments unruffled.

"I suppose you will be glad to see your friend Mr. Demorest when you go back," she said pleasantly; "for of course he will be at Hymettus awaiting you."

He turned eagerly, as he always did at the name. But even then he felt that Demorest was no longer of such importance to him. He felt, too, that he was not yet quite sure of his voice or even what to say. As he hesitated she went on half playfully: "It seems hard that you had to come all the way here on such a bootless errand. You haven't even seen your wife yet."

The mention of his wife recalled him to himself, oddly enough, when Demorest's name had failed. But very differently. Out of his whirling consciousness came the instinctive feeling that he could not see her now. He turned, crossed the room, sat down on the sofa beside Mrs. Horncastle, and without, however, looking at her, said, with his eyes on the floor, "No; and I've been thinking that it's hardly worth while to disturb her so early to-morrow as I should have to go. So I think it's a good deal better to let her have a good night's rest, remain here quietly with you to-morrow until the stage leaves, and that both of you come over together. My horse is still saddled, and I will be back at Hymettus before Demorest has gone to bed."

He was obliged to look up at her as he rose. Mrs. Horncastle was sitting erect, beautiful and dazzling as even he had never seen her before. For his resolution had suddenly lifted a great weight from her shoulders,—the dangerous meeting of husband and wife the next morning, and its results, whatever they might be, had been quietly averted. She felt, too, a half-frightened joy even in the constrained manner in which he had imparted his determination. That frankness which even she had sometimes found so crushing was gone.

"I really think you are quite right," she said, rising also, "and, besides, you see, it will give me a chance to talk to her as you wished."

"To talk to her as I wished?" echoed Barker abstractedly.

"Yes, about Van Loo, you know," said Mrs. Horncastle, smiling.

"Oh, certainly—about Van Loo, of course," he returned hurriedly.

"And then," said Mrs. Horncastle brightly, "I'll tell her. Stay!" she interrupted herself hurriedly. "Why need I say anything about your having been here AT ALL? It might only annoy her, as you yourself suggest." She stopped breathlessly with parted lips.

"Why, indeed?" said Barker vaguely. Yet all this was so unlike his usual truthfulness that he slightly hesitated.

"Besides," continued Mrs. Horncastle, noticing it, "you know you can always tell her later, if necessary." And she added with a charming mischievousness, "As she didn't tell you she was coming, I really don't see why you are bound to tell her that you were here."

The sophistry pleased Barker, even though it put him into a certain retaliating attitude towards his wife which he was not aware of feeling. But, as Mrs. Horncastle put it, it was only a playful attitude.

"Certainly," he said. "Don't say anything about it."

He moved to the door with his soft, broad-brimmed hat swinging between his fingers. She noticed for the first time that he looked taller in his long black serape and riding-boots, and, oddly enough, much more like the hero of an amorous tryst than Van Loo. "I know," she said brightly, "you are eager to get back to your old friend, and it would be selfish for me to try to keep you longer. You have had a stupid evening, but you have made it pleasant to me by telling me what you thought of me. And before you go I want you to believe that I shall try to keep that good opinion." She spoke frankly in contrast to the slight worldly constraint of Barker's manner; it seemed as if they had changed characters. And then she extended her hand.

With a low bow, and without looking up, he took it. Again their pulses seemed to leap together with one accord and the same mysterious understanding. He could not tell if he had unconsciously pressed her hand or if she had returned the pressure. But when their hands unclasped it seemed as if it were the division of one flesh and spirit.

She remained standing by the open door until his footsteps passed down the staircase. Then she suddenly closed and locked the door with an instinct that Mrs. Barker might at once return now that he was gone, and she wished to be a moment alone to recover herself. But she presently opened it again and listened. There was a noise in the courtyard, but it sounded like the rattle of wheels more than the clatter of a horseman. Then she was overcome—a sudden sense of pity for the unfortunate woman still hiding from her husband— and felt a momentary chivalrous exaltation of spirit. Certainly she had done "good" to that wretched "Kitty;" perhaps she had earned the epithet that Barker had applied to her. Perhaps that was the meaning of all this happiness to her, and the result was to be only the happiness and reconciliation of the wife and husband. This was to be her reward. I grieve to say that the tears had come into her beautiful eyes at this satisfactory conclusion, but she dashed them away and ran out into the hall. It was quite dark, but there was a faint glimmer on the opposite wall as if the door of Mrs. Barker's bedroom were ajar to an eager listener. She flew towards the glimmer, and pushed the door open: the room was empty. Empty of Mrs. Barker, empty of her dressing-box, her reticule and shawl. She was gone.

Still, Mrs. Horncastle lingered; the woman might have got frightened and retreated to some further room at the opening of the door and the coming out of her husband. She walked along the passage, calling her name softly. She even penetrated the dreary, half-lit public parlor, expecting to find her crouching there. Then a sudden wild idea took possession of her: the miserable wife had repented of her act and of her concealment, and had crept downstairs to await her husband in the office. She had told him some new lie, had begged him to take her with him, and Barker, of course, had assented. Yes, she now knew why she had heard the rattling wheels instead of the clattering hoofs she had listened for. They had gone together, as he first proposed, in the buggy.

She ran swiftly down the stairs and entered the office. The overworked clerk was busy and querulously curt. These women were always asking such idiotic questions. Yes, Mr. Barker had just gone.

"With Mrs. Barker in the buggy?" asked Mrs. Horncastle.

"No, as he came—on horseback. Mrs. Barker left HALF AN HOUR AGO."

"Alone?"

This was apparently too much for the long-suffering clerk. He lifted his eyes to the ceiling, and then, with painful precision, and accenting every word with his pencil on the desk before him, said deliberately, "Mrs. George Barker—left—here— with her—escort—the—man she—was—always—asking— for—in—the—buggy—at exactly—9.35." And he plunged into his work again.

Mrs. Horncastle turned, ran up the staircase, re-entered the sitting-room, and slamming the door behind her, halted in the centre of the room, panting, erect, beautiful, and menacing.

And she was alone in this empty room—this deserted hotel. From this very room her husband had left her with a brutality on his lips. From this room the fool and liar she had tried to warn had gone to her ruin with a swindling hypocrite. And from this room the only man in the world she ever cared for had gone forth bewildered, wronged, and abused, and she knew now she could have kept and comforted him.

CHAPTER IV

When Philip Demorest left the stagecoach at the cross-roads he turned into the only wayside house, the blacksmith's shop, and, declaring his intention of walking over to Hymettus, asked permission to leave his hand-bag and wraps until they could be sent after him. The blacksmith was surprised that this "likely mannered," distinguished-looking "city man" should WALK eight miles when he could ride, and tried to dissuade him, offering his own buggy. But he was still more surprised when Demorest, laying aside his duster, took off his coat, and, slinging it on his arm, prepared to set forth with the good-humored assurance that he would do the distance in a couple of hours and get in in time for supper. "I wouldn't be too sure of that," said the blacksmith grimly, "or even of getting a room. They're a stuck-up lot over there, and they ain't goin' to hump themselves over a chap who comes traipsin' along the road like any tramp, with nary baggage." But Demorest laughingly accepted the risk, and taking his stout stick in one hand, pressed a gold coin into the blacksmith's palm, which was, however, declined with such reddening promptness that Demorest as promptly reddened and apologized. The habits of European travel had been still strong on him, and he felt a slight patriotic thrill as he said, with a grave smile, "Thank you, then; and thank you still more for reminding me that I am among my own 'people,'" and stepped lightly out into the road.

The air was still deliciously cool, but warmer currents from the heated pines began to alternate with the wind from the summit. He found himself sometimes walking through a stratum of hot air which seemed to exhale from the wood itself, while his head and breast were swept by the mountain breeze. He felt the old intoxication of the balmy-scented air again, and the five years of care and hopelessness laid upon his shoulders since he had last breathed its fragrance slipped from them like a burden. There had been but little change here; perhaps the road was wider and the dust lay thicker, but the great pines still mounted in serried ranks on the slopes as before, with no gaps in their unending files. Here was the spot where the stagecoach had passed them that eventful morning when they were coming out of their camp-life into the world of civilization; a little further back, the spot where Jack Hamlin had forced upon him that grim memento of the attempted robbery of their cabin, which he had kept ever since. He half smiled again at the superstitious interest that had made him keep it, with the intention of some day returning to bury it, with all recollections of the deed, under the site of the old cabin. As he went on in the vivifying influence of the air and scene, new life seemed to course through his veins; his step seemed to grow as elastic as in the old days of their bitter but hopeful struggle for fortune, when he had gayly returned from his weekly tramp to Boomville laden with the scant provision procured by their scant earnings and dying credit. Those were the days when HER living image still inspired his heart with faith and hope; when everything was yet possible to youth and love, and before the irony of fate had given him fortune with one hand only to withdraw HER with the other. It was strange and cruel that coming back from his quest of rest and forgetfulness he should find only these youthful and sanguine dreams revive with his reviving vigor. He walked on more hurriedly as if to escape them, and was glad to be diverted by one or two carryalls and char-a-bancs filled with gayly

dressed pleasure parties—evidently visitors to Hymettus—
which passed him on the road. Here were the first signs of
change. He recalled the train of pack-mules of the old days,
the file of pole-and-basket carrying Chinese, the squaw with
the papoose strapped to her shoulder, or the wandering and
foot-sore prospector, who were the only wayfarers he used to
meet. He contrasted their halts and friendly greetings with
the insolent curiosity or undisguised contempt of the carriage
folk, and smiled as he thought of the warning of the
blacksmith. But this did not long divert him; he found
himself again returning to his previous thought. Indeed, the
face of a young girl in one of the carriages had quite startled
him with its resemblance to an old memory of his lost love
as he saw her,—her frail, pale elegance encompassed in laces
as she leaned back in her drive through Fifth Avenue, with
eyes that lit up and became transfigured only as he passed.
He tried to think of his useless quest in search of her last
resting-place abroad; how he had been baffled by the
opposition of her surviving relations, already incensed by the
thought that her decline had been the effect of her hopeless
passion. He tried to recall the few frigid lines that
reconveyed to him the last letter he had sent her, with the
announcement of her death and the hope that "his
persecutions" would now cease. A wild idea had sometimes
come to him out of the very insufficiency of his knowledge
of this climax, but he had always put it aside as a precursor
of that madness which might end his ceaseless thought. And
now it was returning to him, here, thousands of miles away
from where she was peacefully sleeping, and even filling
him with the vigor of youthful hope.

The brief mountain twilight was giving way now to the
radiance of the rising moon. He endeavored to fix his
thoughts upon his partners who were to meet him at
Hymettus after these long years of separation.

Hymettus! He recalled now the odd coincidence that he had mischievously used as a gag to his questioning fellow traveler; but now he had really come from a villa near Athens to find his old house thus classically rechristened after it, and thought of it with a gravity he had not felt before. He wondered who had named it. There was no suggestion of the soft, sensuous elegance of the land he had left in those great heroics of nature before him. Those enormous trees were no woods for fauns or dryads; they had their own godlike majesty of bulk and height, and as he at last climbed the summit and saw the dark-helmeted head of Black Spur before him, and beyond it the pallid, spiritual cloud of the Sierras, he did not think of Olympus. Yet for a moment he was startled, as he turned to the right, by the Doric-columned facade of a temple painted by the moonbeams and framed in an opening of the dark woods before him. It was not until he had reached it that he saw that it was the new wooden post-office of Heavy Tree Hill.

And now the buildings of the new settlement began to faintly appear. But the obscurity of the shadow and the equally disturbing unreality of the moonlight confused him in his attempts to recognize the old landmarks. A broad and well-kept winding road had taken the place of the old steep, but direct trail to his cabin. He had walked for some moments in uncertainty, when a sudden sweep of the road brought the full crest of the hill above and before him, crowned with a tiara of lights, overtopping a long base of flashing windows. That was all that was left of Heavy Tree Hill. The old foreground of buckeye and odorous ceanothus was gone. Even the great grove of pines behind it had vanished.

There was already a stir of life in the road, and he could see figures moving slowly along a kind of sterile, formal terrace spread with a few dreary marble vases and plaster statues which had replaced the natural slope and the great quartz buttresses of outcrop that supported it. Presently he entered a gate, and soon found himself in the carriage drive leading to the hotel veranda. A number of fair promenaders were facing the keen mountain night wind in wraps and furs. Demorest had replaced his coat, but his boots were red with dust, and as he ascended the steps he could see that he was eyed with some superciliousness by the guests and with considerable suspicion by the servants. One of the latter was approaching him with an insolent smile when a figure darted from the vestibule, and, brushing the waiter aside, seized Demorest's two hands in his and held him at arm's length.

"Demorest, old man!"

"Stacy, old chap!"

"But where's your team? I've had all the spare hostlers and hall-boys listening for you at the gate. And where's Barker? When he found you'd given the dead-cut to the railroad— HIS railroad, you know—he loped over to Boomville after you."

Demorest briefly explained that he had walked by the old road and probably missed him. But by this time the waiters, crushed by the spectacle of this travel-worn stranger's affectionate reception by the great financial magnate, were wildly applying their brushes and handkerchiefs to his trousers and boots until Stacy again swept them away.

"Get off, all of you! Now, Phil, you come with me. The house is full, but I've made the manager give you a lady's drawing-room suite. When you telegraphed you'd meet us HERE there was no chance to get anything else. It's really Mrs. Van Loo's family suite; but they were sent for to go to Marysville yesterday, and so we'll run you in for the night."

"But"—protested Demorest.

"Nonsense!" said Stacy, dragging him away. "We'll pay for it; and I reckon the old lady won't object to taking her share of the damage either, or she isn't Van Loo's mother. Come."

Demorest felt himself hurried forward by the energetic Stacy, preceded by the obsequious manager, through a corridor to a handsomely furnished suite, into whose bathroom Stacy incontinently thrust him.

"There! Wash up; and by the time you're ready Barker ought to be back, and we'll have supper. It's waiting for us in the other room."

"But how about Barker, the dear boy?" persisted Demorest, holding open the door. "Tell me, is he well and happy?"

"About as well as we all are," said Stacy quickly, yet with a certain dry significance. "Never mind now; wait until you see him."

The door closed. When Demorest had finished washing, and wiped away the last red stain of the mountain road, he found Stacy seated by the window of the larger sitting-room. In the centre a table was spread for supper. A bright fire of hickory logs burnt on a marble hearth between two large windows that gave upon the distant outline of Black Spur. As Stacy turned towards him, by the light of the shaded lamp and flickering fire, Demorest had a good look at the face of his old friend and partner. It was as keen and energetic as ever, with perhaps an even more hawk-like activity visible in the eye and nostril; but it was more thoughtful and reticent in the lines of the mouth under the closely clipped beard and mustache, and when he looked up, at first there were two deep lines or furrows across his low broad forehead.

Demorest fancied, too, that there was a little of the old fighting look in his eye, but it softened quickly as his friend approached, and he burst out with his curt but honest single-syllabled laugh. "Ha! You look a little less like a roving Apache than you did when you came. I really thought the waiters were going to chuck you. And you ARE tanned! Darned if you don't look like the profile stamped on a Continental penny! But here's luck and a welcome back, old man!"

Demorest passed his arm around the neck of his seated partner, and grasping his upraised hand said, looking down with a smile, "And now about Barker."

"Oh, Parker, d—n him! He's the same unshakable, unchangeable, ungrow-upable Barker! With the devil's own luck, too! Waltzing into risks and waltzing out of 'em. With fads enough to put him in the insane asylum if people did not prefer to keep him out of it to help 'em. Always believing in everybody, until they actually believe in themselves, and shake him! And he's got a wife that's making a fool of herself, and I shouldn't wonder in time—of him!"

Demorest pressed his hand over his partner's mouth. "Come, Jim! You know you never really liked that marriage, simply because you thought that old man Carter made a good thing of it. And you never seem to have taken into consideration the happiness Barker got out of it, for he DID love the girl. And he still is happy, is he not?" he added quickly, as Stacy uttered a grunt.

"As happy as a man can be who has his child here with a nurse while his wife is gallivanting in San Francisco, and throwing her money—and Lord knows what else—away at the bidding of a smooth-tongued, shady operator."

"Does HE complain of it?" asked Demorest.

"Not he; the fool trusts her!" said Stacy curtly.

Demorest laughed. "That is happiness! Come, Jim! don't let us begrudge him that. But I've heard that his affairs have again prospered."

"He built this railroad and this hotel. The bank owns both now. He didn't care to keep money in them after they were a success; said he wasn't an engineer nor a hotel-keeper, and drew it out to find something new. But here he comes," he added, as a horseman dashed into the drive before the hotel. "Question him yourself. You know you and he always get along best without me."

In another moment Barker had burst into the room, and in his first tempestuous greeting of Demorest the latter saw little change in his younger partner as he held him at arm's length to look at him. "Why, Barker boy, you haven't got a bit older since the day when—you remember—you went over to Boomville to cash your bonds, and then came back and burst upon us like this to tell us you were a beggar."

"Yes," laughed Barker, "and all the while you fellows were holding four aces up your sleeve in the shape of the big strike."

"And you, Georgy, old boy," returned Demorest, swinging Barker's two hands backwards and forwards, "were holding a royal flush up yours in the shape of your engagement to Kitty."

The fresh color died out of Barker's cheek even while the frank laugh was still on his mouth. He turned his face for a moment towards the window, and a swift and almost involuntary glance passed between the others. But he almost as quickly turned his glistening eyes back to Demorest again, and said eagerly, "Yes, dear Kitty! You shall see her and the baby to-morrow."

Then they fell upon the supper with the appetites of the Past, and for some moments they all talked eagerly and even noisily together, all at the same time, with even the spirits of the Past. They recalled every detail of their old life; eagerly and impetuously recounted the old struggles, hopes, and disappointments, gave the strange importance of schoolboys to unimportant events, and a mystic meaning to a shibboleth of their own; roared over old jokes with a delight they had never since given to new; reawakened idiotic nicknames and bywords with intense enjoyment; grew grave, anxious, and agonized over forgotten names, trifling dates, useless distances, ineffective records, and feeble chronicles of their domestic economy. It was the thoughtful and melancholy Demorest who remembered the exact color and price paid for a certain shirt bought from a Greaser peddler amidst the envy of his companions; it was the financial magnate, Stacy, who could inform them what were the exact days they had saleratus bread and when flapjacks; it was the thoughtless and mercurial Barker who recalled with unheard-of accuracy, amidst the applause of the others, the full name of the Indian squaw who assisted at their washing. Even then they were almost feverishly loath to leave the subject, as if the Past, at least, was secure to them still, and they were even doubtful of their own free and full accord in the Present. Then they slipped rather reluctantly into their later experiences, but with scarcely the same freedom or spontaneity; and it was noticeable that these records were elicited from Barker by Stacy or from Stacy by Barker for the information of Demorest, often with chaffing and only under good-humored protest. "Tell Demorest how you broke the 'Copper Ring,'" from the admiring Barker, or, "Tell Demorest how your d—d foolishness in buying up the right and plant of the Ditch Company got you control of the railroad," from the mischievous Stacy, were challenges in point. Presently they left the table, and, to the astonishment of the waiters who removed the cloth, common brier-wood pipes, thoughtfully provided by Barker in commemoration of the Past, were lit, and they ranged themselves in armchairs before the fire quite unconsciously in their old attitudes. The two windows on either side of the hearth gave them the same view that the open door of the old cabin had made familiar to them, the league-long valley below the shadowy bulk of the Black Spur rising in the distance, and, still more remote, the pallid snow-line that soared even beyond its crest.

As in the old time, they were for many moments silent; and then, as in the old time, it was the irrepressible Barker who broke the silence. "But Stacy does not tell you anything about his friend, the beautiful Mrs. Horncastle. You know he's the guardian of one of the finest women in California—a woman as noble and generous as she is handsome. And think of it! He's protecting her from her brute of a husband, and looking after her property. Isn't it good and chivalrous of him?"

The irrepressible laughter of the two men brought only wonder and reproachful indignation into the widely opened eyes of Barker. HE was perfectly sincere. He had been thinking of Stacy's admiration for Mrs. Horncastle in his ride from Boomville, and, strange to say, yet characteristic of his nature, it was equally the natural outcome of his interview with her and the singular effect she had upon him. That he (Barker) thoroughly sympathized with her only convinced him that Stacy must feel the same for her, and that, no doubt, she must respond to him equally. And how noble it was in his old partner, with his advantages of position in the world and his protecting relations to her, not to avail himself of this influence upon her generous nature. If he himself—a married man and the husband of Kitty—was so conscious of her charm, how much greater it must be to the free and INEXPERIENCED Stacy.

The italics were in Barker's thought; for in those matters he felt that Stacy and even Demorest, occupied in other things, had not his knowledge. There was no idea or consciousness of heroically sacrificing himself or Mrs. Horncastle in this. I am afraid there was not even an idea of a superior morality in himself in giving up the possibility of loving her. Ever since Stacy had first seen her he had fancied that Stacy liked her,—indeed, Kitty fancied it, too,—and it seemed almost providential now that he should know how to assist his old partner to happiness. For it was inconceivable that Stacy should not be able to rescue this woman from her shameful bonds, or that she should not consent to it through his (Barker's) arguments and entreaties. To a "champion of dames" this seemed only right and proper. In his unfailing optimism he translated Stacy's laugh as embarrassment and Demorest's as only ignorance of the real question. But Demorest had noticed, if he had not, that Stacy's laugh was a little nervously prolonged for a man of his temperament, and that he had cast a very keen glance at Barker. A messenger arriving with a telegram brought from Boomville called Stacy momentarily away, and Barker was not slow to take advantage of his absence.

"I wish, Phil," he said, hitching his chair closer to Demorest, "that you would think seriously of this matter, and try to persuade Stacy—who, I believe, is more interested in Mrs. Horncastle than he cares to show—to put a little of that determination in love that he has shown in business. She's an awfully fine woman, and in every way suited to him, and he is letting an absurd sense of pride and honor keep him from influencing her to get rid of her impossible husband. There's no reason," continued Barker in a burst of enthusiastic simplicity, "that BECAUSE she has found some one she likes better, and who would treat her better, that she should continue to stick to that beast whom all California would gladly see her divorced from. I never could understand that kind of argument, could you?"

Demorest looked at his companion's glowing cheek and kindling eye with a smile. "A good deal depends upon the side from which you argue. But, frankly, Barker boy, though I think I know you in all your phases, I am not prepared yet to accept you as a match-maker! However, I'll think it over, and find out something more of this from your goddess, who seems to have bewitched you both. But what does Mistress Kitty say to your admiration?"

Barker's face clouded, but instantly brightened. "Oh, they're the best of friends; they're quite like us, you know, even to larks they have together." He stopped and colored at his slip. But Demorest, who had noticed his change of expression, was more concerned at the look of half incredulity and half suspicion with which Stacy, who had re-entered the room in time to hear Barker's speech, was regarding his unconscious younger partner.

"I didn't know that Mrs. Horncastle and Mrs. Barker were such friends," he said dryly as he sat down again. But his face presently became so abstracted that Demorest said gayly:—

"Well, Jim, I'm glad I'm not a Napoleon of Finance! I couldn't stand it to have my privacy or my relaxation broken in upon at any moment, as yours was just now. What confounded somersault in stocks has put that face on you?"

Stacy looked up quickly with his brief laugh. "I'm afraid

you'd be none the wiser if I told you. That was a pony express messenger from New York. You remember how Barker, that night of the strike, when we were sitting together here, or very near here, proposed that we ought to have a password or a symbol to call us together in case of emergency, for each other's help? Well, let us say I have two partners, one in Europe and one in New York. That was my password."

"And, I hope, no more serious than ours," added Demorest.

Stacy laughed his short laugh. Nevertheless, the conversation dragged again. The feverish gayety of the early part of the evening was gone, and they seemed to be suffering from the reaction. They fell into their old attitudes, looking from the firelight to the distant bulk of Black Spur without a word. The occasional sound of the voices of promenaders on the veranda at last ceased; there was the noise of the shutting of heavy doors below, and Barker rose.

"You'll excuse me, boys; but I must go and say good-night to little Sta, and see that he's all right. I haven't seen him since I got back. But"—to Demorest—"you'll see him to-morrow, when Kitty comes. It is as much as my life is worth to show him before she certifies him as being presentable." He paused, and then added: "Don't wait up, you fellows, for me; sometimes the little chap won't let me go. It's as if he thought, now Kitty's away, I was all he had. But I'll be up early in the morning and see you. I dare say you and Stacy have a heap to say to each other on business, and you won't miss me. So I'll say good-night." He laughed lightly, pressed the hands of his partners in his usual hearty fashion, and went out of the room, leaving the gloom a little deeper than before. It was so unusual for Barker to be the first to leave anybody or anything in trouble that they both noticed it. "But for that," said Demorest, turning to Stacy as the door closed,

"I should say the dear fellow was absolutely unchanged. But he seemed a little anxious to-night."

"I shouldn't wonder. He's got two women on his mind,—as if one was not enough."

"I don't understand. You say his wife is foolish, and this other"—

"Never mind that now," interrupted Stacy, getting up and putting down his pipe. "Let's talk a little business. That other stuff will keep."

"By all means," said Demorest, with a smile, settling down into his chair a little wearily, however. "I forgot business. And I forgot, my dear Jim, to congratulate you. I've heard all about you, even in New York. You're the man who, according to everybody, now holds the finances of the Pacific Slope in his hands. And," he added, leaning affectionately towards his old partner, "I don't know any one better equipped in honesty, straightforwardness, and courage for such a responsibility than you."

"I only wish," said Stacy, looking thoughtfully at Demorest, "that I didn't hold nearly a million of your money included in the finances of the Pacific Slope."

"Why," said the smiling Demorest, "as long as I am satisfied?"

"Because I am not. If you're satisfied, I'm a wretched idiot and not fit for my position. Now, look here, Phil. When you wrote me to sell out your shares in the Wheat Trust I was a little staggered. I knew your gait, my boy, and I knew, too, that, while you didn't know enough to trust your own opinions or feeling, you knew too much to trust any one's opinion that wasn't first-class. So I reckoned you had the straight tip; but I didn't see it. Now, I ought not to have been staggered if I was fit for your confidence, or, if I was staggered, I ought to have had enough confidence in myself not to mind you. See?"

"I admit your logic, old man," said Demorest, with an amused face, "but I don't see your premises. WHEN did I tell you to sell out?"

"Two days ago. You wrote just after you arrived."

"I have never written to you since I arrived. I only telegraphed to you to know where we should meet, and received your message to come here."

"You never wrote me from San Francisco?"

"Never."

Stacy looked concernedly at his friend. Was he in his right mind? He had heard of cases where melancholy brooding on a fixed idea had affected the memory. He took from his pocket a letter-case, and selecting a letter handed it to Demorest without speaking.

Demorest glanced at it, turned it over, read its contents, and in a grave voice said, "There is something wrong here. It is like my handwriting, but I never wrote the letter, nor has it been in my hand before."

Stacy sprang to his side. "Then it's a forgery!"

"Wait a moment." Demorest, who, although very grave, was the more collected of the two, went to a writing-desk, selected a sheet of paper, and took up a pen. "Now," he said, "dictate that letter to me."

Stacy began, Demorest's pen rapidly following him:—

"DEAR JIM,—On receipt of this get rid of my Wheat Trust shares at whatever figure you can. From the way things pointed in New York"—

"Stop!" interrupted Demorest.

"Well?" said Stacy impatiently.

"Now, my dear Jim," said Demorest plaintively, "when did you ever know me to write such a sentence as 'the way things pointed'?"

"Let me finish reading," said Stacy. This literary sensitiveness at such a moment seemed little short of puerility to the man of business.

"From the way things pointed in New York," continued Stacy, "and from private advices received, this seems to be the only prudent course before the feathers begin to fly. Longing to see you again and the dear old stamping-ground at Heavy Tree. Love to Barker. Has the dear old boy been at any fresh crank lately?

"Yours, PHIL DEMOREST."

The dictation and copy finished together. Demorest laid the freshly written sheet beside the letter Stacy had produced. They were very much alike and yet quite distinct from each other. Only the signature seemed identical.

"That's the invariable mistake with the forger," said Demorest; "he always forgets that signatures ought to be identical with the text rather than with each other."

But Stacy did not seem to hear this or require further proof. His face was quite gray and his lips compressed until lost in his closely set beard as he gazed fixedly out of the window. For the first time, really concerned and touched, Demorest laid his hand gently on his shoulder.

"Tell me, Jim, how much does this mean to you apart from me? Don't think of me."

"I don't know yet," said Stacy slowly. "That's the trouble. And I won't know until I know who's at the bottom of it. Does anybody know of your affairs with me?"

"No one."

"No confidential friend, eh?"

"None."

"No one who has access to your secrets? No—no—woman? Excuse me, Phil," he said, as a peculiar look passed over Demorest's face, "but this is business."

"No," he returned, with that gentleness that used to frighten them in the old days, "it's ignorance. You fellows always say 'Cherchez la femme' when you can't say anything else. Come now," he went on more brightly, "look at the letter. Here's a man, commercially educated, for he has used the usual business formulas, 'on receipt of this,' and 'advices received,' which I won't merely say I don't use, but which few but commercial men use. Next, here's a man who uses slang, not only ineptly, but artificially, to give the letter the easy, familiar turn it hasn't from beginning to end. I need only say, my dear Stacy, that I don't write slang to you, but that nobody who understands slang ever writes it in that way. And then the knowledge of my opinion of Barker is such as might be gained from the reading of my letters by a person who couldn't comprehend my feelings. Now, let me play inquisitor for a few moments. Has anybody access to my letters to YOU?"

"No one. I keep them locked up in a cabinet. I only make memorandums of your instructions, which I give to my clerks, but never your letters."

"But your clerks sometimes see you make memorandums from them?"

"Yes, but none of them have the ability to do this sort of thing, nor the opportunity of profiting by it."

"Has any woman—now this is not retaliation, my dear Jim, for I fancy I detect a woman's cleverness and a woman's stupidity in this forgery—any access to your secrets or my letters? A woman's villainy is always effective for the moment, but always defective when probed."

The look of scorn which passed over Stacy's face was quite as distinct as Demorest's previous protest, as he said contemptuously, "I'm not such a fool as to mix up petticoats with my business, whatever I do."

"Well, one thing more. I have told you that in my opinion the forger has a commercial education or style, that he doesn't know me nor Barker, and don't understand slang. Now, I have to add what must have occurred to you, Jim, that the forger is either a coward, or his object is not altogether mercenary: for the same ability displayed in this letter would on the signature alone—had it been on a check or draft— have drawn from your bank twenty times the amount concerned. Now, what is the actual loss by this forgery?"

"Very little; for you've got a good price for your stocks, considering the depreciation in realizing suddenly on so large an amount. I told my broker to sell slowly and in small quantities to avoid a panic. But the real loss is the control of the stock."

"But the amount I had was not enough to affect that," said Demorest.

"No, but I was carrying a large amount myself, and together we controlled the market, and now I have unloaded, too."

"You sold out! and with your doubts?" said Demorest.

"That's just it," said Stacy, looking steadily at his companion's face, "because I HAD doubts, and it won't do for me to have them. I ought either to have disobeyed your letter and kept your stock and my own, or have done just what I did. I might have hedged on my own stock, but I don't believe in hedging. There is no middle course to a man in my business if he wants to keep at the top. No great success, no great power, was ever created by it."

Demorest smiled. "Yet you accept the alternative also, which is ruin?"

"Precisely," said Stacy. "When you returned the other day you were bound to find me what I was or a beggar. But nothing between. However," he added, "this has nothing to do with the forgery, or," he smiled grimly, "everything to do with it. Hush! Barker is coming."

There was a quick step along the corridor approaching the room. The next moment the door flew open to the bounding step and laughing face of Barker. Whatever of thoughtfulness or despondency he had carried from the room with him was completely gone. With his amazing buoyancy and power of reaction he was there again in his usual frank, cheerful simplicity.

"I thought I'd come in and say goodnight," he began, with a laugh. "I got Sta asleep after some high jinks we had together, and then I reckoned it wasn't the square thing to leave just you two together, the first night you came. And I remembered I had some business to talk over, too, so I thought I'd chip in again and take a hand. It's only the shank of the evening yet," he continued gayly, "and we ought to sit up at least long enough to see the old snow-line vanish, as we did in old times. But I say," he added suddenly, as he glanced from the one to the other, "you've been having it pretty strong already. Why, you both look as you did that night the backwater of the South Fork came into our cabin. What's up?"

"Nothing," said Demorest hastily, as he caught a glance of Stacy's impatient face. "Only all business is serious, Barker boy, though you don't seem to feel it so."

"I reckon you're right there," said Barker, with a chuckle. "People always laugh, of course, when I talk business, so it might make it a little livelier for you and more of a change if I chipped in now. Only I don't know which you'll do. Hand me a pipe. Well," he continued, filling the pipe Demorest shoved towards him, "you see, I was in Sacramento yesterday, and I went into Van Loo's branch office, as I heard he was there, and I wanted to find out something about Kitty's investments, which I don't think he's managing exactly right. He wasn't there, however, but as I was waiting I heard his clerks talk about a drop in the Wheat Trust, and that there was a lot of it put upon the market. They seemed to think that something had happened, and it was going down still further. Now I knew it was your pet scheme, and that Phil had a lot of shares in it, too, so I just slipped out and went to a broker's and told him to buy all he could of it. And, by Jove! I was a little taken aback when I found what I was in for, for everybody seemed to have unloaded, and I found I hadn't money enough to pay margins, but I knew that Demorest was here, and I reckoned on his seeing me through." He stopped and colored, but added hopefully, "I reckon I'm safe, anyway, for just as the thing was over those same clerks of Van Loo's came bounding into the office to buy up everything. And offered to take it off my hands and pay the margins."

"And you?" said both men eagerly, and in a breath.

Barker stared at them, and reddened and paled by turns. "I held on," he stammered. "You see, boys"—

Both men had caught him by the arms. "How much have you got?" they said, shaking him as if to precipitate the answer.

"It's a heap!" said Barker. "It's a ghastly lot now I think of it. I'm afraid I'm in for fifty thousand, if a cent."

To his infinite astonishment and delight he was alternately hugged and tossed backwards and forwards between the two men quite in the fashion of the old days. Breathless but laughing, he at length gasped out, "What does it all mean?"

"Tell him everything, Jim,—EVERYTHING," said Demorest quickly.

Stacy briefly related the story of the forgery, and then laid the letter and its copy before him. But Barker only read the forgery.

"How could YOU, Stacy—one of the three partners of Heavy Tree—be deceived! Don't you see it's Phil's handwriting—but it isn't PHIL!"

"But have you any idea WHO it is?" said Stacy.

"Not me," said Barker, with widely opened eyes. "You see it must be somebody whom we are familiar with. I can't imagine such a scoundrel."

"How did YOU know that Demorest had stock?" asked Stacy.

"He told me in one of his letters and advised me to go into it. But just then Kitty wanted money, I think, and I didn't go in."

"I remember it," struck in Demorest. "But surely it was no secret. My name would be on the transfer books for any one to see."

"Not so," said Stacy quickly. "You were one of the original shareholders; there was no transfer, and the books as well as the shares of the company were in my hands."

"And your clerks?" added Demorest.

Stacy was silent. After a pause he asked, "Did anybody ever see that letter, Barker?"

"No one but myself and Kitty."

"And would she be likely to talk of it?" continued Stacy.

"Of course not. Why should she? Whom could she talk to?" Yet he stopped suddenly, and then with his characteristic reaction added, with a laugh, "Why no, certainly not."

"Of course, everybody knew that you had bought the shares at Sacramento?"

"Yes. Why, you know I told you the Van Loo clerks came to me and wanted to take it off my hands."

"Yes, I remember; the Van Loo clerks; they knew it, of course," said Stacy with a grim smile. "Well, boys," he said, with sudden alacrity, "I'm going to turn in, for by sun-up to-morrow I must be on my way to catch the first train at the Divide for 'Frisco. We'll hunt this thing down together, for I reckon we're all concerned in it," he added, looking at the others, "and once more we're partners as in the old times. Let us even say that I've given Barker's signal or password," he added, with a laugh, "and we'll stick together. Barker boy," he went on, grasping his younger partner's hand, "your instinct has saved us this time; d—d if I don't sometimes think it better than any other man's sabe; only," he dropped his voice slightly, "I wish you had it in other things than FINANCE. Phil, I've a word to say to you alone before I go. I may want you to follow me."

"But what can I do?" said Barker eagerly. "You're not going to leave me out."

"You've done quite enough for us, old man," said Stacy, laying his hand on Barker's shoulder. "And it may be for US to do something for YOU. Trot off to bed now, like a good boy. I'll keep you posted when the time comes."

Shoving the protesting and leave-taking Barker with paternal familiarity from the room, he closed the door and faced Demorest.

"He's the best fellow in the world," said Stacy quietly, "and has saved the situation; but we mustn't trust too much to him for the present—not even seem to."

"Nonsense, man!" said Demorest impatiently. "You're letting your prejudices go too far. Do you mean to say that you suspect his wife."

"D—n his wife!" said Stacy almost savagely. "Leave her out of this. It's Van Loo that I suspect. It was Van Loo who I knew was behind it, who expected to profit by it, and now we have lost him."

"But how?" said Demorest, astonished.

"How?" repeated Stacy impatiently. "You know what Barker said? Van Loo, either through stupidity, fright, or the wish to get the lowest prices, was too late to buy up the market. If he had, we might have openly declared the forgery, and if it was known that he or his friends had profited by it, even if we could not have proven his actual complicity, we could at least have made it too hot for him in California. But," said Stacy, looking intently at his friend, "do you know how the case stands now?"

"Well," said Demorest, a little uneasily under his friend's keen eyes, "we've lost that chance, but we've kept control of the stock."

"You think so? Well, let me tell you how the case stands and the price we pay for it," said Stacy deliberately, as he folded his arms and gazed at Demorest. "You and I, well known as old friends and former partners, for no apparent reason—for we cannot prove the forgery now—have thrown upon the market all our stock, with the usual effect of depreciating it. Another old friend and former partner has bought it in and sent up the price. A common trick, a vulgar trick, but not a trick worthy of James Stacy or Stacy's Bank!"

"But why not simply declare the forgery without making any specific charge against Van Loo?"

"Do you imagine, Phil, that any man would believe it, and the story of a providentially appointed friend like Barker who saved us from loss? Why, all California, from Cape Mendocino to Los Angeles, would roar with laughter over it! No! We must swallow it and the reputation of 'jockeying' with the Wheat Trust, too. That Trust's as good as done for, for the present! Now you know why I didn't want poor Barker to know it, nor have much to do with our search for the forger."

"It would break the dear fellow's heart if he knew it," said Demorest.

"Well, it's to save him from having his heart broken further that I intend to find out this forger," said Stacy grimly. "Good-night, Phil! I'll telegraph to you when I want you, and then COME!"

With another grip of the hand he left Demorest to his thoughts. In the first excitement of meeting his old partners, and in the later discovery of the forgery, Demorest had been diverted from his old sorrow, and for the time had forgotten it in sympathetic interest with the present. But, to his horror, when alone again, he found that interest growing as remote and vapid as the stories they had laughed over at the table, and even the excitement of the forged letter and its consequences began to be as unreal, as impotent, as shadowy, as the memory of the attempted robbery in the old cabin on that very spot. He was ashamed of that selfishness which still made him cling to this past, so much his own, that he knew it debarred him from the human sympathy of his comrades. And even Barker, in whose courtship and marriage he had tried to resuscitate his youthful emotions and condone his selfish errors—even the suggestion of his unhappiness only touched him vaguely. He would no longer be a slave to the Past, or the memory that had deluded him a few hours ago. He walked to the window; alas, there was the same prospect that had looked upon his dreams, had lent itself to his old visions. There was the eternal outline of the hills; there rose the steadfast pines; there was no change in THEM. It was this surrounding constancy of nature that had affected him. He turned away and entered the bedroom. Here he suddenly remembered that the mother of this vague enemy, Van Loo,—for his feeling towards him was still vague, as few men really hate the personality they don't know,—had only momentarily vacated it, and to his distaste of his own intrusion was now added the profound irony of his sleeping in the same bed lately occupied by the mother of the man who was suspected of having forged his name. He smiled faintly and looked around the apartment. It was handsomely furnished, and although it still had much of the characterlessness of the hotel room, it was distinctly flavored by its last occupant, and still brightened by that mysterious instinct of the sex which is inevitable. Where a man would have simply left his forgotten slippers or collars there was a glass of still unfaded flowers; the cold marble top of the dressing-table was littered with a few linen and silk toilet covers; and on the mantel-shelf was a sheaf of photographs. He walked towards them mechanically, glanced at them abstractedly, and then stopped suddenly with a beating heart. Before him was the picture of his past, the photograph of the one woman who had filled his life!

He cast a hurried glance around the room as if he half expected to see the original start up before him, and then eagerly seized it and hurried with it to the light. Yes! yes! It was SHE,—she as she had lived in his actual memory; she as she had lived in his dream. He saw her sweet eyes, but the frightened, innocent trouble had passed from them; there was the sensitive elegance of her graceful figure in evening dress; but the figure was fuller and maturer. Could he be mistaken by some wonderful resemblance acting upon his too willing brain? He turned the photograph over. No; there on the other side, written in her own childlike hand, endeared and familiar to his recollection, was her own name, and the date! It was surely she!

How did it come there? Did the Van Loos know her? It was taken in Venice; there was the address of the photographers. The Van Loos were foreigners, he remembered; they had traveled; perhaps had met her there in 1858: that was the date in her handwriting; that was the date on the photographer's address—1858. Suddenly he laid the photograph down, took with trembling fingers a letter-case from his pocket, opened it, and laid his last letter to her, indorsed with the cruel announcement of her death, before him on the table. He passed his hand across his forehead and opened the letter. It was dated 1856! The photograph must have been taken two years AFTER her alleged death!

He examined it again eagerly, fixedly, tremblingly. A wild impulse to summon Barker or Stacy on the spot was restrained with difficulty and only when he remembered that they could not help him. Then he began to oscillate between a joy and a new fear, which now, for the first time, began to dawn upon him. If the news of her death had been a fiendish trick of her relations, why had SHE never sought him? It was not ill health, restraint, nor fear; there was nothing but happiness and the strength of youth and beauty in that face and figure. HE had not disappeared from the world; he was known of men; more, his memorable good fortune must have reached her ears. Had he wasted all these miserable years to find himself abandoned, forgotten, perhaps even a dupe? For the first time the sting of jealousy entered his soul. Perhaps, unconsciously to himself, his strange and varying feelings that afternoon had been the gathering climax of his mental condition; at all events, in the sudden revulsion there was a shaking off of his apathetic thought; there was activity, even if it was the activity of pain. Here was a mystery to be solved, a secret to be discovered, a past wrong to be exposed, an enemy or, perhaps, even a faithless love to be punished. Perhaps he had even saved his reason at the expense of his love. He quickly replaced the photograph on the mantel-shelf, returned the letter carefully to his pocket-book,—no longer a souvenir of the past, but a proof of treachery,—and began to mechanically undress himself. He was quite calm now, and went to bed with a strange sense of relief, and slept as he had not slept since he was a boy.

The whole hotel had sunk to rest by this time, and then began the usual slow, nightly invasion and investment of it by nature. For all its broad verandas and glaring terraces, its long ranges of windows and glittering crest of cupola and tower, it gradually succumbed to the more potent influences around it, and became their sport and playground. The mountain breezes from the distant summit swept down upon its flimsy structure, shook the great glass windows as with a strong hand, and sent the balm of bay and spruce through every chink and cranny. In the great hall and corridors the carpets billowed with the intruding blast along the floors; there was the murmur of the pines in the passages, and the damp odor of leaves in the dining-room. There was the cry of night birds in the creaking cupola, and the swift rush of dark wings past bedroom windows. Lissome shapes crept along the terraces between the stolid wooden statues, or, bolder, scampered the whole length of the great veranda. In the lulling of the wind the breath of the woods was every-where; even the aroma of swelling sap—as if the ghastly stumps on the deforested slope behind the hotel were bleeding afresh in the dewless night—stung the eyes and nostrils of the sleepers.

It was, perhaps, from such cause as this that Barker was awakened suddenly by the voice of the boy from the crib beside him, crying, "Mamma! mamma!" Taking the child in his arms, he comforted him, saying she would come that morning, and showed him the faint dawn already veiling with color the ghostly pallor of the Sierras. As they looked at it a great star shot forth from its brethren and fell. It did not fall perpendicularly, but seemed for some seconds to slip along the slopes of Black Spur, gleaming through the trees like a chariot of fire. It pleased the child to say that it was the light of mamma's buggy that was fetching her home, and it pleased the father to encourage the boy's fancy. And talking thus in confidential whispers they fell asleep once more, the father—himself a child in so many things—holding the smaller and frailer hand in his.

They did not know that on the other side of the Divide the wife and mother, scared, doubting, and desperate, by the side of her scared, doubting, and desperate accomplice, was flying down the slope on her night-long road to ruin. Still less did they know that, with the early singing birds, a careless horseman, emerging from the trail as the dust-stained buggy dashed past him, glanced at it with a puzzled air, uttered a quiet whistle of surprise, and then, wheeling his horse, gayly cantered after it.

Bret Harte

CHAPTER V

In the exercise of his arduous profession, Jack Hamlin had sat up all night in the magnolia saloon of the Divide, and as it was rather early to go to bed, he had, after his usual habit, shaken off the sedentary attitude and prepared himself for sleep by a fierce preliminary gallop in the woods. Besides, he had been a large winner, and on those occasions he generally isolated himself from his companions to avoid foolish altercations with inexperienced players. Even in fighting Jack was fastidious, and did not like to have his stomach for a real difficulty distended and vitiated by small preliminary indulgences.

He was just emerging from the wood into the highroad when a buggy dashed past him, containing a man and a woman. The woman wore a thick veil; the man was almost undistinguishable from dust. The glimpse was momentary, but dislike has a keen eye, and in that glimpse Mr. Hamlin recognized Van Loo. The situation was equally clear. The bent heads and averted faces, the dust collected in the heedlessness of haste, the early hour,—indicating a night-long flight,—all made it plain to him that Van Loo was running away with some woman. Mr. Hamlin had no moral scruples, but he had the ethics of a sportsman, which he knew Mr. Van Loo was not. Whether the woman was an innocent schoolgirl or an actress, he was satisfied that Van

Loo was doing a mean thing meanly. Mr. Hamlin also had a taste for mischief, and whether the woman was or was not fair game, he knew that for HIS purposes Van Loo was. With the greatest cheerfulness in the world he wheeled his horse and cantered after them.

They were evidently making for the Divide and a fresh horse, or to take the coach due an hour later. It was Mr. Hamlin's present object to circumvent this, and, therefore, it was quite in his way to return. Incidentally, however, the superior speed of his horse gave him the opportunity of frequently lunging towards them at a furious pace, which had the effect of frantically increasing their own speed, when he would pull up with a silent laugh before he was fairly discovered, and allow the sound of his rapid horse's hoofs to die out. In this way he amused himself until the straggling town of the Divide came in sight, when, putting his spurs to his horse again, he managed, under pretense of the animal becoming ungovernable, to twice "cross the bows" of the fugitives, compelling them to slacken speed. At the second of these passages Van Loo apparently lost prudence, and slashing out with his whip, the lash caught slightly on the counter of Hamlin's horse. Mr. Hamlin instantly acknowledged it by lifting his hat gravely, and speeded on to the hotel, arriving at the steps and throwing himself from the saddle exactly as the buggy drove up. With characteristic audacity, he actually assisted the frightened and eager woman to alight and run into the hotel. But in this action her veil was accidentally lifted. Mr. Hamlin instantly recognized the pretty woman who had been pointed out to him in San Francisco as Mrs. Barker, the wife of one of the partners whose fortunes had interested him five years ago. It struck him that this was an additional reason for his interference on Barker's account, although personally he could not conceive why a man should ever try to prevent a woman from running away from him. But then Mr. Hamlin's personal experiences had been quite the other way.

It was enough, however, to cause him to lay his hand lightly on Van Loo's arm as the latter, leaping down, was about to follow Mrs. Barker into the hotel. "You'll have time enough now," said Hamlin.

"Time for what?" said Van Loo savagely.

"Time to apologize for having cut my horse with your whip," said Jack sweetly. "We don't want to quarrel before a woman."

"I've no time for fooling!" said Van Loo, endeavoring to pass.

But Jack's hand had slipped to Van Loo's wrist, although he still smiled cheerfully. "Ah! Then you DID mean it, and you propose to give me satisfaction?"

Van Loo paled slightly; he knew Jack's reputation as a duelist. But he was desperate. "You see my position," he said hurriedly. "I'm in a hurry; I have a lady with me. No man of honor"—

"You do me wrong," interrupted Jack, with a pained expression,—"you do, indeed. You are in a hurry—well, I have plenty of time. If you cannot attend to me now, why I will be glad to accompany you and the lady to the next station. Of course," he added, with a smile, "at a proper distance, and without interfering with the lady, whom I am pleased to recognize as the wife of an old friend. It would be more sociable, perhaps, if we had some general conversation on the road; it would prevent her being alarmed. I might even be of some use to YOU. If we are overtaken by her husband on the road, for instance, I should certainly claim the right to have the first shot at you. Boy!" he called to the hostler, "just sponge out Pancho's mouth, will you, to be ready when the buggy goes?" And, loosening his grip of Van Loo's wrist, he turned away as the other quickly entered the hotel.

But Mr. Van Loo did not immediately seek Mrs. Barker. He had already some experience of that lady's nerves and irascibility on the drive, and had begun to see his error in taking so dangerous an impediment to his flight from the country. And another idea had come to him. He had already effected his purpose of compromising her with him in that flight, but it was still known only to few. If he left her behind for the foolish, doting husband, would not that devoted man take her back to avoid a scandal, and even forbear to pursue HIM for his financial irregularities? What were twenty thousand dollars of Mrs. Barker's money to the scandal of Mrs. Barker's elopement? Again, the failure to realize the forgery had left him safe, and Barker was sufficiently potent with the bank and Demorest to hush up that also. Hamlin was now the only obstacle to his flight; but even he would scarcely pursue HIM if Mrs. Barker were left behind. And it would be easier to elude him if he did.

In his preoccupation Van Loo did not see that he had entered the bar-room, but, finding himself there, he moved towards the bar; a glass of spirits would revive him. As he drank it he saw that the room was full of rough men, apparently miners or packers—some of them Mexican, with here and there a Kanaka or Australian. Two men more ostentatiously clad, though apparently on equal terms with the others, were standing in the corner with their backs towards him. From the general silence as he entered he imagined that he had been the subject of conversation, and that his altercation with Hamlin had been overheard. Suddenly one of the two men turned and approached him. To his consternation he recognized Steptoe,—Steptoe, whom he had not seen for five years until last night, when he had avoided him in the courtyard of the Boomville Hotel. His first instinct was to retreat, but it was too late. And the spirits had warmed him into temporary recklessness.

"You ain't goin' to be backed down by a short-card gambler, are yer?" said Steptoe, with coarse familiarity.

"I have a lady with me, and am pressed for time," said Van Loo quickly. "He knows it, otherwise he would not have dared"—

"Well, look here," said Steptoe roughly. "I ain't particularly sweet on you, as you know; but I and these gentlemen," he added, glancing around the room, "ain't particularly sweet on Mr. Jack Hamlin neither, and we kalkilate to stand by you if you say so. Now, I reckon you want to get away with the woman, and the quicker the better, as you're afraid there'll be somebody after you afore long. That's the way it pans out, don't it? Well, when you're ready to go, and you just tip us the wink, we'll get in a circle round Jack and cover him, and if he starts after you we'll send him on a little longer journey!—eh, boys?"

The men muttered their approval, and one or two drew their revolvers from their belts. Van Loo's heart, which had leaped at first at this proposal of help, sank at this failure of his little plan of abandoning Mrs. Barker. He hesitated, and then stammered, "Thank you! Haste is everything with us now; but I shouldn't mind leaving the lady among CHIVALROUS GENTLEMEN like yourselves for a few hours only, until I could communicate with my friends and return to properly chastise this scoundrel."

Steptoe drew in his breath with a slight whistle, and gazed at

Van Loo. He instantly understood him. But the plea did not suit Steptoe, who, for purposes of his own, wished to put Mrs. Barker beyond her husband's possible reach. He smiled grimly. "I think you'd better take the woman with you," he said. "I don't think," he added in a lower voice, "that the boys would like your leaving her. They're very high-toned, they are!" he concluded ironically.

"Then," said Van Loo, with another desperate idea, "could you not let us have saddle-horses instead of the buggy? We could travel faster, and in the event of pursuit and anything happening to ME," he added loftily, "SHE at least could escape her pursuer's vengeance."

This suited Steptoe equally well, as long as the guilty couple fled TOGETHER, and in the presence of witnesses. But he was not deceived by Van Loo's heroic suggestion of self-sacrifice. "Quite right," he said sarcastically, "it shall be done, and I've no doubt ONE of you will escape. I'll send the horses round to the back door and keep the buggy in front. That will keep Jack there, TOO,—with the boys handy."

But Mr. Hamlin had quite as accurate an idea of Mr. Van Loo's methods and of his OWN standing with Steptoe's gang of roughs as Mr. Steptoe himself. More than that, he also had a hold on a smaller but more devoted and loyal following than Steptoe's. The employees and hostlers of the hotel worshiped him. A single word of inquiry revealed to him the fact that the buggy was NOT going on, but that Mr. Van Loo and Mrs. Barker WERE—on two horses, a temporary side-saddle having been constructed out of a mule's pack-tree. At which Mr. Hamlin, with his usual audacity, walked into the bar-room, and going to the bar leaned carelessly against it. Then turning to the lowering faces around him, he said, with a flash of his white teeth, "Well, boys, I'm calculating to leave the Divide in a few minutes to follow some friends in the buggy, and it seems to me only the square thing to stand the liquor for the crowd, without prejudice to any feeling or roughness there may be against me. Everybody who knows me knows that I'm generally there when the band plays, and I'm pretty sure to turn up for THAT sort of thing. So you'll just consider that I've had a good game on the Divide, and I'm reckoning it's only fair to leave a little of it behind me here, to 'sweeten the pot' until I call again. I only ask you, gentlemen, to drink success to my friends in the buggy as early and as often as you can." He flung two gold pieces on the counter and paused, smiling.

He was right in his conjecture. Even the men who would have willingly "held him up" a moment after, at the bidding of Steptoe, saw no reason for declining a free drink "without prejudice." And it was a part of the irony of the situation that Steptoe and Van Loo were also obliged to participate to keep in with their partisans. It was, however, an opportune diversion to Van Loo, who managed to get nearer the door leading to the back entrance of the hotel, and to Mr. Jack Hamlin, who was watching him, as the men closed up to the bar.

The toast was drunk with acclamation, followed by another and yet another. Steptoe and Van Loo, who had kept their heads cool, were both wondering if Hamlin's intention were to intoxicate and incapacitate the crowd at the crucial moment, and Steptoe smiled grimly over his superior knowledge of their alcoholic capacity. But suddenly there was the greater diversion of a shout from the road, the on-coming of a cloud of red dust, and the halt of another vehicle before the door. This time it was no jaded single horse and dust-stained buggy, but a double team of four spirited trotters, whose coats were scarcely turned with foam, before a light station wagon containing a single man. But that man was instantly recognized by every one of the outside loungers and stable-boys as well as the staring crowd within the saloon. It was James Stacy, the millionaire and banker. No one but himself knew that he had covered half the distance of a night-long ride from Boomville in two hours. But before they could voice their astonishment Stacy had thrown a letter to the obsequious landlord, and then gathering up the reins had sped away to the railroad station half a mile distant.

"Looks as if the Boss of Creation was in a hurry," said one of the eager gazers in the doorway. "Somebody goin' to get smashed, sure."

"More like as if he was just humpin' himself to keep from getting smashed," said Steptoe. "The bank hasn't got over the effect of their smart deal in the Wheat Trust. Everything they had in their hands tumbled yesterday in Sacramento. Men like me and you ain't goin' to trust their money to be 'jockeyed' with in that style. Nobody but a man with a swelled head like Stacy would have even dared to try it on. And now, by G-d! he's got to pay for it."

The harsh, exultant tone of the speaker showed that he had quite forgotten Van Loo and Hamlin in his superior hatred of the millionaire, and both men noticed it. Van Loo edged still nearer to the door, as Steptoe continued, "Ever since he made that big strike on Heavy Tree five years ago, the country hasn't been big enough to hold him. But mark my words, gentlemen, the time ain't far off when he'll find a two-foot ditch again and a pick and grub wages room enough and to spare for him and his kind of cattle."

"You're not drinking," said Jack Hamlin cheerfully.

Steptoe turned towards the bar, and then started. "Where's Van Loo?" he demanded of Jack sharply.

Jack jerked his thumb over his shoulder. "Gone to hurry up his girl, I reckon. I calculate he ain't got much time to fool away here."

Steptoe glanced suspiciously at Jack. But at the same moment they were all startled—even Jack himself—at the apparition of Mrs. Barker passing hurriedly along the veranda before the windows in the direction of the still waiting buggy. "D—n it!" said Steptoe in a fierce whisper to the man next him. "Tell her not THERE—at the back door!" But before the messenger reached the door there was a sudden rattle of wheels, and with one accord all except Hamlin rushed to the veranda, only to see Mrs. Barker driving rapidly away alone. Steptoe turned back into the room, but Jack also had disappeared.

For in the confusion created at the sight of Mrs. Barker, he had slipped to the back door and found, as he suspected, only one horse, and that with a side-saddle on. His intuitions were right. Van Loo, when he disappeared from the saloon, had instantly fled, taking the other horse and abandoning the woman to her fate. Jack as instantly leaped upon the remaining saddle and dashed after him. Presently he caught a glimpse of the fugitive in the distance, heard the half-angry, half-ironical shouts of the crowd at the back door, and as he reached the hilltop saw, with a mingling of satisfaction and perplexity, Mrs. Barker on the other road, still driving frantically in the direction of the railroad station. At which Mr. Hamlin halted, threw away his encumbering saddle, and, good rider that he was, remounted the horse, barebacked but for his blanket-pad, and thrusting his knees in the loose girths, again dashed forwards,—with such good results that, as Van Loo galloped up to the stagecoach office, at the next station, and was about to enter the waiting coach for Marysville, the soft hand of Mr. Hamlin was laid on his shoulder.

"I told you," said Jack blandly, "that I had plenty of time. I would have been here BEFORE and even overtaken you, only you had the better horse and the only saddle."

Van Loo recoiled. But he was now desperate and reckless. Beckoning Jack out of earshot of the other passengers, he said with tightened lips, "Why do you follow me? What is your purpose in coming here?"

"I thought," said Hamlin dryly, "that I was to have the pleasure of getting satisfaction from you for the insult you gave me."

"Well, and if I apologize for it, what then?" he said quickly.

Hamlin looked at him quietly. "Well, I think I also said something about the lady being the wife of a friend of mine."

"And I have left her BEHIND. Her husband can take her back without disgrace, for no one knows of her flight but you and me. Do you think your shooting me will save her? It will spread the scandal far and wide. For I warn you, that as I have apologized for what you choose to call my personal insult, unless you murder me in cold blood without witness, I shall let them know the REASON of your quarrel. And I can tell you more: if you only succeed in STOPPING me here, and make me lose my chance of getting away, the scandal to your friend will be greater still."

Mr. Hamlin looked at Van Loo curiously. There was a certain amount of conviction in what he said. He had never met this kind of creature before. He had surpassed even Hamlin's first intuition of his character. He amused and interested him. But Mr. Hamlin was also a man of the world, and knew that Van Loo's reasoning might be good. He put his hands in his pockets, and said gravely, "What IS your little game?"

Van Loo had been seized with another inspiration of desperation. Steptoe had been partly responsible for this situation. Van Loo knew that Jack and Steptoe were not friends. He had certain secrets of Steptoe's that might be of importance to Jack. Why should he not try to make friends with this powerful free-lance and half-outlaw?

"It's a game," he said significantly, "that might be of interest to your friends to hear."

Hamlin took his hands out of his pockets, turned on his heel, and said, "Come with me."

"But I must go by that coach now," said Van Loo desperately, "or—I've told you what would happen."

"Come with me," said Jack coolly. "If I'm satisfied with what you tell me, I'll put you down at the next station an hour before that coach gets there."

"You swear it?" said Van Loo hesitatingly.

"I've SAID it," returned Jack. "Come!" and Van Loo followed Mr. Hamlin into the station hotel.

CHAPTER VI

The abrupt disappearance of Jack Hamlin and the strange lady and gentleman visitor was scarcely noticed by the other guests of the Divide House, and beyond the circle of Steptoe and his friends, who were a distinct party and strangers to the town, there was no excitement. Indeed, the hotel proprietor might have confounded them together, and, perhaps, Van Loo was not far wrong in his belief that their identity had not been suspected. Nor were Steptoe's followers very much concerned in an episode in which they had taken part only at the suggestion of their leader, and which had terminated so tamely. That they would have liked a "row," in which Jack Hamlin would have been incidentally forced to disgorge his winnings, there was no doubt, but that their interference was asked solely to gratify some personal spite of Steptoe's against Van Loo was equally plain to them. There was some grumbling and outspoken criticism of his methods.

This was later made more obvious by the arrival of another guest for whom Steptoe and his party were evidently waiting. He was a short, stout man, whose heavy red beard was trimmed a little more carefully than when he was first known to Steptoe as Alky Hall, the drunkard of Heavy Tree Hill. His dress, too, exhibited a marked improvement in quality and style, although still characterized in the waist and chest by the unbuttoned freedom of portly and slovenly middle age. Civilization had restricted his potations or limited them to certain festivals known as "sprees," and his face was less puffy and sodden. But with the accession of sobriety he had lost his good humor, and had the irritability and intolerance of virtuous restraint.

"Ye needn't ladle out any of your forty-rod whiskey to me," he said querulously to Steptoe, as he filed out with the rest of the party through the bar-room into the adjacent apartment. "I want to keep my head level till our business is over, and I reckon it wouldn't hurt you and your gang to do the same. They're less likely to blab; and there are few doors that whiskey won't unlock," he added, as Steptoe turned the key in the door after the party had entered.

The room had evidently been used for meetings of directors or political caucuses, and was roughly furnished with notched and whittled armchairs and a single long deal table, on which were ink and pens. The men sat down around it with a half-embarrassed, half-contemptuous attitude of formality, their bent brows and isolated looks showing little community of sentiment and scarcely an attempt to veil that individual selfishness that was prominent. Still less was there any essay of companionship or sympathy in the manner of Steptoe as he suddenly rapped on the table with his knuckles.

"Gentlemen," he said, with a certain deliberation of utterance, as if he enjoyed his own coarse directness, "I reckon you all have a sort of general idea what you were picked up for, or you wouldn't be here. But you may or may not know that for the present you are honest, hard-working miners,—the backbone of the State of Californy,—and that you have formed yourselves into a company called the 'Blue Jay,' and you've settled yourselves on the Bar below Heavy Tree Hill, on a deserted claim of the Marshall Brothers, not half a mile from where the big strike was made five years ago. That's what you ARE, gentlemen; that's what you'll continue TO BE until the job's finished; and," he added, with a sudden dominance that they all felt, "the man who forgets it will have to reckon with me. Now," he continued, resuming his former ironical manner, "now, what are the cold facts of the case? The Marshalls worked this claim ever since '49, and never got anything out of it; then they dropped off or died out, leaving only one brother, Tom Marshall, to work what was left of it. Well, a few days ago HE found indications of a big lead in the rock, and instead of rushin' out and yellin' like an honest man, and callin' in the boys to drink, he sneaks off to 'Frisco, and goes to the bank to get 'em to take a hand in it. Well, you know, when Jim Stacy takes a hand in anything, IT'S BOTH HANDS, and the bank wouldn't see it until he promised to guarantee possession of the whole abandoned claim,—'dips, spurs, and angles,'—and let them work the whole thing, which the d—d fool DID, and the bank agreed to send an expert down there to-morrow to report. But while he was away some one on our side, who was an expert also, got wind of it, and made an examination all by himself, and found it was a vein sure enough and a big thing, and some one else on our side found out, too, all that Marshall had promised the bank and what the bank had promised him. Now, gentlemen, when the bank sends down that expert to-morrow I expect that he will find YOU IN POSSESSION of every part of the deserted claim except the spot where Tom is still working."

"And what good is that to us?" asked one of the men contemptuously.

"Good?" repeated Steptoe harshly. "Well, if you're not as d—d a fool as Marshall, you'll see that if he has struck a lead or vein it's bound to run across OUR CLAIMS, and what's to keep us from sinking for it as long as Marshall hasn't worked the other claims for years nor pre-empted them for this lead?"

"What'll keep him from preempting now?"

"Our possession."

"But if he can prove that the brothers left their claims to him to keep, he'll just send the sheriff and his posse down upon us," persisted the first speaker.

"It will take him three months to do that by law, and the sheriff and his posse can't do it before as long as we're in peaceable possession of it. And by the time that expert and Marshall return they'll find us in peaceful possession, unless we're such blasted fools as to stay talking about it here!"

"But what's to prevent Marshall from getting a gang of his own to drive us off?"

"Now your talkin' and not yelpin'," said Steptoe, with slow insolence. "D—d if I didn't begin to think you kalkilated I was goin' to employ you as lawyers! Nothing is to prevent him from gettin' up HIS gang, and we hope he'll do it, for you see it puts us both on the same level before the law, for we're both BREAKIN' IT. And we kalkilate that we're as good as any roughs they can pick up at Heavy Tree."

"I reckon!" "Ye can count us in!" said half a dozen voices eagerly.

"But what's the job goin' to pay us?" persisted a Sydney man. "An' arter we've beat off this other gang, are we going to scrub along on grub wages until we're yanked out by process-sarvers three months later? If that's the ticket I'm not in it. I aren't no b—y quartz miner."

"We ain't going to do no more MINING there than the bank," said Steptoe fiercely. "And the bank ain't going to wait no three months for the end of the lawsuit. They'll float the stock of that mine for a couple of millions, and get out of it with a million before a month. And they'll have to buy us off to do that. What they'll pay will depend upon the lead; but we don't move off those claims for less than five thousand dollars, which will be two hundred and fifty dollars to each man. But," said Steptoe in a lower but perfectly distinct voice, "if there should be a row,—and they BEGIN it,—and in the scuffle Tom Marshall, their only witness, should happen to get in the way of a revolver or have his head caved in, there might be some difficulty in their holdin' ANY OF THE MINE against honest, hardworking miners in possession. You hear me?"

There was a breathless silence for the moment, and a slight movement of the men in their chairs, but never in fear or protest. Every one had heard the speaker distinctly, and every man distinctly understood him. Some of them were criminals, one or two had already the stain of blood on their hands; but even the most timid, who at other times might have shrunk from suggested assassination, saw in the speaker's words only the fair removal of a natural enemy.

"All right, boys. I'm ready to wade in at once. Why ain't we on the road now? We might have been but for foolin' our time away on that man Van Loo."

"Van Loo!" repeated Hall eagerly,—"Van Loo! Was he here?"

"Yes," said Steptoe shortly, administering a kick under the table to Hall, as he had no wish to revive the previous irritability of his comrades. "He's gone, but," turning to the others, "you'd have had to wait for Mr. Hall's arrival, anyhow. And now you've got your order you can start. Go in two parties by different roads, and meet on the other side of the hotel at Hymettus. I'll be there before you. Pick up some shovels and drills as you go; remember you're honest miners, but don't forget your shootin'-irons for all that. Now scatter."

It was well that they did, vacating the room more cheerfully and sympathetically than they had entered it, or Hall's manifest disturbance over Van Loo's visit would have been noticed. When the last man had disappeared Hall turned quickly to Steptoe. "Well, what did he say? Where has he gone?"

"Don't know," said Steptoe, with uneasy curtness. "He was running away with a woman—well, Mrs. Barker, if you want to know," he added, with rising anger, "the wife of one of those cursed partners. Jack Hamlin was here, and was jockeying to stop him, and interfered. But what the devil has that job to do with our job?" He was losing his temper; everything seemed to turn upon this infernal Van Loo!

"He wasn't running away with Mrs. Barker," gasped Hall,— "it was with her MONEY! and the fear of being connected with the Wheat Trust swindle which he organized, and with our money which I lent him for the same purpose. And he knows all about that job, for I wanted to get him to go into it with us. Your name and mine ain't any too sweet-smelling for the bank, and we ought to have a middleman who knows business to arrange with them. The bank daren't object to him, for they've employed him in even shadier transactions than this when THEY didn't wish to appear. I knew he was in difficulties along with Mrs. Barker's speculations, but I never thought him up to this. And," he added, with sudden desperation, "YOU trusted him, too."

In an instant Steptoe caught the frightened man by the shoulders and was bearing him down on the table. "Are you a traitor, a liar, or a besotted fool?" he said hoarsely. "Speak.

WHEN and WHERE did I trust him?"

"You said in your note—I was—to—help him," gasped Hall.

"My note," repeated Steptoe, releasing Hall with astonished eyes.

"Yes," said Hall, tremblingly searching in his vest pocket. "I brought it with me. It isn't much of a note, but there's your signature plain enough."

He handed Steptoe a torn piece of paper folded in a three-cornered shape. Steptoe opened it. He instantly recognized the paper on which he had written his name and sent up to his wife at the Boomville Hotel. But, added to it, in apparently the same hand, in smaller characters, were the words, "Help Van Loo all you can."

The blood rushed into his face. But he quickly collected himself, and said hurriedly, "All right, I had forgotten it. Let the d—d sneak go. We've got what's a thousand times better in this claim at Marshall's, and it's well that he isn't in it to scoop the lion's share. Only we must not waste time getting there now. You go there first, and at once, and set those rascals to work. I'll follow you before Marshall comes up. Get; I'll settle up here."

His face darkened once more as Hall hurried away, leaving him alone. He drew out the piece of paper from his pocket and stared at it again. Yes; it was the one he had sent to his wife. How did Van Loo get hold of it? Was he at the hotel that night? Had he picked it up in the hall or passage when the servant dropped it? When Hall handed him the paper and he first recognized it a fiendish thought, followed by a spasm of more fiendish rage, had sent the blood to his face. But his crude common sense quickly dismissed that suggestion of his wife's complicity with Van Loo. But had she seen him passing through the hotel that night, and had sought to draw from him some knowledge of his early intercourse with the child, and confessed everything, and even produced the paper with his signature as a proof of identity? Women had been known to do such desperate things. Perhaps she disbelieved her son's aversion to her, and was trying to sound Van Loo. As for the forged words by Van Loo, and the use he had put them to, he cared little. He believed the man was capable of forgery; indeed, he suddenly remembered that in the old days his son had spoken innocently, but admiringly, of Van Loo's wonderful chirographical powers and his faculty of imitating the writings of others, and how he had even offered to teach him. A new and exasperating thought came into his feverish consciousness. What if Van Loo, in teaching the boy, had even made use of him as an innocent accomplice to cover up his own tricks! The suggestion was no question of moral ethics to Steptoe, nor of his son's possible contamination, although since the night of the big strike he had held different views; it was simply a fierce, selfish jealousy that ANOTHER might have profited by the lad's helplessness and inexperience. He had been tormented by this jealousy before in his son's liking for Van Loo. He had at first encouraged his admiration and imitative regard for this smooth swindler's graces and accomplishments, which, though he scorned them himself, he was, after the common parental infatuation, willing that the boy should profit by. Incapable, through his own consciousness, of distinguishing between Van Loo's superficial polish and the true breeding of a gentleman, he had only looked upon it as an equipment for his son which might be serviceable to himself. He had told his wife the truth when he informed her of Van Loo's fears of being reminded of their former intimacy; but he had not told her how its discontinuance after they had left Heavy Tree Hill had affected her son, and how he still cherished his old admiration for that specious rascal.

Nor had he told her how this had stung him, through his own selfish greed of the boy's affection. Yet now that it was possible that she had met Van Loo that evening, she might have become aware of Van Loo's power over her child. How she would exult, for all her pretended hatred of Van Loo! How, perhaps, they had plotted together! How Van Loo might have become aware of the place where his son was kept, and have been bribed by the mother to tell her! He stopped in a whirl of giddy fancies. His strong common sense in all other things had been hitherto proof against such idle dreams or suggestions; but the very strength of his parental love and jealousy had awakened in him at last the terrors of imagination.

His first impulse had been to seek his wife, regardless of discovery or consequences, at Hymettus, where she had said she was going. It was on his way to the rendezvous at Marshall's claim. But this he as instantly set aside, it was his SON he must find; SHE might not confess, or might deceive him—the boy would not; and if his fears were correct, she could be arraigned afterwards. It was possible for him to reach the little Mission church and school, secluded in a remote valley by the old Franciscan fathers, where he had placed the boy for the last few years unknown to his wife. It would be a long ride, but he could still reach Heavy Tree Hill afterwards before Marshall and the expert arrived. And he had a feeling he had never felt before on the eve of a desperate adventure,—that he must see the boy first. He remembered how the child had often accompanied him in his flight, and how he had gained strength, and, it seemed to him, a kind of luck, from the touch of that small hand in his. Surely it was necessary now that at least his mind should be at rest regarding HIM on the eve of an affair of this moment. Perhaps he might never see him again. At any other time, and under the influence of any other emotion, he would have scorned such a sentimentalism—he who had never troubled himself either with preparation for the future or consideration for the past. But at that moment he felt both. He drew a long breath. He could catch the next train to the Three Boulders and ride thence to San Felipe. He hurriedly left the room, settled with the landlord, and galloped to the station. By the irony of circumstances the only horse available for that purpose was Mr. Hamlin's own.

By two o'clock he was at the Three Boulders, where he got a fast horse and galloped into San Felipe by four. As he descended the last slope through the fastnesses of pines towards the little valley overlooked in its remoteness and purely pastoral simplicity by the gold-seeking immigrants,— its seclusion as one of the furthest northern Californian missions still preserved through its insignificance and the efforts of the remaining Brotherhood, who used it as an infirmary and a school for the few remaining Spanish families,—he remembered how he once blundered upon it with the boy while hotly pursued by a hue and cry from one of the larger towns, and how he found sanctuary there. He remembered how, when the pursuit was over, he had placed the boy there under the padre's charge. He had lied to his wife regarding the whereabouts of her son, but he had spoken truly regarding his free expenditure for the boy's maintenance, and the good fathers had accepted, equally for the child's sake as for the Church's sake, the generous "restitution" which this coarse, powerful, ruffianly looking father was apparently seeking to make. He was quite aware of it at the time, and had equally accepted it with grim cynicism; but it now came back to him with a new and smarting significance. Might THEY, too, not succeed in weaning the boy's affection from him, or if the mother had interfered, would they not side with her in claiming an equal right? He had sometimes laughed to himself over the security of this hiding-place, so unknown and so unlikely to be discovered by her, yet within easy reach of her friends and his enemies; he now ground his teeth over the mistake which his doting desire to keep his son accessible to him had caused him to make. He put spurs to his horse, dashed down the little, narrow, ill-paved street, through the deserted plaza, and pulled up in a cloud of dust before the only remaining tower, with its cracked belfry, of the half-ruined Mission church. A new dormitory and school-building had been extended from its walls, but in a subdued, harmonious, modest way, quite unlike the usual glaring white-pine glories of provincial towns. Steptoe laughed to himself bitterly. Some of his money had gone in it.

He seized the horsehair rope dangling from a bell by the wall and rang it sharply. A soft-footed priest appeared,—Father Dominico. "Eddy Horncastle? Ah! yes. Eddy, dear child, is gone."

"Gone!" shouted Steptoe in a voice that startled the padre. "Where? When? With whom?"

"Pardon, senor, but for a time—only a pasear to the next village. It is his saint's day—he has half-holiday. He is a good boy. It is a little pleasure for him and for us."

"Oh!" said Steptoe, softened into a rough apology. "I forgot. All right. Has he had any visitors lately—lady, for instance?"

Father Dominico cast a look half of fright, half of reproval upon his guest.

"A lady HERE!"

In his relief Steptoe burst into a coarse laugh. "Of course; you see I forgot that, too. I was thinking of one of his woman folks, you know—relatives—aunts. Was there any other visitor?"

"Only one. Ah! we know the senor's rules regarding his son."

"One?" repeated Steptoe. "Who was it?"

"Oh, quite an hidalgo—an old friend of the child's—most polite, most accomplished, fluent in Spanish, perfect in deportment. The Senor Horncastle surely could find nothing to object to. Father Pedro was charmed with him. A man of affairs, and yet a good Catholic, too. It was a Senor Van Loo—Don Paul the boy called him, and they talked of the boy's studies in the old days as if—indeed, but for the stranger being a caballero and man of the world—as if he had been his teacher."

It was a proof of the intensity of the father's feelings that they had passed beyond the power of his usual coarse, brutal expression, and he only stared at the priest with a dull red face in which the blood seemed to have stagnated. Presently he said thickly, "When did he come?"

"A few days ago."

"Which way did Eddy go?"

"To Brown's Mills, scarcely a league away. He will be here—even now—on the instant. But the senor will come into the refectory and take some of the old Mission wine from the Catalan grape, planted one hundred and fifty years ago, until the dear child returns. He will be so happy."

"No! I'm in a hurry. I will go on and meet him." He took off his hat, mopped his crisp, wet hair with his handkerchief, and in a thick, slow, impeded voice, more suggestive than the outburst he restrained, said, "And as long as my son remains here that man, Van Loo, must not pass this gate, speak to him, or even see him. You hear me? See to it, you and all the others. See to it, I say, or"—He stopped abruptly, clapped his hat on the swollen veins of his forehead, turned quickly, passed out without another word through the archway into the road, and before the good priest could cross himself or recover from his astonishment the thud of his horse's hoofs came from the dusty road.

It was ten minutes before his face resumed its usual color. But in that ten minutes, as if some of the struggle of his rider had passed into him, his horse was sweating with exhaustion and fear. For in that ten minutes, in this new imagination with which he was cursed, he had killed both Van Loo and his son, and burned the refectory over the heads of the treacherous priests. Then, quite himself again, a voice came to him from the rocky trail above the road with the hail of "Father!" He started quickly as a lad of fifteen or sixteen came bounding down the hillside, and ran towards him.

"You passed me and I called to you, but you did not seem to hear," said the boy breathlessly. "Then I ran after you. Have you been to the Mission?"

Steptoe looked at him quite as breathlessly, but from a deeper emotion. He was, even at first sight, a handsome lad, glowing with youth and the excitement of his run, and, as the father looked at him, he could see the likeness to his mother in his clear-cut features, and even a resemblance to himself in his square, compact chest and shoulders and crisp, black curls. A thrill of purely animal paternity passed over him, the fierce joy of his flesh over his own flesh! His own son, by God! They could not take THAT from him; they might plot, swindle, fawn, cheat, lie, and steal away his affections, but there he was, plain to all eyes, his own son, his very son!

"Come here," he said in a singular, half-weary and half-protesting voice, which the boy instantly recognized as his father's accents of affection.

The boy hesitated as he stood on the edge of the road and pointed with mingled mischief and fastidiousness to the depths of impalpable red dust that lay between him and the horseman. Steptoe saw that he was very smartly attired in holiday guise, with white duck trousers and patent leather shoes, and, after the Spanish fashion, wore black kid gloves. He certainly was a bit of a dandy, as he had said. The father's whole face changed as he wheeled and came before the lad, who lifted up his arms expectantly. They had often ridden together on the same horse.

"No rides to-day in that toggery, Eddy," he said in the same voice. "But I'll get down and we'll go and sit somewhere under a tree and have some talk. I've got a bit of a job that's hurrying me, and I can't waste time."

"Not one of your old jobs, father? I thought you had quite given that up?"

The boy spoke more carelessly than reproachfully, or even wonderingly; yet, as he dismounted and tethered his horse, Steptoe answered evasively, "It's a big thing, sonny; maybe we'll make our eternal fortune, and then we'll light out from this hole and have a gay time elsewhere. Come along."

He took the boy's gloved right hand in his own powerful grasp, and together they clambered up the steep hillside to a rocky ledge on which a fallen pine from above had crashed, snapped itself in twain, and then left its withered crown to hang half down the slope, while the other half rested on the ledge. On this they sat, looking down upon the road and the tethered horse. A gentle breeze moved the treetops above their heads, and the westering sun played hide-and-seek with the shifting shadows. The boy's face was quick and alert with all that moved round him, but without thought the father's face was heavy, except for the eyes that were fixed upon his son.

"Van Loo came to the Mission," he said suddenly.

The boy's eyes glittered quickly, like a steel that pierced the father's heart. "Oh," he said simply, "then it was the padre told you?"

"How did he know you were here?" asked Steptoe.

"I don't know," said the boy quietly. "I think he said something, but I've forgotten it. But it was mighty good of him to come, for I thought, you know, that he did not care to see me after Heavy Tree, and that he'd gone back on us."

"What did he tell you?" continued Steptoe. "Did he talk of me or of your mother?"

"No," said the boy, but without any show of interest or sympathy; "we talked mostly about old times."

"Tell ME about those old times, Eddy. You never told me anything about them."

The boy, momentarily arrested more by something in the tone of his father's voice—a weakness he had never noticed before—than by any suggestion of his words, said with a laugh, "Oh, only about what we used to do when I was very little and used to call myself his 'little brother,'—don't you remember, long before the big strike on Heavy Tree? They were gay times we had then."

"And how he used to teach you to imitate other people's handwriting?" said Steptoe.

"What made you think of that, pop?" said the boy, with a slight wonder in his eyes. "Why, that's the very thing we DID talk about."

"But you didn't do it again; you ain't done it since," said Steptoe quickly.

"Lord! no," said the boy contemptuously. "There ain't no chance now, and there wouldn't be any fun in it. It isn't like the old times when him and me were all alone, and we used to write letters as coming from other people to all the boys round Heavy Tree and the Bar, and sometimes as far as Boomville, to get them to do things, and they'd think the letters were real, and they'd do 'em. And there'd be the biggest kind of a row, and nobody ever knew who did it."

Steptoe stared at this flesh of his own flesh half in relief, half in frightened admiration. Sitting astride the log, his elbows on his knees and his gloved hands supporting his round cheeks, the boy's handsome face became illuminated with an impish devilry which the father had never seen before. With dancing eyes he went on. "It was one of those very games we played so long ago that he wanted to see me about and wanted me to keep mum about, for some of the folks that he played it on were around here now. It was a game we got off on one of the big strike partners long before the strike. I'll tell YOU, dad, for you know what happened afterwards, and you'll be glad. Well, that partner—Demorest—was a kind of silly, you remember—a sort of Miss Nancyish fellow— always gloomy and lovesick after his girl in the States. Well, we'd written lots of letters to girls from their chaps before, and got lots of fun out of it; but we had even a better show for a game here, for it happened that Van Loo knew all about the girl—things that even the man's own partners didn't, for Van Loo's mother was a sort of a friend of the girl's family, and traveled about with her, and knew that the girl was spoony over this Demorest, and that they corresponded. So, knowing that Van Loo was employed at Heavy Tree, she wrote to him to find out all about Demorest and how to stop their foolish nonsense, for the girl's parents didn't want her to marry a broken-down miner like him. So we thought we'd do it our own way, and write a letter to her as if it was from him, don't you see? I wanted to make him call her awful names, and say that he hated her, that he was a murderer and a horse-thief, and that he had killed a policeman, and that he was thinking of becoming a Digger Injin, and having a Digger squaw for a wife, which he liked better than her. Lord! dad, you ought to have seen what stuff I made up." The boy burst into a shrill, half-feminine laugh, and Steptoe, catching the infection, laughed loudly in his own coarse, brutal fashion.

For some moments they sat there looking in each other's faces, shaking with sympathetic emotion, the father forgetting the purpose of his coming there, his rage over Van Loo's visit, and even the rendezvous to which his horse in the road below was waiting to bring him; the son forgetting their retreat from Heavy Tree Hill and his shameful vagabond wanderings with that father in the years that followed. The sinking sun stared blankly in their faces; the protecting pines above them moved by a stronger gust shook a few cones upon them; an enormous crow mockingly repeated the father's coarse laugh, and a squirrel scampered away from the strangely assorted pair as Steptoe, wiping his eyes and forehead with his pocket-handkerchief, said:—

"And did you send it?"

"Oh! Van Loo thought it too strong. Said that those sort of love-sick fools made more fuss over little things than they did over big things, and he sort of toned it down, and fixed it up himself. But it told. For there were never any more letters in the post-office in her handwriting, and there wasn't any posted to her in his."

They both laughed again, and then Steptoe rose. "I must be getting along," he said, looking curiously at the boy. "I've got to catch a train at Three Boulders Station."

"Three Boulders!" repeated the boy. "I'm going there, too, on Friday, to meet Father Cipriano."

"I reckon my work will be all done by Friday," said Steptoe musingly. Standing thus, holding his boy's hand, he was thinking that the real fight at Marshall's would not take place at once, for it might take a day or two for Marshall to gather forces. But he only pressed his son's hand gently.

"I wish you would sometimes take me with you as you used to," said the boy curiously. "I'm bigger now, and wouldn't be in your way."

Steptoe looked at the boy with a choking sense of satisfaction and pride. But he said, "No;" and then suddenly with simulated humor, "Don't you be taken in by any letters from ME, such as you and Van Loo used to write. You hear?"

The boy laughed.

"And," continued Steptoe, "if anybody says I sent for you, don't you believe them."

"No," said the boy, smiling.

"And don't you even believe I'm dead till you see me so. You understand. By the way, Father Pedro has some money of mine kept for you. Now hurry back to school and say you met me, but that I was in a great hurry. I reckon I may have been rather rough to the priests."

They had reached the lower road again, and Steptoe silently unhitched his horse. "Good-by," he said, as he laid his hand on the boy's arm.

"Good-by, dad."

He mounted his horse slowly. "Well," he said smilingly, looking down the road, "you ain't got anything more to say to me, have you?"

"No, dad."

"Nothin' you want?"

"Nothin', dad."

"All right. Good-by."

He put spurs to his horse and cantered down the road without looking back. The boy watched him with idle curiosity until he disappeared from sight, and then went on his way, whistling and striking off the heads of the wayside weeds with his walking-stick.

CHAPTER VII

The sun arose so brightly over Hymettus on the morning after the meeting of the three partners that it was small wonder that Barker's impressionable nature quickly responded to it, and, without awakening the still sleeping child, he dressed hurriedly, and was the first to greet it in the keen air of the slope behind the hotel. To his pantheistic spirit it had always seemed as natural for him to early welcome his returning brothers of the woods and hills as to say good-morning to his fellow mortals. And, in the joy of seeing Black Spur rising again to his level in the distance before him, he doffed his hat to it with a return of his old boyish habit, laid his arm caressingly around the great girth of the nearest pine, clapped his hands to the scampering squirrels in his path, and whistled to the dipping jays. In this way he quite forgot the more serious affairs of the preceding night, or, rather, saw them only in the gilding of the morning, until, looking up, he perceived the tall figure of Demorest approaching him; and then it struck him with his first glance at his old partner's face that his usual suave, gentle melancholy had been succeeded by a critical cynicism of look and a restrained bitterness of accent. Barker's loyal heart smote him for his own selfishness; Demorest had been hard hit by the discovery of the forgery and Stacy's concern in it, and had doubtless passed a restless night, while he (Barker) had forgotten all about it. "I thought of knocking at your door, as I passed," he said, with sympathetic apology, "but I was afraid I might disturb you. Isn't it glorious here? Quite like the old hill. Look at that lizard; he hasn't moved since he first saw me. Do you remember the one who used to steal our sugar, and then stiffen himself into stone on the edge of the bowl until he looked like an ornamental handle to it?" he continued, rebounding again into spirits.

"Barker," said Demorest abruptly, "what sort of woman is this Mrs. Van Loo, whose rooms I occupy?"

"Oh," said Barker, with optimistic innocence, "a most proper woman, old chap. White-haired, well-dressed, with a little foreign accent and a still more foreign courtesy. Why, you don't suppose we'd"—

"But what is she like?" said Demorest impatiently.

"Well," said Barker thoughtfully, "she's the kind of woman who might be Van Loo's mother, I suppose."

"You mean the mother of a forger and a swindler?" asked Demorest sharply.

"There are no mothers of swindlers and forgers," said Barker gravely, "in the way you mean. It's only those poor devils," he said, pointing, nevertheless, with a certain admiration to a circling sparrow-hawk above him, "who have inherited instincts. What I mean is that she might be Van Loo's mother, because he didn't SELECT her."

"Where did she come from? and how long has she been here?" asked Demorest.

"She came from abroad, I believe. And she came here just after you left. Van Loo, after he became secretary of the

Ditch Company, sent for her and her daughter to keep house for him. But you'll see her to-day or to-morrow probably, when she returns. I'll introduce you; she'll be rather glad to meet some one from abroad, and all the more if he happens to be rich and distinguished, and eligible for her daughter." He stopped suddenly in his smile, remembering Demorest's lifelong secret. But to his surprise his companion's face, instead of darkening as it was wont to do at any such allusion, brightened suddenly with a singular excitement as he answered dryly, "Ah well, if the girl is pretty, who knows!"

Indeed, his spirits seemed to have returned with strange vivacity as they walked back to the hotel, and he asked many other questions regarding Mrs. Van Loo and her daughter, and particularly if the daughter had also been abroad. When they reached the veranda they found a few early risers eagerly reading the Sacramento papers, which had just arrived, or, in little knots, discussing the news. Indeed, they would probably have stopped Barker and his companion had not Barker, anxious to relieve his friend's curiosity, hurried with him at once to the manager's office.

"Can you tell me exactly when you expect Mrs. Van Loo to return?" asked Barker quickly.

The manager with difficulty detached himself from the newspaper which he, too, was anxiously perusing, and said, with a peculiar smile, "Well no! she WAS to return to-day, but if you're wanting to keep her rooms, I should say there wouldn't be any trouble about it, as she'll hardly be coming back here NOW. She's rather high and mighty in style, I know, and a determined sort of critter, but I reckon she and her daughter wouldn't care much to be waltzing round in public after what has happened."

"I don't understand you," said Demorest impatiently. "WHAT has happened?"

"Haven't you heard the news?" said the manager in surprise. "It's in all the Sacramento papers. Van Loo is a defaulter—has hypothecated everything he had and skedaddled."

Barker started. He was not thinking of the loss of his wife's money—only of HER disappointment and mortification over it. Poor girl! Perhaps she was also worrying over his resentment,—as if she did not know him! He would go to her at once at Boomville. Then he remembered that she was coming with Mrs. Horncastle, and might be already on her way here by rail or coach, and he would miss her. Demorest in the meantime had seized a paper, and was intently reading it.

"There's bad news, too, for your friend, your old partner," said the manager half sympathetically, half interrogatively. "There has been a drop out in everything the bank is carrying, and everybody is unloading. Two firms failed in 'Frisco yesterday that were carrying things for the bank, and have thrown everything back on it. There was an awful panic last night, and they say none of the big speculators know where they stand. Three of our best customers in the hotel rushed off to the bay this morning, but Stacy himself started before daylight, and got the through night express to stop for him on the Divide on signal. Shall I send any telegrams that may come to your room?"

Demorest knew that the manager suspected him of being interested in the bank, and understood the purport of the question. He answered, with calm surprise, that he was expecting no telegrams, and added, "But if Mrs. Van Loo returns I beg you to at once let me know," and taking Barker's arm he went in to breakfast. Seated by themselves, Demorest looked at his companion. "I'm afraid, Barker boy, that this thing is more serious to Jim than we expected last night, or than he cared to tell us. And you, old man, I fear are hurt a little by Van Loo's flight. He had some money of your wife's, hadn't he?"

Barker, who knew that the bulk of Demorest's fortune was in Stacy's hands, was touched at this proof of his unselfish thought, and answered with equal unselfishness that he was concerned only by the fear of Mrs. Barker's disappointment. "Why, Lord! Phil, whether she's lost or saved her money it's nothing to me. I gave it to her to do what she liked with it, but I'm afraid she'll be worrying over what I think of it,—as if she did not know me! And I'm half a mind, if it were not for missing her, to go over to Boomville, where she's stopping."

"I thought you said she was in San Francisco?" said Demorest abstractedly.

Barker colored. "Yes," he answered quickly. "But I've heard since that she stopped at Boomville on the way."

"Then don't let ME keep you here," returned Demorest. "For if Jim telegraphs to me I shall start for San Francisco at once, and I rather think he will. I did not like to say so before those panic-mongers outside who are stampeding everything; so run along, Barker boy, and ease your mind about the wife. We may have other things to think about soon."

Thus adjured, Barker rose from his half-finished breakfast and slipped away. Yet he was not quite certain what to do. His wife must have heard the news at Boomville as quickly as he had, and, if so, would be on her way with Mrs. Horncastle; or she might be waiting for him—knowing, too, that he had heard the news—in fear and trembling. For it was Barker's custom to endow all those he cared for with his own sensitiveness, and it was not like him to reflect that the woman who had so recklessly speculated against his opinion would scarcely fear his reproaches in her defeat. In the fullness of his heart he telegraphed to her in case she had not yet left Boomville: "All right. Have heard news. Understand perfectly. Don't worry. Come to me." Then he left the hotel by the stable entrance in order to evade the guests who had congregated on the veranda, and made his way to a little wooded crest which he knew commanded a view of the two roads from Boomville. Here he determined to wait and intercept her before she reached the hotel. He knew that many of the guests were aware of his wife's speculations with Van Loo, and that he was her broker. He wished to spare her running the gauntlet of their curious stares and comments as she drove up alone. As he was climbing the slope the coach from Sacramento dashed past him on the road below, but he knew that it had changed horses at Boomville at four o'clock, and that his tired wife would not have availed herself of it at that hour, particularly as she could not have yet received the fateful news. He threw himself under a large pine, and watched the stagecoach disappear as it swept round into the courtyard of the hotel.

He sat there for some moments with his eyes bent upon the two forks of the red road that diverged below him, but which appeared to become whiter and more dazzling as he searched their distance. There was nothing to be seen except an occasional puff of dust which eventually revealed a horseman or a long trailing cloud out of which a solitary mule, one of a pack-train of six or eight, would momentarily emerge and be lost again. Then he suddenly heard his name called, and, looking up, saw Mrs. Horncastle, who had halted a few paces from him between two columns of the long-drawn aisle of pines.

In that mysterious half-light she seemed such a beautiful and goddess-like figure that his consciousness at first was unable to grasp anything else. She was always wonderfully well dressed, but the warmth and seclusion of this mountain morning had enabled her to wear a light gown of some delicate fabric which set off the grace of her figure, and even pardoned the rural coquetry of a silken sash around her still slender waist. An open white parasol thrown over her shoulder made a nimbus for her charming head and the thick coils of hair under her lace-edged hat. He had never seen her look so beautiful before. And that thought was so plainly in his frank face and eyes as he sprang to his feet that it brought a slight rise of color to her own cheek.

"I saw you climbing up here as I passed in the coach a few minutes ago," she said, with a smile, "and as soon as I had shaken the dust off I followed you."

"Where's Kitty?" he stammered.

The color faded from her face as it had come, and a shade of something like reproach crept into her dark eyes. And whatever it had been her purpose to say, or however carefully she might have prepared herself for this interview, she was evidently taken aback by the sudden directness of the inquiry. Barker saw this as quickly, and as quickly referred it to his own rudeness. His whole soul rushed in apology to his face as he said, "Oh, forgive me! I was anxious about Kitty; indeed, I had thought of coming again to Boomville, for you've heard the news, of course? Van Loo is a defaulter, and has run away with the poor child's money."

Mrs. Horncastle had heard the news at the hotel. She paused a moment to collect herself, and then said slowly and tentatively, with a watchful intensity in her eyes, "Mrs. Barker went, I think, to the Divide"—

But she was instantly interrupted by the eager Barker. "I see. I thought of that at once. She went directly to the company's offices to see if she could save anything from the wreck before she saw me. It was like her, poor girl! And you— you," he went on eagerly, his whole face beaming with gratitude,—"you, out of your goodness, came here to tell me." He held out both hands and took hers in his.

For a moment Mrs. Horncastle was speechless and vacillating. She had often noticed before that it was part of the irony of the creation of such a simple nature as Barker's that he was not only open to deceit, but absolutely seemed to invite it. Instead of making others franker, people were inclined to rebuke his credulity by restraint and equivocation on their own part. But the evasion thus offered to her, although only temporary, was a temptation she could not resist. And it prolonged an interview that a ruthless revelation of the truth might have shortened.

"She did not tell me she was going there," she replied still evasively; "and, indeed," she added, with a burst of candor still more dangerous, "I only learned it from the hotel clerk after she was gone. But I want to talk to you about her relations to Van Loo," she said, with a return of her former intensity of gaze, "and I thought we would be less subject to interruption here than at the hotel. Only I suppose everybody knows this place, and any of those flirting couples are likely to come here. Besides," she added, with a little half-hysterical laugh and a slight shiver, as she looked up at the high interlacing boughs above her head, "it's as public as the aisles of a church, and really one feels as if one were 'speaking out' in meeting. Isn't there some other spot a little more secluded, where we could sit down," she went on, as she poked her parasol into the usual black gunpowdery deposit of earth which mingled with the carpet of pine-needles beneath her feet, "and not get all sticky and dirty?"

Barker's eyes sparkled. "I know every foot of this hill, Mrs. Horncastle," he said, "and if you will follow me I'll take you to one of the loveliest nooks you ever dreamed of. It's an old Indian spring now forgotten, and I think known only to me and the birds. It's not more than ten minutes from here; only"—he hesitated as he caught sight of the smart French bronze buckled shoe and silken ankle which Mrs. Horncastle's gathering up of her dainty skirts around her had disclosed—"it may be a little rough and dusty going to your feet."

But Mrs. Horncastle pointed out that she had already irretrievably ruined her shoes and stockings in climbing up to him,—although Barker could really distinguish no diminution of their freshness,—and that she might as well go on. Whereat they both passed down the long aisle of slope to a little hollow of manzanita, which again opened to a view of Black Spur, but left the hotel hidden.

"What time did Kitty go?" began Barker eagerly, when they were half down the slope.

But here Mrs. Horncastle's foot slipped upon the glassy pine-needles, and not only stopped an answer, but obliged Barker to give all his attention to keep his companion from falling again until they reached the open. Then came the plunge through the manzanita thicket, then a cool wade through waist-deep ferns, and then they emerged, holding each other's hand, breathless and panting before the spring.

It did not belie his enthusiastic description. A triangular hollow, niched in a shelf of the mountain-side, narrowed to a point from which the overflow of the spring percolated through a fringe of alder, to fall in what seemed from the valley to be a green furrow down the whole length of the mountain-side. Overhung by pines above, which met and mingled with the willows that everywhere fringed it, it made the one cooling shade in the whole basking expanse of the mountain, and yet was penetrated throughout by the intoxicating spice of the heated pines. Flowering reeds and long lush grasses drew a magic circle round an open bowl-like pool in the centre, that was always replenished to the slow murmur of an unseen rivulet that trickled from a white-quartz cavern in the mountain-side like a vein opened in its flank. Shadows of timid wings crossed it, quick rustlings disturbed the reeds, but nothing more. It was silent, but breathing; it was hidden to everything but the sky and the illimitable distance.

They threaded their way around it on the spongy carpet, covered by delicate lace-like vines that seemed to caress rather than trammel their moving feet, until they reached an open space before the pool. It was cushioned and matted with disintegrated pine bark, and here they sat down. Mrs. Horncastle furled her parasol and laid it aside; raised both hands to the back of her head and took two hat-pins out, which she placed in her smiling mouth; removed her hat, stuck the hat-pins in it, and handed it to Barker, who gently placed it on the top of a tall reed, where during the rest of that momentous meeting it swung and drooped like a flower; removed her gloves slowly; drank still smilingly and gratefully nearly a wineglassful of the water which Barker brought her in the green twisted chalice of a lily leaf; looked the picture of happiness, and then burst into tears.

Barker was astounded, dismayed, even terror-stricken. Mrs. Horncastle crying! Mrs. Horncastle, the imperious, the collected, the coldly critical, the cynical, smiling woman of the world, actually crying! Other women might cry—Kitty had cried often—but Mrs. Horncastle! Yet, there she was, sobbing; actually sobbing like a schoolgirl, her beautiful shoulders rising and falling with her grief; crying unmistakably through her long white fingers, through a lace pocket-handkerchief which she had hurriedly produced and shaken from behind her like a conjurer's trick; her beautiful eyes a thousand times more lustrous for the sparkling beads that brimmed her lashes and welled over like the pool before her.

"Don't mind me," she murmured behind her handkerchief. "It's very foolish, I know. I was nervous—worried, I suppose; I'll be better in a moment. Don't notice me, please."

But Barker had drawn beside her and was trying, after the fashion of his sex, to take her handkerchief away in apparently the firm belief that this action would stop her tears. "But tell me what it is. Do Mrs. Horncastle, please," he pleaded in his boyish fashion. "Is it anything I can do? Only say the word; only tell me SOMETHING!"

But he had succeeded in partially removing the handkerchief, and so caught a glimpse of her wet eyes, in which a faint smile struggled out like sunshine through rain. But they clouded again, although she didn't cry, and her breath came and went with the action of a sob, and her hands still remained against her flushed face.

"I was only going to talk to you of Kitty" (sob)—"but I suppose I'm weak" (sob)—"and such a fool" (sob) "and I got to thinking of myself and my own sorrows when I ought to be thinking only of you and Kitty."

"Never mind Kitty," said Barker impulsively. "Tell me about yourself—your own sorrows. I am a brute to have bothered you about her at such a moment; and now until you have told me what is paining you so I shall not let you speak of her." He was perfectly sincere. What were Kitty's possible and easy tears over the loss of her money to the unknown agony that could wrench a sob from a woman like this? "Dear Mrs.

Horncastle," he went on as breathlessly, "think of me now not as Kitty's husband, but as your true friend. Yes, as your BEST and TRUEST friend, and speak to me as you would speak to him."

"You will be my friend?" she said suddenly and passionately, grasping his hand, "my best and truest friend? and if I tell you all,—everything, you will not cast me from you and hate me?"

Barker felt the same thrill from her warm hand slowly possess his whole being as it had the evening before, but this time he was prepared and answered the grasp and her eyes together as he said breathlessly, "I will be—I AM your friend."

She withdrew her hand and passed it over her eyes. After a moment she caught his hand again, and, holding it tightly as if she feared he might fly from her, bit her lip, and then slowly, without looking at him, said, "I lied to you about myself and Kitty that night; I did not come with her. I came alone and secretly to Boomville to see—to see the man who is my husband."

"Your husband!" said Barker in surprise. He had believed, with the rest of the world, that there had been no communication between them for years. Yet so intense was his interest in her that he did not notice that this revelation was leaving now no excuse for his wife's presence at Boomville.

Mrs. Horncastle went on with dogged bitterness, "Yes, my husband. I went to him to beg and bribe him to let me see my child. Yes, MY child," she said frantically, tightening her hold upon his hand, "for I lied to you when I once told you I had none. I had a child, and, more than that, a child who at his birth I did not dare to openly claim."

She stopped breathlessly, stared at his face with her former intensity as if she would pluck the thought that followed from his brain. But he only moved closer to her, passed his arm over her shoulders with a movement so natural and protecting that it had a certain dignity in it, and, looking down upon her bent head with eyes brimming with sympathy, whispered, "Poor, poor child!"

Whereat Mrs. Horncastle again burst into tears. And then, with her head half drawn towards his shoulder, she told him all,—all that had passed between her and her husband,— even all that they had then but hinted at. It was as if she felt she could now, for the first time, voice all these terrible memories of the past which had come back to her last night when her husband had left her. She concealed nothing, she veiled nothing; there were intervals when her tears no longer flowed, and a cruel hardness and return of her old imperiousness of voice and manner took their place, as if she was doing a rigid penance and took a bitter satisfaction in laying bare her whole soul to him. "I never had a friend," she whispered; "there were women who persecuted me with their jealous sneers; there were men who persecuted me with their selfish affections. When I first saw YOU, you seemed something so apart and different from all other men that, although I scarcely knew you, I wanted to tell you, even then, all that I have told you now. I wanted you to be my friend; something told me that you could,—that you could separate me from my past; that you could tell me what to do; that you could make me think as you thought, see life as YOU saw it, and trust always to some goodness in people as YOU did. And in this faith I thought that you would understand me now, and even forgive me all."

She made a slight movement as if to disengage his arm, and,

possibly, to look into his eyes, which she knew instinctively were bent upon her downcast head. But he only held her the more tightly until her cheek was close against his breast. "What could I do?" she murmured. "A man in sorrow and trouble may go to a woman for sympathy and support and the world will not gainsay or misunderstand him. But a woman—weaker, more helpless, credulous, ignorant, and craving for light—must not in her agony go to a man for succor and sympathy."

"Why should she not?" burst out Barker passionately, releasing her in his attempt to gaze into her face. "What man dare refuse her?"

"Not THAT," she said slowly, but with still averted eyes, "but because the world would say she LOVED him."

"And what should she care for the opinion of a world that stands aside and lets her suffer? Why should she heed its wretched babble?" he went on in flashing indignation.

"Because," she said faintly, lifting her moist eyes and moist and parted lips towards him,—"because it would be TRUE!"

There was a silence so profound that even the spring seemed to withhold its song as their eyes and lips met. When the spring recommenced its murmur, and they could hear the droning of a bee above them and the rustling of the reed, she was murmuring, too, with her face against his breast: "You did not think it strange that I should follow you—that I should risk everything to tell you what I have told you before I told you anything else? You will never hate me for it, George?"

There was another silence still more prolonged, and when he looked again into the flushed face and glistening eyes he was saying, "I have ALWAYS loved you. I know now I loved you from the first, from the day when I leaned over you to take little Sta from your lap and saw your tenderness for him in your eyes. I could have kissed you THEN, dearest, as I do now."

"And," she said, when she had gained her smiling breath again, "you will always remember, George, that you told me this BEFORE I told you anything of her."

"HER? Of whom, dearest?" he asked, leaning over her tenderly.

"Of Kitty—of your wife," she said impatiently, as she drew back shyly with her former intense gaze.

He did not seem to grasp her meaning, but said gravely, "Let us not talk of her NOW. Later we shall have MUCH to say of her. For," he added quietly, "you know I must tell her all."

The color faded from her cheek. "Tell her all!" she repeated vacantly; then suddenly she turned upon him eagerly, and said, "But what if she is gone?"

"Gone?" he repeated.

"Yes; gone. What if she has run away with Van Loo? What if she has disgraced you and her child?"

"What do you mean?" he said, seizing both her hands and gazing at her fixedly.

"I mean," she said, with a half-frightened eagerness, "that she has already gone with Van Loo. George! George!" she burst out suddenly and passionately, falling upon her knees before him, "do you think that I would have followed you here and told you what I did if I thought that she had now the slightest claim upon your love or honor? Don't you understand me? I came to tell you of her flight to Boomville with that man; how I accidentally intercepted them there; how I tried to save her from him, and even lied to you to try to save her from your indignation; but how she deceived me as she has you, and even escaped and joined her lover while you were with me. I came to tell you that and nothing more, George, I swear it. But when you were kind to me and pitied me, I was mad—wild! I wanted to win you first out of your own love. I wanted you to respond to MINE before you knew your wife was faithless. Yet I would have saved her if I could. Listen, George! A moment more before you speak!"

Then she hurriedly told him all; the whole story of his wife's dishonor, from her entrance into the sitting-room with Van Loo, her later appeal for concealment from her husband's unexpected presence, to the use she made of that conceal-ment to fly with her lover. She spared no detail, and even repeated the insult Mrs. Barker had cast upon her with the triumphant reproach that her husband would not believe her. "Perhaps," she added bitterly, "you may not believe me now. I could even stand that from you, George, if it could make you happier; but you would still have to believe it from others. The people at the Boomville Hotel saw them leave it together."

"I do believe you," he said slowly, but with downcast eyes, "and if I did not love you before you told me this I could love you now for the part you have taken; but"—He stopped.

"You love her still," she burst out, "and I might have known it. Perhaps," she went on distractedly, "you love her the more that you have lost her. It is the way of men—and women."

"If I had loved her truly," said Barker, lifting his frank eyes to hers, "I could not have touched YOUR lips. I could not even have wished to—as I did three years ago—as I did last night. Then I feared it was my weakness, now I know it was my love. I have thought of it ever since, even while waiting my wife's return here, knowing that I did not and never could have loved her. But for that very reason I must try to save her for her own sake, if I cannot save her for mine; and if I fail, dearest, it shall not be said that we climbed to happiness over her back bent with the burden of her shame. If I loved you and told you so, thinking her still guiltless and innocent, how could I profit now by her fault?"

Mrs. Horncastle saw too late her mistake. "Then you would take her back?" she said frenziedly.

"To my home—which is hers—yes. To my heart—no. She never was there."

"And I," said Mrs. Horncastle, with a quivering lip,—"where do I go when you have settled this? Back to my past again? Back to my husbandless, childless life?"

She was turning away, but Barker caught her in his arms again. "No!" he said, his whole face suddenly radiating with hope and youthful enthusiasm. "No! Kitty will help us; we will tell her all. You do not know her, dearest, as I do—how good and kind she is, in spite of all. We will appeal to her; she will devise some means by which, without the scandal of a divorce, she and I may be separated. She will take dear little Sta with her—it is only right, poor girl; but she will let me come and see him. She will be a sister to us, dearest. Courage! All will come right yet. Trust to me."

An hysterical laugh came to Mrs. Horncastle's lips and then stopped. For as she looked up at him in his supreme hopefulness, his divine confidence in himself and others—at his handsome face beaming with love and happiness, and his clear gray eyes glittering with an almost spiritual prescience—she, woman of the world and bitter experience, and perfectly cognizant of her own and Kitty's possibilities, was, nevertheless, completely carried away by her lover's optimism. For of all optimism that of love is the most convincing. Dear boy!—for he was but a boy in experience—only his love for her could work this magic. So she gave him kiss for kiss, largely believing, largely hoping, that Mrs. Barker was in love with Van Loo and would NOT return. And in this hope an invincible belief in the folly of her own sex soothed and sustained her.

"We must go now, dearest," said Barker, pointing to the sun already near the meridian. Three hours had fled, they knew not how. "I will bring you back to the hill again, but there we had better separate, you taking your way alone to the hotel as you came, and I will go a little way on the road to the Divide and return later. Keep your own counsel about Kitty for her sake and ours; perhaps no one else may know the truth yet." With a farewell kiss they plunged again hand in hand through the cool bracken and again through the hot manzanita bushes, and so parted on the hilltop, as they had never parted before, leaving their whole world behind them.

Barker walked slowly along the road under the flickering shade of wayside sycamore, his sensitive face also alternating with his thought in lights and shadows. Presently there crept towards him out of the distance a halting, vacillating, deviating buggy, trailing a cloud of dust after it like a broken wing. As it came nearer he could see that the horse was spent and exhausted, and that the buggy's sole occupant—a woman—was equally exhausted in her monotonous attempt to urge it forward with whip and reins that rose and fell at intervals with feeble reiteration. Then he stepped out of the shadow and stood in the middle of the sunlit road to await it. For he recognized his wife.

The buggy came nearer. And then the most exquisite pang he had ever felt before at his wife's hands shot through him. For as she recognized him she made a wild but impotent attempt to dash past him, and then as suddenly pulled up in the ditch.

He went up to her. She was dirty, she was disheveled, she was haggard, she was plain. There were rings of dust round her tear-swept eyes and smudges of dust-dried perspiration over her fair cheek. He thought of the beauty, freshness, and elegance of the woman he had just left, and an infinite pity swept the soul of this weak-minded gentleman. He ran towards her, and tenderly lifting her in her shame-stained garments from the buggy, said hurriedly, "I know it all, poor Kitty! You heard the news of Van Loo's flight, and you ran over to the Divide to try and save some of your money. Why didn't you wait? Why didn't you tell me?"

There was no mistaking the reality of his words, the genuine pity and tenderness of his action; but the woman saw before her only the familiar dupe of her life, and felt an infinite relief mingled with a certain contempt for his weakness and anger at her previous fears of him.

"You might have driven over, then, yourself," she said in a high, querulous voice, "if you knew it so well, and have spared ME this horrid, dirty, filthy, hopeless expedition, for I have not saved anything—there! And I have had all this disgusting bother!"

For an instant he was sorely tempted to lift his eyes to her face, but he checked himself; then he gently took her dust-coat from her shoulders and shook it out, wiped the dust from her face and eyes with his own handkerchief, held her hat and blew the dust from it with a vivid memory of performing the same service for Mrs. Horncastle only an hour before, while she arranged her hair; and then, lifting her again into the buggy, said quietly, as he took his seat beside her and grasped the reins:—

"I will drive you to the hotel by way of the stables, and you can go at once to your room and change your clothes. You are tired, you are nervous and worried, and want rest. Don't tell me anything now until you feel quite yourself again."

He whipped up the horse, who, recognizing another hand at the reins, lunged forward in a final effort, and in a few minutes they were at the hotel.

As Mrs. Horncastle sat at luncheon in the great dining-room, a little pale and abstracted, she saw Mrs. Barker sweep confidently into the room, fresh, rosy, and in a new and ravishing toilette. With a swift glance of conscious power towards the other guests she walked towards Mrs. Horncastle. "Ah, here you are, dear," she said in a voice that could easily reach all ears, "and you've arrived only a little before me, after all. And I've had such an AWFUL drive to the Divide! And only think! poor George telegraphed to me at Boomville not to worry, and his dispatch has only just come back here."

And with a glance of complacency she laid Barker's gentle and forgiving dispatch before the astonished Mrs. Horncastle.

Bret Harte

CHAPTER VIII

As the day advanced the excitement over the financial crisis increased at Hymettus, until, in spite of its remote and peaceful isolation, it seemed to throb through all its verandas and corridors with some pulsation from the outer world. Besides the letters and dispatches brought by hurried messengers and by coach from the Divide, there was a crowd of guests and servants around the branch telegraph at the new Heavy Tree post-office which was constantly augmenting. Added to the natural anxiety of the deeply interested was the stimulated fever of the few who wished to be "in the fashion." It was early rumored that a heavy operator, a guest of the hotel, who was also a director in the telegraph company, had bought up the wires for his sole use, that the dispatches were doctored in his interests as a "bear," and there was wild talk of lynching by the indignant mob. Passengers from Sacramento, San Francisco, and Marysville brought incredible news and the wildest sensations. Firm after firm had failed in the great cities. Old established houses that dated back to the "spring of '49," and had weathered the fires and inundations of their perilous Californian infancy, collapsed before this mysterious, invisible, impalpable breath of panic. Companies rooted in respectability and sneered at for old-fashioned ways were discovered to have shamelessly speculated with trusts! An eminent deacon and pillar of the church was found dead in his room with a bullet in his heart and a damning confession on the desk before him! Foreign bankers were sending their gold out of the country; government would be appealed to to open the vaults of the Mint; there would be an embargo on all bullion shipment! Nothing was too wild or preposterous to be repeated or credited.

And with this fever of sordid passion the summer temperature had increased. For the last two weeks the thermometer had stood abnormally high during the day-long sunshine; and the metallic dust in the roads over mineral ranges pricked the skin like red-hot needles. In the deepest woods the aromatic sap stood in beads on felled logs and splintered tree-shafts; even the mountain night breeze failed to cool these baked and heated fastnesses. There were ominous clouds of smoke by day that were pillars of fire by night along the distant valleys. Some of the nearer crests were etched against the midnight sky by dull red creeping lines like a dying firework. The great hotel itself creaked and crackled and warped though all its painted, blistered, and veneered expanse, and was filled with the stifling breath of desiccation. The stucco cracked and crumbled away from the cornices; there were yawning gaps in the boarded floors beneath the Turkey carpets. Plate-glass windows became hopelessly fixed in their warped and twisted sashes, and added to the heat; there was a warm incense of pine sap in the dining-room that flavored all the cuisine. And yet the babble of stocks and shares went on, and people pricked their ears over their soup to catch the gossip of the last arrival.

Demorest, loathing it all in his new-found bitterness, was nevertheless impatient in his inaction, and was eagerly awaiting a telegram from Stacy; Barker had disappeared since luncheon. Suddenly there was a commotion on the veranda as a carriage drove up with a handsome, gray-haired woman. In the buzzing of voices around him Demorest heard the name of Mrs. Van Loo. In further comments, made in more smothered accents, he heard that Van Loo had been stopped at Canyon Station, but that no warrant had yet been issued against him; that it was generally believed that the bank dared not hold him; that others openly averred that he had been used as a scapegoat to avert suspicion from higher guilt. And certainly Mrs. Van Loo's calm, confident air seemed to corroborate these assertions.

He was still wondering if the strange coincidence which had brought both mother and son into his own life was not merely a fancy, as far as SHE was concerned, when a waiter brought a message from Mrs. Van Loo that she would be glad to see him for a few moments in her room. Last night he could scarcely have restrained his eagerness to meet her and elucidate the mystery of the photograph; now he was conscious of an equally strong revulsion of feeling, and a dull premonition of evil. However, it was no doubt possible that the man had told her of his previous inquiries, and she had merely acknowledged them by that message.

Demorest found Mrs. Van Loo in the private sitting-room where he and his old partners had supped on the preceding night. She received him with unmistakable courtesy and even a certain dignity that might or might not have been assumed. He had no difficulty in recognizing the son's mechanical politeness in the first, but he was puzzled at the second.

"The manager of this hotel," she began, with a foreigner's precision of English, "has just told me that you were at present occupying my rooms at his invitation, but that you wished to see me at once on my return, and I believe that I was not wrong in apprehending that you preferred to hear my wishes from my own lips rather than from an innkeeper. I had intended to keep these rooms for some weeks, but, unfortunately for me, though fortunately for you, the present terrible financial crisis, which has most unjustly brought my son into such scandalous prominence, will oblige me to return to San Francisco until his reputation is fully cleared of these foul aspersions. I shall only ask you to allow me the undisturbed possession of these rooms for a couple of hours until I can pack my trunks and gather up a few souvenirs that I almost always keep with me."

"Pray, consider that your wishes are my own in respect to that, my dear madam," returned Demorest gravely, "and that, indeed, I protested against even this temporary intrusion upon your apartments; but I confess that now that you have spoken of your souvenirs I have the greatest curiosity about one of them, and that even my object in seeking this interview was to gratify it. It is in regard to a photograph which I saw on the chimney-piece in your bedroom, which I think I recognized as that of some one whom I formerly knew."

There was a sudden look of sharp suspicion and even hard aggressiveness that quite changed the lady's face as he mentioned the word "souvenir," but it quickly changed to a smile as she put up her fan with a gesture of arch deprecation, and said:

"Ah! I see. Of course, a lady's photograph."

The reply irritated Demorest. More than that, he felt a sudden sense of the absolute sentimentality of his request, and the consciousness that he was about to invite the familiar confidence of this strange woman—whose son had forged his name—in regard to HER!

"It was a Venetian picture," he began, and stopped, a singular disgust keeping him from voicing the name.

But Mrs. Van Loo was less reticent. "Oh, you mean my dearest friend—a lovely picture, and you know her? Why, yes, surely. You are THE Mr. Demorest who—Of course, that old love-affair. Well, you are a marvel! Five years ago, at least, and you have not forgotten! I really must write and tell her."

"Write and tell her!" Then it was all a lie about her death! He felt not only his faith, his hope, his future leaving him, but even his self-control. With an effort he said.—

"I think you have already satisfied my curiosity. I was told five years ago that she was dead. It was because of the date of the photograph—two years later—that I ventured to intrude upon you. I was anxious only to know the truth."

"She certainly was very much living and of the world when I saw her last, two years ago," said Mrs. Van Loo, with an easy smile. "I dare say that was a ruse of her relatives—a very stupid one—to break off the affair, for I think they had other plans. But, dear me! now I remember, was there not some little quarrel between you before? Some letter from you that was not very kind? My impression is that there was something of the sort, and that the young lady was indignant. But only for a time, you know. She very soon forgot it. I dare say if you wrote something very charming to her it might not be too late. We women are very forgiving, Mr. Demorest, and although she is very much sought after, as are all young American girls whose fathers can give them a comfortable 'dot', her parents might be persuaded to throw over a poor prince for a rich countryman in the end. Of course, you know, to you Republicans there is always something fascinating in titles and blood, and our dear friend is like other girls. Still, it is worth the risk. And five years of waiting and devotion really ought to tell. It's quite a romance! Shall I write to her and tell her I have seen you, looking well and prosperous? Nothing more. Do let me! I should be delighted."

"I think it hardly worth while for you to give yourself that trouble," said Demorest quietly, looking in Mrs. Van Loo's smiling eyes, "now that I know the story of the young lady's death was a forgery. And I will not intrude further on your time. Pray give yourself no needless hurry over your packing. I may go to San Francisco this afternoon, and not even require the rooms to-night."

"At least, let me make you a present of the souvenir as an acknowledgment of your courtesy," said Mrs. Van Loo, passing into her bedroom and returning with the photograph. "I feel that with your five years of constancy it is more yours than mine." As a gentleman Demorest knew he could not refuse, and taking the photograph from her with a low bow, with another final salutation he withdrew.

Alone by himself in a corner of the veranda he was surprised that the interview had made so little impression on him, and had so little altered his conviction. His discovery that the announcement of his betrothed's death was a fiction did not affect the fact that though living she was yet dead to him, and apparently by her own consent. The contrast between her life and his during those five years had been covertly accented by Mrs. Van Loo, whether intentionally or not, and he saw again as last night the full extent of his sentimental folly. He could not even condole with himself that he was the victim of miserable falsehoods that others had invented. SHE had accepted them, and had even excused her desertion of him by that last deceit of the letter.

He drew out her photograph and again examined it, but not as a lover. Had she really grown stouter and more self-complacent? Was the spirituality and delicacy he had worshiped in her purely his own idiotic fancy? Had she always been like this? Yes. There was the girl who could weakly strive, weakly revenge herself, and weakly forget. There was the figure that he had expected to find carved upon the tomb which he had long sought that he might weep over. He laughed aloud.

It was very hot, and he was stifling with inaction. What was Barker doing, and why had not Stacy telegraphed to him? And what were those people in the courtyard doing? Were they discussing news of further disaster and ruin? Perhaps he was even now a beggar. Well, his fortune might go with his faith.

But the crowd was simply looking at the roof of the hotel, and he now saw that a black smoke was drifting across the courtyard, and was conscious of a smell of soot and burning. He stepped down from the veranda among the mingled guests and servants, and saw that the smoke was only pouring from a chimney. He heard, too, that the chimney had been on fire, and that it was Mrs. Van Loo's bedroom chimney, and that when the startled servants had knocked at the locked door she had told them that she was only burning some old letters and newspapers, the refuse of her trunks. There was naturally some indignation that the hotel had been so foolishly endangered, in such scorching weather, and the manager had had a scene with her which resulted in her leaving the hotel indignantly with her half-packed boxes. But even after the smoke had died away and the fire been extinguished in the chimney and hearth, there was an acrid smell of smouldering pine penetrating the upper floors of the hotel all that afternoon.

When Mrs. Van Loo drove away, the manager returned with Demorest to the rooms. The marble hearth was smoked and discolored and still littered with charred ashes of burnt paper.

"My belief is," said the manager darkly, "that the old hag came here just to burn up a lot of incriminating papers that her son had intrusted to her keeping. It looks mighty suspicious. You see she got up an awful lot of side when I told her I didn't reckon to run a smelting furnace in a wooden hotel with the thermometer at one hundred in the office, and I reckon it was just an excuse for getting off in a hurry."

But the continued delay in Stacy's promised telegram had begun to work upon Demorest's usual equanimity, and he scarcely listened in his anxiety for his old partner. He knew that Stacy should have arrived in San Francisco by noon. He had almost determined to take the next train from the Divide when two horsemen dashed into the courtyard. There was the usual stir on the veranda and rush for news, but the two new arrivals turned out to be Barker, on a horse covered with foam, and a dashing, elegantly dressed stranger on a mustang as carefully groomed and as spotless as himself. Demorest instantly recognized Jack Hamlin.

He had not seen Hamlin since that day, five years before, when the latter had accompanied the three partners with their treasure to Boomville, and had handed him the mysterious packet. As the two men dismounted hurriedly and moved towards him, he felt a premonition of something as fateful and important as then. In obedience to a sign from Barker he led them to a more secluded angle of the veranda. He could not help noticing that his younger partner's face was mobile as ever, but more thoughtful and older; yet his voice rang with the old freemasonry of the camp, as he said, with a laugh, "The signal has been given, and it's boot and saddle and away."

"But I have had no dispatch from Stacy," said Demorest in surprise. "He was to telegraph to me from San Francisco in any emergency."

"He never got there at all," said Barker. "Jack ran slap into Van Loo at the Divide, and sent a dispatch to Jim, which stopped him halfway until Jack could reach him, which he nearly broke his neck to do; and then Jack finished up by bringing a message from Stacy to us that we should all meet together on the slope of Heavy Tree, near the Bar. I met Jack just as I was riding into the Divide, and came back with him. He will tell you the rest, and you can swear by what Jack says, for he's white all through," he added, laying his hand affectionately on Hamlin's shoulder.

Hamlin winced slightly. For he had NOT told Barker that his wife was with Van Loo, nor his first reason for interfering. But he related how he had finally overtaken Van Loo at Canyon Station, and how the fugitive had disclosed the conspiracy of Steptoe and Hall against the bank and Marshall as the price of his own release. On this news, remembering that Stacy had passed the Divide on his way to the station, he had first sent a dispatch to him, and then met him at the first station on the road. "I reckon, gentlemen," said Hamlin, with an unusual earnestness in his voice, "that he'd not only got my telegram, but ALL THE NEWS that had been flying around this morning, for he looked like a man to whom it was just a 'toss-up' whether he took his own life then and there or was willing to have somebody else take it for him, for he said, 'I'll go myself,' and telegraphed to have the surveyor stopped from coming. Then he told me to tell you fellows, and ask you to come too." Jack paused, and added half mischievously, "He sort of asked ME what I would take to stand by him in the row, if there was one, and I told him I'd take—whiskey! You see, boys, it's a kind of off-night with me, and I wouldn't mind for the sake of old times to finish the game with old Steptoe that I began a matter of five years ago."

"All right," said Demorest, with a kindling eye; "I suppose

we'd better start at once. One moment," he added. "Barker boy, will you excuse me if I speak a word to Hamlin?" As Barker nodded and walked to the rails of the veranda, Demorest took Hamlin aside, "You and I," he said hurriedly, "are SINGLE men; Barker has a wife and child. This is likely to be no child's play."

But Jack Hamlin was no fool, and from certain leading questions which Barker had already put, but which he had skillfully evaded, he surmised that Barker knew something of his wife's escapade. He answered a little more seriously than his wont, "I don't think as regards HIS WIFE that would make much difference to him or her how stiff the work was."

Demorest turned away with his last pang of bitterness. It needed only this confirmation of all that Stacy had hinted, of what he himself had seen in his brief interview with Mrs. Barker since his return, to shake his last remaining faith. "We'll all go together, then," he said, with a laugh, "as in the old times, and perhaps it's as well that we have no woman in our confidence."

An hour later the three men passed quietly out of the hotel, scarcely noticed by the other guests, who were also oblivious of their absence during the evening. For Mrs. Barker, quite recovered from her fatiguing ride, was in high spirits and the most beautiful and spotless of summer gowns, and was considered quite a heroine by the other ladies as she dwelt upon the terrible heat of her return journey. "Only I knew Mr. Barker would be worried—and the poor man actually walked a mile down the Divide road to meet me—I believe I should have stayed there all day." She glanced round the other groups for Mrs. Horncastle, but that lady had retired early. Possibly she alone had noticed the absence of the two partners.

The guests sat up until quite late, for the heat seemed to grow still more oppressive, and the strange smell of burning wood revived the gossip about Mrs. Van Loo and her stupidity in setting fire to her chimney. Some averred that it would be days before the smell could be got out of the house; others referred it to the fires in the woods, which were now dangerously near. One spoke of the isolated position of the hotel as affording the greatest security, but was met by the assertion of a famous mountaineer that the forest fires were wont to leap from crest to crest mysteriously, without any apparent continuous contact. This led to more or less light-hearted conjecture of present danger and some amusing stories of hotel fires and their ludicrous revelations. There were also some entertaining speculations as to what they would do and what they would try to save in such an emergency.

"For myself," said Mrs. Barker audaciously, "I should certainly let Mr. Barker look after Sta and confine myself entirely to getting away with my diamonds. I know the wretch would never think of them."

It was still later when, exhausted by the heat and some reaction from the excitement of the day, they at last deserted the veranda for their rooms, and for a while the shadowy bulk of the whole building was picked out with regularly spaced lights from its open windows, until now these finally faded and went out one by one. An hour later the whole building had sunk to rest. It was said that it was only four in the morning when a yawning porter, having put out the light in a dark, upper corridor, was amazed by a dull glow from the top of the wall, and awoke to the fact that a red fire, as yet smokeless and flameless, was creeping along the cornice. He ran to the office and gave the alarm; but on returning with assistance was stopped in the corridor by an impenetrable wall of smoke veined with murky flashes. The alarm was given in all the lower floors, and the occupants rushed from their beds half dressed to the courtyard, only to see, as they afterwards averred, the flames burst like cannon discharges from the upper windows and unite above the crackling roof. So sudden and complete was the catastrophe, although slowly prepared by a leak in the overheated chimney between the floors, that even the excitement of fear and exertion was spared the survivors. There was bewilderment and stupor, but neither uproar nor confusion. People found themselves wandering in the woods, half awake and half dressed, having descended from the balconies and leaped from the windows,—they knew not how. Others on the upper floor neither awoke nor moved from their beds, but were suffocated without a cry. From the first an instinctive idea of the hopelessness of combating the conflagration possessed them all; to a blind, automatic feeling to flee the building was added the slow mechanism of the somnambulist; delicate women walked speechlessly, but securely, along ledges and roofs from which they would have fallen by the mere light of reason and of day. There was no crowding or impeding haste in their dumb exodus. It was only when Mrs. Barker awoke disheveled in the courtyard, and with an hysterical outcry rushed back into the hotel, that there was any sign of panic.

Mrs. Horncastle, who was standing near, fully dressed as from some night-long vigil, quickly followed her. The half-frantic woman was making directly for her own apartments, whose windows those in the courtyard could see were already belching smoke. Suddenly Mrs. Horncastle stopped with a bitter cry and clasped her forehead. It had just flashed upon her that Mrs. Barker had told her only a few hours before that Sta had been removed with the nurse to the UPPER FLOOR! It was not the forgotten child that Mrs. Barker was returning for, but her diamonds! Mrs. Horncastle called her; she did not reply. The smoke was already pouring down the staircase. Mrs. Horncastle hesitated for a moment only, and then, drawing a long breath, dashed up the stairs. On the first landing she stumbled over something—the prostrate figure of the nurse. But this saved her, for she found that near the floor she could breathe more freely. Before her appeared to be an open door. She crept along towards it on her hands and knees. The frightened cry of a child, awakened from its sleep in the dark, gave her nerve to rise, enter the room, and dash open the window. By the flashing light she could see a little figure rising from a bed. It was Sta. There was not a moment to be lost, for the open window was beginning to draw the smoke from the passage. Luckily, the boy, by some childish instinct, threw his arms round her neck and left her hands free. Whispering him to hold tight, she clambered out of the window. A narrow ledge of cornice scarcely wide enough for her feet ran along the house to a distant balcony. With her back to the house she zigzagged her feet along the cornice to get away from the smoke, which now poured directly from the window. Then she grew dizzy; the weight of the child on her bosom seemed to be toppling her forward towards the abyss below. She closed her eyes, frantically grasping the child with crossed arms on her breast as she stood on the ledge, until, as seen from below through the twisting smoke, they might have seemed a figure of the Madonna and Child niched in the wall. Then a voice from above called to her, "Courage!" and she felt the flap of a twisted sheet lowered from an upper window against her face. She grasped it eagerly; it held firmly. Then she heard a cry from below, saw them carrying a ladder, and at last was lifted with her burden from the ledge by powerful hands. Then only did she raise her eyes to the upper window whence had come her help. Smoke and flame were pouring from it. The unknown hero who had sacrificed his only chance of escape to her remained forever unknown.

*****

Only four miles away that night a group of men were waiting for the dawn in the shadow of a pine near Heavy Tree Bar. As the sky glowed redly over the crest between them and Hymettus, Hamlin said:—

"Another one of those forest fires. It's this side of Black Spur, and a big one, I reckon."

"Do you know," said Barker thoughtfully, "I was thinking of the time the old cabin burnt up on Heavy Tree. It looks to be about in the same place."

"Hush!" said Stacy sharply.

CHAPTER IX

An abandoned tunnel—an irregular orifice in the mountain flank which looked like a dried-up sewer that had disgorged through its opening the refuse of the mountain in red slime, gravel, and a peculiar clay known as "cement," in a foul streak down its side; a narrow ledge on either side, broken up by heaps of quartz, tailings, and rock, and half hidden in scrub, oak, and myrtle; a decaying cabin of logs, bark, and cobblestones—these made up the exterior of the Marshall claim. To this defacement of the mountain, the rude clearing of thicket and underbrush by fire or blasting, the lopping of tree-boughs and the decapitation of saplings, might be added the debris and ruins of half-civilized occupancy. The ground before the cabin was covered with broken boxes, tin cans, the staves and broken hoops of casks, and the cast-off rags of blankets and clothing. The whole claim in its unsavory, unpicturesque details, and its vulgar story of sordid, reckless, and selfish occupancy and abandonment, was a foul blot on the landscape, which the first rosy dawn only made the more offending. Surely the last spot in the world that men should quarrel and fight for!

So thought George Barker, as with his companions they moved in single file slowly towards it. The little party consisted only of himself, Demorest, and Stacy; Marshall and Hamlin—according to a prearranged plan—were still in ambush to join them at the first appearance of Steptoe and his gang. The claim was yet unoccupied; they had secured their first success. Steptoe's followers, unaware that his design had been discovered, and confident that they could easily reach the claim before Marshall and the surveyor, had lingered. Some of them had held a drunken carouse at their rendezvous at Heavy Tree. Others were still engaged in procuring shovels and picks and pans for their mock equipment as miners, and this, again, gave Marshall's adherents the advantage. THEY knew that their opponents would probably first approach the empty claim encumbered only with their peaceful implements, while they themselves had brought their rifles with them.

Stacy, who by tacit consent led the party, on reaching the claim at once posted Demorest and Barker each behind a separate heap of quartz tailings on the ledge, which afforded them a capital breastwork, and stationed himself at the mouth of the tunnel which was nearest the trail. It had already been arranged what each man was to do. They were in possession. For the rest they must wait. What they thought at that moment no one knew. Their characteristic appearance had slightly changed. The melancholy and philosophic Demorest was alert and bitter. Barker's changeful face had become fixed and steadfast. Stacy alone wore his "fighting look," which the others had remembered.

They had not long to wait. The sounds of rude laughter, coarse skylarking, and voices more or less still confused with half-spent liquor came from the rocky trail. And then Steptoe appeared with part of his straggling followers, who were celebrating their easy invasion by clattering their picks and shovels and beating loudly upon their tins and prospecting-pans. The three partners quickly recognized the stamp of the strangers, in spite of their peaceful implements. They were the waifs and strays of San Francisco wharves, of

Sacramento dens, of dissolute mountain towns; and there was not, probably, a single actual miner among them. A raging scorn and contempt took possession of Barker and Demorest, but Stacy knew their exact value. As Steptoe passed before the opening of the tunnel he heard the cry of "Halt!"

He looked up. He saw Stacy not thirty yards before him with his rifle at half-cock. He saw Barker and Demorest, fully armed, rise from behind their breastworks of rock along the ledge and thus fully occupy the claim. But he saw more. He saw that his plot was known. Outlaw and desperado as he was, he saw that he had lost his moral power in this actual possession, and that from that moment he must be the aggressor. He saw he was fighting no irresponsible hirelings like his own, but men of position and importance, whose loss would make a stir. Against their rifles the few revolvers that his men chanced to have slung to them were of little avail. But he was not cowed, although his few followers stumbled together at this momentary check, half angrily, half timorously like wolves without a leader. "Bring up the other men and their guns," he whispered fiercely to the nearest. Then he faced Stacy.

"Who are YOU to stop peaceful miners going to work on their own claim?" he said coarsely. "I'll tell you WHO, boys," he added, suddenly turning to his men with a hoarse laugh. "It ain't even the bank! It's only Jim Stacy, that the bank kicked out yesterday to save itself,—Jim Stacy and his broken-down pals. And what's the thief doing here—in Marshall's tunnel—the only spot that Marshall can claim? We ain't no particular friends o' Marshall's, though we're neighbors on the same claim; but we ain't going to see Marshall ousted by tramps. Are we, boys?"

"No, by G-d!" said his followers, dropping the pans and

seizing their picks and revolvers. They understood the appeal to arms if not to their reason. For an instant the fight seemed imminent. Then a voice from behind them said:—

"You needn't trouble yourselves about that! I'M Marshall! I sent these gentlemen to occupy the claim until I came here with the surveyor," and two men stepped from a thicket of myrtle in the rear of Steptoe and his followers. The speaker, Marshall, was a thin, slight, overworked, over-aged man; his companion, the surveyor, was equally slight, but red-bearded, spectacled, and professional-looking, with a long traveling-duster that made him appear even clerical. They were scarcely a physical addition to Stacy's party, whatever might have been their moral and legal support.

But it was just this support that Steptoe strangely clung to in his designs for the future, and a wild idea seized him. The surveyor was really the only disinterested witness between the two parties. If Steptoe could confuse his mind before the actual fighting—from which he would, of course, escape as a non-combatant—it would go far afterwards to rehabilitate Steptoe's party. "Very well, then," he said to Marshall, "I shall call this gentleman to witness that we have been attacked here in peaceable possession of our part of the claim by these armed strangers, and whether they are acting on your order or not, their blood will be on your head."

"Then I reckon," said the surveyor, as he tore away his beard, wig, spectacles, and mustache, and revealed the figure of Jack Hamlin, "that I'm about the last witness that Mr. Steptoe-Horncastle ought to call, and about the last witness that he ever WILL call!"

But he had not calculated upon the desperation of Steptoe over the failure of this last hope. For there sprang up in the outlaw's brain the same hideous idea that he voiced to his companions at the Divide. With a hoarse cry to his followers, he crashed his pickaxe into the brain of Marshall, who stood near him, and sprang forward. Three or four shots were exchanged. Two of his men fell, a bullet from Stacy's rifle pierced Steptoe's leg, and he dropped forward on one knee. He heard the steps of his reinforcements with their weapons coming close behind him, and rolled aside on the sloping ledge to let them pass. But he rolled too far. He felt himself slipping down the mountain-side in the slimy shoot of the tunnel. He made a desperate attempt to recover himself, but the treacherous drift of the loose debris rolled with him, as if he were part of its refuse, and, carrying him down, left him unconscious, but otherwise uninjured, in the bushes of the second ledge five hundred feet below.

When he recovered his senses the shouts and outcries above him had ceased. He knew he was safe. The ledge could only be reached by a circuitous route three miles away. He knew, too, that if he could only reach a point of outcrop a hundred yards away he could easily descend to the stage road, down the gentle slope of the mountain hidden in a growth of hazel-brush. He bound up his wounded leg, and dragged himself on his hands and knees laboriously to the outcrop. He did not look up; since his pick had crashed into Marshall's brain he had but one blind thought before him—to escape at once! That his revenge and compensation would come later he never doubted. He limped and crept, rolled and fell, from bush to bush through the sloping thickets, until he saw the red road a few feet below him.

If he only had a horse he could put miles between him and any present pursuit! Why should he not have one? The road was frequented by solitary horsemen—miners and Mexicans. He had his revolver with him; what mattered the life of another man if he escaped from the consequences of the one he had just taken? He heard the clatter of hoofs; two priests on mules rode slowly by; he ground his teeth with disappointment. But they had scarcely passed before another and more rapid clatter came from their rear. It was a lad on horseback. He started. It was his own son!

He remembered in a flash how the boy had said he was coming to meet the padre at the station on that day. His first impulse was to hide himself, his wound, and his defeat from the lad, but the blind idea of escape was still paramount. He leaned over the bank and called to him. The astonished lad cantered eagerly to his side.

"Give me your horse, Eddy," said the father; "I'm in bad luck, and must get."

The boy glanced at his father's face, at his tattered garments and bandaged leg, and read the whole story. It was a familiar page to him. He paled first and then flushed, and then, with an odd glitter in his eyes, said, "Take me with you, father. Do! You always did before. I'll bring you luck."

Desperation is superstitious. Why not take him? They had been lucky before, and the two together might confound any description of their identity to the pursuers. "Help me up, Eddy, and then get up before me."

"BEHIND, you mean," said the boy, with a laugh, as he helped his father into the saddle.

"No," said Steptoe harshly. "BEFORE me,—do you hear? And if anything happens BEHIND you, don't look! If I drop off, don't stop! Don't get down, but go on and leave me. Do you understand?" he repeated almost savagely.

"Yes," said the boy tremulously.

"All right," said the father, with a softer voice, as he passed his one arm round the boy's body and lifted the reins. "Hold tight when we come to the cross-roads, for we'll take the first turn, for old luck's sake, to the Mission."

They were the last words exchanged between them, for as they wheeled rapidly to the left at the cross-roads, Jack Hamlin and Demorest swung as quickly out of another road to the right immediately behind them. Jack's challenge to "Halt!" was only answered by Steptoe's horse springing forward under the sharp lash of the riata.

"Hold up!" said Jack suddenly, laying his hand upon the rifle which Demorest had lifted to his shoulder. "He's carrying some one,—a wounded comrade, I reckon. We don't want HIM. Swing out and go for the horse; well forward, in the neck or shoulder."

Demorest swung far out to the right of the road and raised his rifle. As it cracked Steptoe's horse seemed to have suddenly struck some obstacle ahead of him rather than to have been hit himself, for his head went down with his fore feet under him, and he turned a half-somersault on the road, flinging his two riders a dozen feet away.

Steptoe scrambled to his knees, revolver in hand, but the other figure never moved. "Hands up!" said Jack, sighting his own weapon. The reports seemed simultaneous, but Jack's bullet had pierced Steptoe's brain even before the outlaw's pistol exploded harmlessly in the air.

The two men dismounted, but by a common instinct they both ran to the prostrate figure that had never moved.

"By God! it's a boy!" said Jack, leaning over the body and lifting the shoulders from which the head hung loosely.

"Neck broken and dead as his pal." Suddenly he started, and, to Demorest's astonishment, began hurriedly pulling off the glove from the boy's limp right hand.

"What are you doing?" demanded Demorest in creeping horror.

"Look!" said Jack, as he laid bare the small white hand. The first two fingers were merely unsightly stumps that had been hidden in the padded glove.

"Good God! Van Loo's brother!" said Demorest, recoiling.

"No!" said Jack, with a grim face, "it's what I have long suspected,—it's Steptoe's son!"

"His son?" repeated Demorest.

"Yes," said Jack; and he added, after looking at the two bodies with a long-drawn whistle of concern, "and I wouldn't, if I were you, say anything of this to Barker."

"Why?" said Demorest.

"Well," returned Jack, "when our scrimmage was over down there, and they brought the news to Barker that his wife and her diamonds were burnt up at the hotel, you remember that they said that Mrs. Horncastle had saved his boy."

"Yes," said Demorest; "but what has that to do with it?"

"Nothing, I reckon," said Jack, with a slight shrug of his shoulders, "only Mrs. Horncastle was the mother of the boy that's lying there."

*****

Two years later as Demorest and Stacy sat before the fire in the old cabin on Marshall's claim—now legally their own— they looked from the door beyond the great bulk of Black Spur to the pallid snow-line of the Sierras, still as remote and unchanged to them as when they had gazed upon it from Heavy Tree Hill. And, for the matter of that, they themselves seemed to have been left so unchanged that even now, as in the old days, it was Barker's voice as he greeted them from the darkening trail that alone broke their reverie.

"Well," said Demorest cheerfully, "your usual luck, Barker boy!" for they already saw in his face the happy light they had once seen there on an eventful night seven years ago.

"I'm to be married to Mrs. Horncastle next month," he said breathlessly, "and little Sta loves her already as if she was his own mother. Wish me joy."

A slight shadow passed over Stacy's face; but his hand was the first to grasp Barker's, and his voice the first to say "Amen!"

ABOUT THE AUTHOR

 **Francis Bret Harte** (August 25, 1836–May 6, 1902) was an American author and poet, best remembered for his accounts of pioneering life in California.

Born in Albany, New York, Harte moved to California in 1853, later working there in a number of capacities, including miner, teacher, messenger, and journalist. He spent part of his life in the northern California coast town now known as Arcata, at the time it was just a mining camp on Humboldt Bay.

His first literary efforts, including poetry and prose, appeared in The Californian, an early literary journal edited by Charles Henry Webb. In 1868 he became editor of The Overland Monthly, another new literary magazine, but this one more in tune with the pioneering spirit of excitement in California. His story, "The Luck of Roaring Camp," appeared in the magazine's second edition, propelling Harte to nationwide fame.

As an established literary figure, he was appointed to the position of United States Consul in the town of Krefeld, Germany in 1878 and Glasgow in 1880. In 1885 he settled in London. During the thirty years he spent in Europe, he never abandoned writing, and maintained a prodigious output of stories that retained the freshness of his earlier work. He died in England in 1902.

Other books by this author

Openings in the Old Trail
Sally Dows and Other Stories
Stories in Light and Shadow
Tales of the Argonauts
Tales of Trail and Town
Maruja
Under the Redwoods
By Shore and Sedge
Colonel Starbottle's Client and Other Stories
Clarence
Cressy
Devil's Ford
Frontier Stories
In a Hollow of the Hills
In the Carquinez Woods
Jeff Briggs's Love Story
Snow-Bound at Eagle's
The Argonauts of North Liberty
The Bell-Ringer of Angel's and Other Stories
The Crusade of the Excelsior
The Story of a Mine

Choose from Thousands of 1stWorldLibrary Classics By

A. M. Barnard
Ada Leverson
Adolphus William Ward
Aesop
Agatha Christie
Alexander Aaronsohn
Alexander Kielland
Alexandre Dumas
Alfred Gatty
Alfred Ollivant
Alice Duer Miller
Alice Turner Curtis
Alice Dunbar
Allen Chapman
Alleyne Ireland
Ambrose Bierce
Amelia E. Barr
Amory H. Bradford
Andrew Lang
Andrew McFarland Davis
Andy Adams
Angela Brazil
Anna Alice Chapin
Anna Sewell
Annie Besant
Annie Hamilton Donnell
Annie Payson Call
Annie Roe Carr
Annonaymous
Anton Chekhov
Archibald Lee Fletcher
Arnold Bennett
Arthur C. Benson
Arthur Conan Doyle
Arthur M. Winfield
Arthur Ransome
Arthur Schnitzler
Arthur Train
Atticus
B.H. Baden-Powell
B. M. Bower
B. C. Chatterjee
Baroness Emmuska Orczy
Baroness Orczy
Basil King
Bayard Taylor
Ben Macomber
Bertha Muzzy Bower
Bjornstjerne Bjornson

Booth Tarkington
Boyd Cable
Bram Stoker
C. Collodi
C. E. Orr
C. M. Ingleby
Carolyn Wells
Catherine Parr Traill
Charles A. Eastman
Charles Amory Beach
Charles Dickens
Charles Dudley Warner
Charles Farrar Browne
Charles Ives
Charles Kingsley
Charles Klein
Charles Hanson Towne
Charles Lathrop Pack
Charles Romyn Dake
Charles Whibley
Charles Willing Beale
Charlotte M. Braeme
Charlotte M. Yonge
Charlotte Perkins Stetson
Clair W. Hayes
Clarence Day Jr.
Clarence E. Mulford
Clemence Housman
Confucius
Coningsby Dawson
Cornelis DeWitt Wilcox
Cyril Burleigh
D. H. Lawrence
Daniel Defoe
David Garnett
Dinah Craik
Don Carlos Janes
Donald Keyhoe
Dorothy Kilner
Dougan Clark
Douglas Fairbanks
E. Nesbit
E. P. Roe
E. Phillips Oppenheim
E. S. Brooks
Earl Barnes
Edgar Rice Burroughs
Edith Van Dyne
Edith Wharton

Edward Everett Hale
Edward J. O'Biren
Edward S. Ellis
Edwin L. Arnold
Eleanor Atkins
Eleanor Hallowell Abbott
Eliot Gregory
Elizabeth Gaskell
Elizabeth McCracken
Elizabeth Von Arnim
Ellem Key
Emerson Hough
Emilie F. Carlen
Emily Bronte
Emily Dickinson
Enid Bagnold
Enilor Macartney Lane
Erasmus W. Jones
Ernie Howard Pie
Ethel May Dell
Ethel Turner
Ethel Watts Mumford
Eugene Sue
Eugenie Foa
Eugene Wood
Eustace Hale Ball
Evelyn Everett-green
Everard Cotes
F. H. Cheley
F. J. Cross
F. Marion Crawford
Fannie E. Newberry
Federick Austin Ogg
Ferdinand Ossendowski
Fergus Hume
Florence A. Kilpatrick
Fremont B. Deering
Francis Bacon
Francis Darwin
Frances Hodgson Burnett
Frances Parkinson Keyes
Frank Gee Patchin
Frank Harris
Frank Jewett Mather
Frank L. Packard
Frank V. Webster
Frederic Stewart Isham
Frederick Trevor Hill
Frederick Winslow Taylor

Friedrich Kerst
Friedrich Nietzsche
Fyodor Dostoyevsky
G.A. Henty
G.K. Chesterton
Gabrielle E. Jackson
Garrett P. Serviss
Gaston Leroux
George A. Warren
George Ade
Geroge Bernard Shaw
George Cary Eggleston
George Durston
George Ebers
George Eliot
George Gissing
George MacDonald
George Meredith
George Orwell
George Sylvester Viereck
George Tucker
George W. Cable
George Wharton James
Gertrude Atherton
Gordon Casserly
Grace E. King
Grace Gallatin
Grace Greenwood
Grant Allen
Guillermo A. Sherwell
Gulielma Zollinger
Gustav Flaubert
H. A. Cody
H. B. Irving
H. C. Bailey
H. G. Wells
H. H. Munro
H. Irving Hancock
H. R. Naylor
H. Rider Haggard
H. W. C. Davis
Haldeman Julius
Hall Caine
Hamilton Wright Mabie
Hans Christian Andersen
Harold Avery
Harold McGrath
Harriet Beecher Stowe
Harry Castlemon
Harry Coghill
Harry Houidini

Hayden Carruth
Helent Hunt Jackson
Helen Nicolay
Hendrik Conscience
Hendy David Thoreau
Henri Barbusse
Henrik Ibsen
Henry Adams
Henry Ford
Henry Frost
Henry James
Henry Jones Ford
Henry Seton Merriman
Henry W Longfellow
Herbert A. Giles
Herbert Carter
Herbert N. Casson
Herman Hesse
Hildegard G. Frey
Homer
Honore De Balzac
Horace B. Day
Horace Walpole
Horatio Alger Jr.
Howard Pyle
Howard R. Garis
Hugh Lofting
Hugh Walpole
Humphry Ward
Ian Maclaren
Inez Haynes Gillmore
Irving Bacheller
Isabel Cecilia Williams
Isabel Hornibrook
Israel Abrahams
Ivan Turgenev
J. G.Austin
J. Henri Fabre
J. M. Barrie
J. M. Walsh
J. Macdonald Oxley
J. R. Miller
J. S. Fletcher
J. S. Knowles
J. Storer Clouston
J. W. Duffield
Jack London
Jacob Abbott
James Allen
James Andrews
James Baldwin

James Branch Cabell
James DeMille
James Joyce
James Lane Allen
James Lane Allen
James Oliver Curwood
James Oppenheim
James Otis
James R. Driscoll
Jane Abbott
Jane Austen
Jane L. Stewart
Janet Aldridge
Jens Peter Jacobsen
Jerome K. Jerome
Jessie Graham Flower
John Buchan
John Burroughs
John Cournos
John F. Kennedy
John Gay
John Glasworthy
John Habberton
John Joy Bell
John Kendrick Bangs
John Milton
John Philip Sousa
John Taintor Foote
Jonas Lauritz Idemil Lie
Jonathan Swift
Joseph A. Altsheler
Joseph Carey
Joseph Conrad
Joseph E. Badger Jr
Joseph Hergesheimer
Joseph Jacobs
Jules Vernes
Julian Hawthrone
Julie A Lippmann
Justin Huntly McCarthy
Kakuzo Okakura
Karle Wilson Baker
Kate Chopin
Kenneth Grahame
Kenneth McGaffey
Kate Langley Bosher
Kate Langley Bosher
Katherine Cecil Thurston
Katherine Stokes
L. A. Abbot
L. T. Meade

L. Frank Baum
Latta Griswold
Laura Dent Crane
Laura Lee Hope
Laurence Housman
Lawrence Beasley
Leo Tolstoy
Leonid Andreyev
Lewis Carroll
Lewis Sperry Chafer
Lilian Bell
Lloyd Osbourne
Louis Hughes
Louis Joseph Vance
Louis Tracy
Louisa May Alcott
Lucy Fitch Perkins
Lucy Maud Montgomery
Luther Benson
Lydia Miller Middleton
Lyndon Orr
M. Corvus
M. H. Adams
Margaret E. Sangster
Margret Howth
Margaret Vandercook
Margaret W. Hungerford
Margret Penrose
Maria Edgeworth
Maria Thompson Daviess
Mariano Azuela
Marion Polk Angellotti
Mark Overton
Mark Twain
Mary Austin
Mary Catherine Crowley
Mary Cole
Mary Hastings Bradley
Mary Roberts Rinehart
Mary Rowlandson
M. Wollstonecraft Shelley
Maud Lindsay
Max Beerbohm
Myra Kelly
Nathaniel Hawthrone
Nicolo Machiavelli
O. F. Walton
Oscar Wilde

Owen Johnson
P.G. Wodehouse
Paul and Mabel Thorne
Paul G. Tomlinson
Paul Severing
Percy Brebner
Percy Keese Fitzhugh
Peter B. Kyne
Plato
Quincy Allen
R. Derby Holmes
R. L. Stevenson
R. S. Ball
Rabindranath Tagore
Rahul Alvares
Ralph Bonehill
Ralph Henry Barbour
Ralph Victor
Ralph Waldo Emmerson
Rene Descartes
Ray Cummings
Rex Beach
Rex E. Beach
Richard Harding Davis
Richard Jefferies
Richard Le Gallienne
Robert Barr
Robert Frost
Robert Gordon Anderson
Robert L. Drake
Robert Lansing
Robert Lynd
Robert Michael Ballantyne
Robert W. Chambers
Rosa Nouchette Carey
Rudyard Kipling
Saint Augustine
Samuel B. Allison
Samuel Hopkins Adams
Sarah Bernhardt
Sarah C. Hallowell
Selma Lagerlof
Sherwood Anderson
Sigmund Freud
Standish O'Grady
Stanley Weyman
Stella Benson
Stella M. Francis

Stephen Crane
Stewart Edward White
Stijn Streuvels
Swami Abhedananda
Swami Parmananda
T. S. Ackland
T. S. Arthur
The Princess Der Ling
Thomas A. Janvier
Thomas A Kempis
Thomas Anderton
Thomas Bailey Aldrich
Thomas Bulfinch
Thomas De Quincey
Thomas Dixon
Thomas H. Huxley
Thomas Hardy
Thomas More
Thornton W. Burgess
U. S. Grant
Upton Sinclair
Valentine Williams
Various Authors
Vaughan Kester
Victor Appleton
Victor G. Durham
Victoria Cross
Virginia Woolf
Wadsworth Camp
Walter Camp
Walter Scott
Washington Irving
Wilbur Lawton
Wilkie Collins
Willa Cather
Willard F. Baker
William Dean Howells
William le Queux
W. Makepeace Thackeray
William W. Walter
William Shakespeare
Winston Churchill
Yei Theodora Ozaki
Yogi Ramacharaka
Young E. Allison
Zane Grey